RUNG HO!

He rode as the crusaders once rode.

RUNG HO!

By TALBOT MUNDY.

McKINLAY, STONE & MACKENZIE
NEW YORK

RUNG HO!

RUNG HO!

CHAPTER I

Howrah City bows the knee
More or less to masters three,
    King, and Prince, and Siva.
Howrah City pays in pain
Taxes which the royal twain
Give to priests, to give again
    (More or less) to Siva.

THAT was no time or place for any girl of twenty
to be wandering unprotected. Rosemary McClean
knew it; the old woman, of the sweeper caste, that
is no caste at all,—the hag with the flat breasts and
wrinkled skin, who followed her dogwise, and was
no more protection than a toothless dog,—knew it
well, and growled about it in incessant undertones
that met with neither comment nor response.

"Leave a pearl of price to glisten on the street,
yes!" she grumbled. "Perhaps none might notice
it—perhaps! But her—here—at this time—" She
would continue in a rumbling growl of half-prophetic
catalogues of evil—some that she had seen to happen, some that she imagined, and not any part of
which was in the least improbable.

As the girl passed through the stenching, many-

hued bazaar, the roar would cease for a second and
then rise again. Turbaned and pugreed—Mohammedan and Hindoo—men of all grades of color,
language, and belief, but with only one theory on
women, would stare first at the pony that she rode,
then at her, and then at the ancient grandmother
who trotted in her wake. Low jests would greet
the grandmother, and then the trading and the
gambling would resume, together with the under-
thread of restlessness that was so evidently there
and yet so hard to lay a finger on.

The sun beat down pitilessly—brass—like the din
of cymbals. Beneath the sun helmet that sat so
squarely and straightforwardly on the tidy chestnut curls, her face was pale. She smiled as she
guided her pony in and out amid the roaring throng,
and carefully refused to see the scowls; her brave
little shoulders seconded a pair of quiet, brave gray
eyes in showing an unconquerable courage to the
world, and her clean, neat cotton riding-habit gave
the lie and the laugh in one to poverty; but, as the
crowd had its atmosphere of secret murmuring, she
had another of secret anxiety.

Neither had fear. She did not believe in it. She
was there to help her father fight inhuman wrong,
and die, if need be, in the last ditch. The crowd
had none, for it had begun to realize that it was part
of a two-hundred-million crowd, held down and
compelled by less than a hundred thousand aliens.
And, least of all, had the man who followed her at
a little distance the slightest sense of fear. He was

far more conversant with it than she, but—unlike her, and far more than the seething crowd—he knew the trend of events, and just what likelihood there was of insult or injury to Rosemary McClean being avenged in a generation.

He caused more comment than she, and of a different kind. His rose-pink pugree, with the egret and the diamond brooch to hold the egret in its place—his jewelled sabre—his swaggering, almost ruffianly air—were no more meant to escape attention than his charger that clattered and kicked among the crowd, or his following, who cleared a way for him with the butt ends of their lances. He rode ahead, but every other minute a mounted sepoy would reach out past him and drive his lance-end into the ribs of some one in the way.

There would follow much deep salaaming; more than one head would bow very low indeed; and in many languages, by the names of many gods, he would be cursed in undertones. Aloud, they would bless him and call him "Heaven-born!"

But he took no interest whatever in the crowd. His dark-brown eyes were fixed incessantly on Rosemary McClean's back. Whenever she turned a corner in the crowded maze of streets, he would spur on in a hurry until she was in sight again, and then his handsome, swarthy face would light with pleasure—wicked pleasure—self-assertive, certain, cruel. He would rein in again to let her draw once more ahead.

Rosemary McClean knew quite well who was fol-

lowing her, and knew, too, that she could do nothing
to prevent him. Once, as she passed a species of
caravansary—low-roofed, divided into many lock-
able partitions, and packed tight with babbling
humanity—she caught sight of a pair of long, black
thigh boots, silver-spurred, and of a polished scabbard that moved spasmodically, as though its owner
were impatient.

"Mahommed Gunga!" she muttered to herself.
"I wonder whether he would come to my assistance
if I needed him. He fought once—or so *he* says—
for the British; he might be loyal still. I wonder
what he is doing here, and what— Oh, I wonder!"

She was very careful not to seem to look sideways,
or seek acquaintance with the wearer of the boots;
had she done so, she would have gained nothing,
for the moment that he caught sight of her through
the opened door he drew back into a shadow, and
swore lustily. What he said to himself would have
been little comfort to her.

"By the breath of God!" he growled. "These
preachers of new creeds are the last straw, if one
were wanting! They choose the one soft place
where Mohammedan and Hindoo think alike, and
smite! If I wanted to raise hell from end to end of
Hind, I too would preach a new creed, and turn
good-looking women loose to wander on the countryside!— Ah!" He drew back even further, as he
spied the egret and the sabre and the stallion
cavorting down the street—then thought better of
it and strode swaggering to the doorway, and stood,

crimson-coated, in the sunlight, stroking upward insolently at his black, fierce-barbered beard. There was a row of medal ribbons on his left breast that bore out something at least of his contention; he had been loyal to the British once, whether he was so now or not.

The man on the charger eyed him sideways and passed on. Mahommed Gunga waited. One of the prince's followers rode close to him—leaned low from the saddle—and leered into his face.

"Knowest not enough to salute thy betters?" he demanded.

Mahommed Gunga made a movement with his right hand in the direction of his left hip—one that needed no explanation; the other legged his horse away, and rode on, grinning nastily. To reassure himself of his superiority over everybody but his master, he spun his horse presently so that its rump struck against a tented stall, and upset tent and goods. Then he spent two full minutes in outrageous execration of the men who struggled underneath the gaudy cloth, before cantering away, looking, feeling, riding like a fearless man again. Mahommed Gunga sneered after him, and spat, and turned his back on the sunshine and the street.

"I had a mind to teach that Hindoo who his betters are!" he growled.

"Come in, risaldar-sahib!" said a voice persuasively. "By your own showing the hour is not yet—why spill blood before the hour?"

The Rajput swaggered to the dark door, spurs

jingling, looking back across his shoulder once or twice, as though he half-regretted leaving the Hindoo horseman's head upon his shoulders.

"Come in, sahib," advised the voice again. "They be many. We are few. And, who knows —our roads may lie together yet."

Mahommed Gunga kicked his scabbard clear, and strode through the door. The shadows inside and the hum of voices swallowed him as though he were a big, red, black-legged devil reassimilated in the brewing broth of trouble; but his voice boomed deep and loud after he had disappeared from view.

"When their road and my road lie together, we will travel all feet foremost!" he asserted.

Ten turnings further away by that time, Rosemary McClean pressed on through the hot, dinning swarm of humanity, missing no opportunity to slip her pony through an opening, but trying, too, to seem unaware that she was followed. She chose narrow, winding ways, where the awnings almost met above the middle of the street, and where a caval-cade of horsemen would not be likely to follow her—only to hear a roar behind her, as the prince's escort started slashing at the awnings with their swords.

There was a rush and a din of shouting beside her and ahead, as the frightened merchants scurried to pull down their awnings before the ruthless horse-men could ride down on them; the narrow street transformed itself almost on the instant into an undraped, cleared defile between two walls. And after that she kept to the broader streets, where there was room in the middle for a troop to follow, four abreast, should it choose. She had no mind to seek her own safety at the expense of men whose souls her father was laboring so hard to save.

She got no credit, though, for consideration— only blame for what the swordsmen had already done. One man—a Maharati trader—half-naked, his black hair coiled into a shaggy rope and twisted up above his neck—followed her, side-tracking through the mazy byways of the bewildering mart, and coming out ahead of her—or lurking beside bales of merchandise and waiting his opportunity to leap from shadow into shadow unobserved.

He followed her until she reached the open, where a double row of trees on each side marked the edge of a big square, large enough for the drilling of an army. Along one side of the square there ran the high brick wall, topped with a kind of battlement, that guarded the Maharajah's palace grounds from the eyes of men.

Just as she turned, just as she was starting to canter her pony beside the long wall, he leaped out at her and seized her reins. The old woman screamed, and ran to the wall and cowered there.

Very likely the man only meant to frighten her and heap insults on her, for in '56, though wrath ran deep and strong, men waited. There was to be sudden, swift whelming when the time came, not intermittent outrage. But he had no time to do more than rein her pony back onto its haunches.

There came a clatter of scurrying hoofs behind, and from a whirl of dust, topped by a rose-pink pugree, a steel blade swooped down on her and him. A surge of brown and pink and cream, and a dozen rainbow tints flashed past her; a long boot brushed her saddle on the off side. There was a sickening sound, as something hard swished and whicked home; her pony reeled from the shock of a horse's shoulder, and—none too gently—none too modestly—the prince with the egret and the handsome face reined in on his horse's haunches and saluted her.

There was blood, becoming dull-brown in the dust between them. He shook his sabre, and the blood dripped from it; then he held it outstretched, and a horseman wiped it, before he returned it with a clang.

"The sahiba's servant!" he said magnificently, making no motion to let her pass, but twisting with his sword-hand at his waxed mustache and smiling darkly.

She looked down between them at the thing that but a minute since had lived, and loved perhaps as well as hated.

"Shame on you, Jaimihr-sahib!" she said, shuddering. A year ago she would have fallen from her pony in a swoon, but one year of Howrah and its daily horrors had so hardened her that she could look and loathe without the saving grace of losing consciousness.

"The shame would have been easier to realize,

had I taken more than one stroke!" he answered irritably, still blocking the way on his great horse, still twisting at his mustache point, still looking down at her through eyes that blazed a dozen accumulated centuries' store of lawless ambition. He was proud of that back-handed swipe of his that would cleave a man each time at one blow from shoulder-joint to ribs, severing the backbone. A woman of his own race would have been singing songs in praise of him and his skill in swordsmanship already; but no woman of his own race would have looked him in the eye like that and dared him, nor have done what she did next. She leaned over and swished his charger with her little whip, and slipped past him.

He swore, deep and fiercely, as he spurred and wheeled, and cantered after her. His great stallion could overhaul her pony in a minute, going stride for stride; the wall was more than two miles long with no break in it other than locked gates; there was no hurry. He watched her through half-closed, glowering, appraising eyes as he cantered in her wake, admiring the frail, slight figure in the gray cotton habit, and bridling his desire to make her— seize her reins, and halt, and make her—admit him master of the situation.

As he reached her stirrup, she reined in and faced him, after a hurried glance that told her her duenna had failed her. The old woman was invisible.

"Will you leave that body to lie there in the dust and sun?" she asked indignantly.

"I am no vulture, or jackal, or hyena, sahiba!"
he smiled. "I do not eat carrion!" He seemed to
think that that was a very good retort, for he showed
his wonderful white teeth until his handsome face
was the epitome of self-satisfied amusement. His
horse blocked the way again, and all retreat was
cut off, for his escort were behind her, and three of
them had ridden to the right, outside the row of
trees, to cut off possible escape in that direction.
"Was it not well that I was near, sahiba? Would
it have been better to die at the hands of a Maharati
of no caste——?"

"Than to see blood spilt—than to be beholden
to a murderer? Infinitely better! There was no
need to kill that man—I could have quieted him.
Let me pass, please, Jaimihr-sahib!"

He reined aside; but if she thought that cold
scorn or hot anger would either of them quell his
ardor, she had things reversed. The less she behaved as a native woman would have done—the
more she flouted him—the more enthusiastic he became.

"Sahiba!"—he trotted beside her, his great horse
keeping up easily with her pony's canter— "I
have told you oftener than once that I make a
good friend and a bad enemy!"

"And I have answered oftener than once that I
do not need your friendship, and am not afraid of
you! You forget that the British Government will
hold your royal brother liable for my safety and
my father's!"

"You, too, overlook certain things, sahiba." He spoke evenly, with a little space between each word. With the dark look that accompanied it, with the blood barely dry yet on the dusty road behind, his speech was not calculated to reassure a slip of a girl, gray-eyed or not, stiff-chinned or not, borne up or not by Scots enthusiasm for a cause. "This is a native state. My brother rules. The British——"

"Are near enough, and strong enough, to strike and to bring you and your brother to your knees if you harm a British woman!" she retorted. "You forget—when the British Government gives leave to missionaries to go into a native state, it backs them up with a strong arm!"

"You build too much on the British and my brother, sahiba! Listen—Howrah is as strong as I am, and no stronger. Had he been stronger, he would have slain me long ago. The British are——" He checked himself and trotted beside her in silence for a minute. She affected complete indifference; it was as though she had not heard him; if she could not be rid of him, she at least knew how to show him his utter unimportance in her estimation.

"Have you heard, sahiba, of the Howrah treasure? Of the rubies? Of the pearls? Of the emeralds? Of the bars of gold? It is foolishness, of course; we who are modern-minded see the crime of hoarding all that wealth, and adding to it, for twenty generations. Have you heard of it, sahiba?"

"Yes!" she answered savagely, swishing at his

charger again to make him keep his distance. "You
have told me of it twice. You have told me that
you know where it is, and you have offered to show
it to me. You have told me that you and your
brother Maharajah Howrah and the priests of Siva
are the only men who know where it is, and you
lust for that treasure! I can see you lust! You
think that I lust too, and you make a great mistake,
Jaimihr-sahib! You see, I remember what you have
told me. Now, go away and remember what I tell
you. I care for you and for your treasure exactly
that!" She hit his charger with all her might, and
at the sting of the little whip he shied clear of the
road before the Rajah's brother could rein him in.

Again her effort to destroy his admiration for her
had directly the opposite effect. He swore, and he
swore vengeance; but he swore, too, that there was
no woman in the East so worth a prince's while as
this one, who dared flout him with her riding-whip
before his men!

"Sahiba!" he said, sidling close to her again, and
bowing in the saddle in mock cavalier humility.
"The time will come when your government and
my brother, who—at present—is Maharajah Howrah—will be of little service to you. Then, perhaps, you may care to recall my promise to load all
the jewels you can choose out of the treasure-house
on you. Then, perhaps, you may remember that
I said 'a throne is better than a grave, sahiba.' Or
else——"

"Or else what, Jaimihr-sahib?" She reined again

and wheeled about and faced him—pale—trembling
a little—looking very small and frail beside him on
his great war-horse, but not flinching under his gaze
for a single second.

"Or else, sahiba— I think you saw me slay the
Maharati? Do you think that I would stop at
anything to accomplish what I had set out to do?
See, sahiba—there is a little blood there on your
jacket! Let that be for a pledge between us—for
a sign—for a token of my oath that on the day I
am Maharajah Howrah, you are Maharanee—mistress of all the jewels in the treasure-house!"

She shuddered. She did not look to find the
blood; she took his word for that, if for nothing
else.

"I wonder you dare tell me that you plot against
your brother!" That was more a spoken thought
than a statement or a question.

"I would be very glad if you would warn my
brother!" he answered her; and she knew like a
flash, and on the instant, that what he said was
true. She had been warned before she came to
bear no tales to any one. No Oriental would believe
the tale, coming from her; the Maharajah would
arrest her promptly, glad of the excuse to vent his
hatred of Christian missionaries. Jaimihr would
attempt a rescue; it was common knowledge that
he plotted for the throne. There would be instant
civil war, in which the British Government would
perforce back up the alleged protector of a defence-
less woman. There would be a new Maharajah;

then, in a little while, and in all likelihood, she would have disappeared forever while the war raged. There would be, no doubt, a circumstantial story of her death from natural causes.

She did not answer. She stared back at him, and he smiled down at her, twisting at his mustache.

"Think!" he said, nodding. "A throne, sahiba, is considerably better than a grave!" Then he wheeled like a sudden dust-devil and decamped in a cloud of dust, followed at full pelt by his clattering escort. She watched their horses leap one after the other the corpse of the Maharati that lay by the corner where it fell, and she saw the last of them go clattering, whirling up the street through the bazaar. The old hag rose out of a shadow and trotted after her again as she turned and rode on, pale-faced and crying now a little, to the little begged school place where her father tried to din the alphabet into a dozen low-caste fosterlings.

"Father!" she cried, and she all but fell out of the saddle into his arms as the tall, lean Scotsman came to the door to meet her and stood blinking in the sunlight. "Father, I've seen another man killed! I've had another scene with Jaimihr! I can't endure it! I—I— Oh, why did I ever come?"

"I don't know, dear," he answered. "But you *would* come, wouldn't you?"

CHAPTER II

'Twixt loot and law—'tween creed and caste—
Through slough this people wallows,
To where we choose our road at last.
I choose the RIGHT! Who follows?

HEMMED in amid the stifling stench and babel of
the caravansary, secluded by the very denseness of
the many-minded swarm, five other Rajputs and
Mahommed Gunga—all six, according to their turbans, followers of Islam—discussed matters that
appeared to bring them little satisfaction.

They sat together in a dark, low-ceilinged room;
its open door—it was far too hot to close anything
that admitted air—gave straight onto the street,
and the one big window opened on a courtyard,
where a pair of game-cocks fought in and out between the restless legs of horses, while a yelling
horde betted on them. On a heap of grass fodder
in a corner of the yard an all-but-naked expert
in inharmony thumped a skin tom-tom with his
knuckles, while at his feet the own-blood brother to
the screech-owls wailed of hell's torments on a wind
instrument.

Din — glamour — stink — incessant movement —
interblended poverty and riches rubbing shoulders—
noisy self-interest side by side with introspective

revery, where stray priests nodded in among the
traders,—many-peopled India surged in miniature
between the four hot walls and through the passage to the overflowing street; changeable and unexplainable, in ever-moving flux, but more con-
servative in spite of it than the very rocks she rests
on—India who is sister to Aholibah and mother
of all fascination.

In that room with the long window, low-growled,
the one thin thread of clear-sighted unselfishness
was reeling out to very slight approval. Mahommed Gunga paced the floor and kicked his toes
against the walls, as he turned at either end, until
his spurs jingled, and looked with blazing dark-
brown eyes from one man to the other.

"What good ever came of listening to priests?"
he asked. "All priests are alike—ours, and theirs,
and padre-sahibs! They all preach peace and goad
the lust that breeds war and massacre! Does a
priest serve any but himself? Since when? There
will come this rising that the priests speak of—yes!
Of a truth, there will, for the priests will see to it!
There is a padre-sahib here in Howrah now for
the Hindoo priests to whet their hate on. You saw
the woman ride past here a half-hour gone? There
is a pile of tinder ready here, and any fool of a priest
can make a spark! There will be a rising, and a big
one!"

"There will! Of a truth, there will!" Alwa,
his cousin, crossed one leg above the other with a
clink of spurs and scabbard. He had no objection

to betraying interest, but declined for the present
to betray his hand.

"There will be a blood-letting that will do no
harm to us Rajputs!" said another man, whose
eyes gleamed from the darkest corner; he, too,
clanked his scabbard as though the sound were an
obbligato to his thoughts. "Sit still and say nothing is my advice; we will be all ready to help our-
selves when the hour comes!"

"It is this way," said Mahommed Gunga, standing straddle-legged to face all five of them, with his
back to the window. He stroked his black beard
upward with one hand and fingered with the other
at his sabre-hilt. "Without aid when the hour does
come, the English will be smashed—worn down—
starved out—surrounded—stamped out—annihilated
—so!" He stamped with his heel descriptively on
the hard earth floor. "And then, what?"

"Then, the plunder!" said Alwa, showing a
double row of wonderful white teeth. The other
four grinned like his reflections.

"Ay, there will be plunder—for the priests!
And we Rajputs will have new masters over us!
Now, as things are, we have honorable men. They
are fools, for any man is a fool who will not see and
understand the signs. But they are honest. They
ride straight! They look us straight between the
eyes, and speak truth, and fear nobody! Will the
Hindoo priests, who will rule India afterward, be
thus? Nay! Here is one sword for the British when
the hour comes!"

"I have yet to see a Hindoo priest rule me or plunder me!" said Alwa with a grin.

"You will live to see it!" said Mahommed Gunga.
"Truly, you will live to see it, unless you throw your
weight into the other scale! What are we Rajputs
without a leader whom we all trust? What have
we ever been?" He swung on his heels suddenly
—angrily—and began to pace the floor again—then
stopped.

"Divided, and again subdivided—one-fifth Mohammedan and four-fifths Hindoo—clan within clan,
and each against the other. Do we own Rajputana?
Nay! Do we rule it? Nay! What were we until
Cunnigan-bahadur came?"

"Ah!" All five men rose with a clank in honor
to the memory of that man. "Cunnigan-bahadur!
Show us such another man as he was, and I and
mine ride at his back!" said Alwa. "Not all the
English are like Cunnigan! A Cunnigan could have
five thousand men the minute that he asked for
them!"

"Am I a wizard? Can I cast spells and bring
dead men's spirits from the dead again? I know
of no man to take his place," said Mahommed
Gunga sadly.

He was the poorest of them, but they were all,
comparatively speaking, poor men; for the long
peace had told its tale on a race of men who are
first gentlemen, then soldiers, and last—least of all
—and only as a last resource, landed proprietors.
The British, for whom they had often fought be-

cause that way honor seemed to lie, had impoverished them afterward by passing and enforcing zemindary laws that lifted nine-tenths of the burden from the necks of starving tenants. The new law was just, as the Rajputs grudgingly admitted, but it pinched their pockets sadly; like the old-time English squires, they would give their best blood and their last rack-rent-wrung rupee for the cause that they believed in, but they resented interference with the rack-rents! Mahommed Gunga had had influence enough with these five landlord relations of his to persuade them to come and meet him in Howrah City to discuss matters; the mere fact that he had thought it worth his while to leave his own little holding in the north had satisfied them that he would be well worth listening to—for no man rode six hundred miles on an empty errand. But they needed something more than words before they pledged the word that no Rajput gentleman will ever break.

"Find us a Cunnigan—bring him to us—prove him to us—and if a blade worth having from end to end of Rajputana is not at his service, I myself will gut the Hindoo owner of it! That is my given word!" said Alwa.

"He had a son," said Mahommed Gunga quietly.

"True. Are all sons like their fathers? Take Maharajah Howrah here; his father was a man with whom any soldier might be proud to pick a quarrel. The present man is afraid of his own shadow on the wall—divided between love for the

treasure-chests he dare not broach and fear of a
brother whom he dare not kill. He is priest-ridden,
priest-taught, and fit to be nothing but a priest.
Who knows how young Cunnigan will shape?
Where is he? Overseas yet! He must prove himself, as his father did, before he can hope to lead a
free regiment of horse!"

"Then Cunnigan-bahadur's watch-word 'For the
peace of India,' is dead—died with him?" asked Mahommed Gunga. "We are each for our own again?"

"I have spoken!" answered Alwa. As the biggest clan-chief left on all that countryside, he had a
right to speak before the others, and he knew that
what he said would carry weight when they had all
ridden home again, and the report had gone abroad
in ever-widening rings. "If the English can hold
India, let them! I will not fight against them, for
they are honest men for all their madness. If they
cannot, then I am for Rajputana, not India—India
may burn or rot or burst to pieces, so long as Rajputana stands! But—" He paused a moment,
and looked at each man in turn, and tapped his
sabre-hilt, "—if a Cunnigan-bahadur were among
us—a man whom I could trust to lead me and mine
and every man—I would lend him my sword for
the sheer honor of helping him hack truth out of
corruption! I have nothing more to say!"

"One word more, cousin!" said Mahommed
Gunga. "I was risaldar in Cunnigan-bahadur's
regiment of horse. There was more than mere discipline between us. I ate his salt. Once—when he

might have saved himself the trouble without any daring to reproach him—he risked his own life, and a troop, and his reputation to save a woman of my family from capture, and something worse. There was never a Rajput or any other native woman wronged while he was with us."

"Well?"

"I am no friend of Christian priests—of padres. But——"

"She who rode by just now? What, then?"

"I ride northward now, and then very likely south again. I can do nothing in the matter, yet— were he in my shoes, and she a native woman at the mercy of the troops—Cunnigan-bahadur would have assigned a guard for her."

"Ho! So I am thy sepoy?" sneered Alwa, standing sideways—looking sideways—and throwing out his chest. "I am to do thy bidding, guarding stray padres" (he spoke the word as though it were a bad taste he was spitting from his mouth), "and herding women without purdah, while thou ridest on assignations Allah knows where? Since when?"

"I have yet to refuse to guard thy back, or thy good name, Alwa!" Mahommed Gunga eyed him straight, and thrust his hilt out. "The woman is nothing to me—the padre-sahib less. It is because of the debt I owe to Cunnigan that I ask this favor."

"Oh. It is granted! Should she appeal to me, I will rip Howrah into rags and burn this city to protect her if need be! She must first ask, though, even as thou didst."

Mahommed Gunga saluted him, bolt-upright as a lance, and without the slightest change in his expression.

"The word is sufficient, cousin!"

Alwa returned his salute, and raised his voice in a gruff command. A saice outside the window woke as though struck by a stick—sprang to his feet—and passed the order on. A dozen horses clattered in the courtyard and filed through the arched passage to the street, and Alwa mounted. The others, each with his escort, followed suit, and a moment later, with no further notice of one another, but with as much pomp and noise as though they owned the whole of India, the five rode off, each on his separate way, through the scattering crowd.

Then Mahommed Gunga called for his own horse and the lone armed man of his own race who acted squire to him.

"Did any overhear our talk?" he asked.

"No, sahib."

"Not the saice, even?"

"No, sahib. He slept."

"He awoke most suddenly, and at not much noise."

"For that reason I know he slept, sahib. Had he been pretending, he would have wakened slowly."

"Thou art no idiot!" said Mahommed Gunga. "Wait here until I return, and lie a few lies if any ask thee why we six came together, and of what we spoke!"

Then he mounted and rode off slowly, picking his

way through the throng much more cautiously and
considerately than his relatives had done, though
not, apparently, because he loved the crowd. He
used some singularly biting insults to help clear the
way, and frowned as though every other man he
looked at were either an assassin or—what a good
Mohammedan considers worse—an infidel. He
reached the long brick wall at last—broke into a
canter—scattered the pariah dogs that were nosing
and quarrelling about the corpse of the Maharati,
and drew rein fifteen minutes later by the door of
the tiny school place that Miss McClean had entered.

CHAPTER III

For service truly rendered, and for duty dumbly done—
For men who neither tremble nor forget—
There is due reward, my henchman. There is honor to be won.
There is watch and ward and sterner duty yet.

No sound came from within the schoolhouse. The little building, coaxed from a grudging Maharajah, seemed to strain for light and air between two overlapping, high-walled brick warehouses. Before the door, in a spot where the scorching sun-rays came but fitfully between a mesh of fast-decaying thatch, the old hag who had followed Rosemary McClean lay snoozing, muttering to herself, and blinking every now and then as a street dog blinks at the passers-by. She took no notice of Mahommed Gunga until he swore at her.

"Miss-sahib hai?" he growled; and the woman jumped up in a hurry and went inside. A moment later Rosemary McClean stood framed in the doorway still in her cotton riding-habit, very pale—evidently frightened at the summons—but strangely, almost ethereally, beautiful. Her wealth of chestnut hair was loosely coiled above her neck, as though she had been caught in the act of dressing it. She looked like the wan, wasted spirit of human pity—he like a great, grim war-god.

26

"Salaam, Miss Maklin-sahib!"

He dismounted as he spoke and stood at attention, then stared truculently, too inherently chivalrous to deny her civility—he would have cut his throat as soon as address her from horseback while she stood—and too contemptuous of her father's calling to be more civil than he deemed in keeping with his honor.

"Salaam, Mohammed Gunga!" She seemed very much relieved, although doubtful yet. "Not letters again?"

"No, Miss-sahib. I am no mail-carrier! I brought those letters as a favor to Franklin-sahib at Peshawur; I was coming hither, and he had no man to send. I will take letters, since I am now going, if there are letters ready; I ride to-night."

"Thank you, Mahommed Gunga. I have letters for England. They are not yet sealed. May I send them to you before you start?"

"I will send my man for them. Also, Miss Maklin-sahib" (heavens! how much cleaner and better that sounded than the prince's ironical "sahiba"!) "if you wish it, I will escort you to Peshawur, or to any city between here and there."

"But—but why?"

"I saw Jaimihr. I know Jaimihr."

"And——"

"And—this is no place for a padre, or for the daughter of a padre."

What he said was true, but it was also insolent, said insolently.

"Mahommed Gunga-sahib, what are those ribbons on your breast?" she asked him.

He glanced down at them, and his expression changed a trifle; it was scarcely perceptible, but underneath his fierce mustache the muscles of his mouth stiffened.

"They are medal ribbons—for campaigns," he answered.

"Three—four—five! Then, you were a soldier a long time? Did you—did you desert your post when there was danger?"

He flushed, and raised his hand as though about to speak.

"Or did people insult you when you chose to remain on duty?"

"Miss-sahib, I have not insulted you!" said Mahommed Gunga. "I came here for another purpose."

"You came, very kindly, to ask whether there were letters. Thank you, Mahommed Gunga-sahib, for your courtesy. There are letters, and I will give them to your man, if you will be good enough to send him for them."

He still stood there, staring at her with eyes that did not blink. He was too much of a soldier to admit himself at a loss what to say, yet he had no intention of leaving Howrah without saying it, for that, too, would have been unsoldierly.

"The reason why your countrymen have found men of this land before now to fight for them—one reason, at least—" he said gruffly, "is that hitherto they have not meddled with our religions. It is not safe! It would be better to come away, Miss-sahib."

"Would you like to say that to my father? He is——"

"Allah forbid that I should argue with him! I spoke to you, on your account!"

"You forget, I think," she answered him gently, "that we had permission from the British Government to come here; it has not been withdrawn. We are doing no harm here—trying only to do good. There is always danger when——"

"I would speak of that," he interrupted. "You will not come away?"

She shook her head.

"Your father could remain."

She shook her head again. "I stay with him," she answered.

"At present, Jaimihr is the danger, Miss-sahib; but I think that at present he will dare do nothing. The Maharajah dare do nothing either, yet. Should either of them make a move to interfere with you, it would not be safe to appeal to the other one. You will not understand, but it is so. In that event, there is a way to safety of which I would warn you."

"Thank you, Mahommed Gunga. What is it?"

"There are men more than a day's ride away from here who are to be depended on—by you, at least—under all circumstances. Is that old woman to be trusted?"

"How should I know?" she smiled. "I believe she is fond of me."

"That should be enough. I would like, if the Miss-sahib will permit, to speak with her."

At a word from Miss McClean the old hag came out into the sun again and blinked at the Rajput, very much afraid of him. Mahommed Gunga saluted Miss McClean—swore at the old woman —pointed a wordless order with his right arm— watched her shuffle half a hundred yards up-street —followed her, and growled at her for about five minutes, while she nodded. Finally, he drew from the pocket of his crimson coat a small handful of gold mohurs—fat, dignified coins that glittered— and held them out toward her with an air as though they meant nothing to him—positively nothing. Her eyes gleamed. He let her take a good look at the money before replacing it, then tossed her a silver quarter-rupee piece, saluted Miss McClean again—for she was watching the pantomime from the doorway still—and mounted and rode off, his back looking like the back of one who has neither care nor fear nor master.

At the caravansary his squire came running out to hold his stirrup.

"Picket the horse in the yard," said Mahommed Gunga, "then find me another servant and bring him to me in the room here!"

"Another servant? But, sahib——"

"I said another servant! Has deafness overcome thee?" He used a word in the dialect which left no

room for doubt as to his meaning; it was to be a
different servant—a substitute for the squire he had
already. The squire bowed his head in disciplined
obedience and led the horse away.

An hour later—evening was drawing on—he came
back, followed by a somewhat ruffianly-looking half-
breed Rajput-Punjaubi. The new man was rather
ragged and lacked one eye, but with the single eye
he had he looked straight at his prospective master.
Mahommed Gunga glared at him, but the man did
not quail or shrink.

"This fellow wishes honorable service, sahib."
The squire spoke as though he were calling his
master's attention to a horse that was for sale. "I
have seen his family; I have inquired about him;
and I have explained to him that unless he serves
thee faithfully his wife and his man child will die
at my hands in his absence."

"Can he groom a horse?"

"So he says, sahib, and so say others."

"Can he fight?"

"He slew the man with his bare hands who pricked
his eye out with a sword."

"Oh! What payment does he ask?"

"He leaves that matter to your honor's pleasure."

"Good. Instruct him, then. Set him to clean-
ing my horse and then return here."

The squire was back again within five minutes
and stood before Mahommed Gunga in silent ex-
pectation.

"I shall miss thee," said Mahommed Gunga

after five minutes' reflection. "It is well that I have other servants in the north."

"In what have I offended, sahib?"

"In nothing. Therefore there is a trust imposed."

The man salaamed. Mahommed Gunga produced his little handful of gold mohurs and divided it into two equal portions; one he handed to the squire.

"Stay here. Be always either in the caravansary, or else at call. Should the old woman who serves Miss Maklin-sahib, the padre-sahib's daughter, come and ask thy aid, then saddle swiftly the three horses I will leave with thee, and bear Miss Maklin-sahib and her father to my cousin Alwa's place. Present two of the gold mohurs to the hag, should that happen."

"But, sahib—two mohurs? I could buy ten such hags outright for the price!"

"She has my word in the matter! It is best to have her eager to win great reward. The hag will stay awake, but see to it that thou sleepest not!"

"And for how long must I stay here, sahib?"

"One month—six months—a year—who knows? Until the hag summons thee, or I, by writing or by word of mouth, relieve thee of thy trust."

At sunset he sent the squire to Miss McClean for the letters he had promised to deliver; and at one hour after sunset, when the heat of the earth had begun to rise and throw back a hot blast to the darkened sky and the little eddies of luke-warm surface wind made movement for horse and man less like a fight with scorching death, he rode off, with his new servant, on the two horses left to him of the five with which he came.

A six-hundred-mile ride without spare horses, in the heat of northern India, was an undertaking to have made any strong man flinch. The stronger the man, and the more soldierly, the better able he would be to realize the effort it would call for. But Mahommed Gunga rode as though he were starting on a visit to a near-by friend; he was not given to crossing bridges before he reached them, nor to letting prospects influence his peace of mind. He was a soldier. He took precautions first, when and where such were possible, then rode and looked fate in the eye.

He appeared to take no more notice of the glowering looks that followed him from stuffy balconies and dense-packed corners than of the mosquitoes and the heat. Without hurry he picked his way through the thronged streets, where already men lay in thousands to escape the breathlessness of walled interiors; the gutters seemed like trenches where the dead of a devastated city had been laid; the murmur was like the voice of storm-winds gathering, and the little lights along the housetops were the vent-holes on the lid of a tormented underworld.

But he rode on at his ease. Ahead of him lay that which he considered duty. He could feel the long-kept peace of India disintegrating all around him, and he knew—he was certain—as sometimes a brave man can see what cleverer men all overlook —that the right touch by the right man at the right moment, when the last taut-held thread should break, would very likely swing the balance in favor of peace again, instead of individual self-seeking anarchy.

He knew what "Cunnigan-bahadur" would have done. He swore by Cunnigan-bahadur. And by the memory of that same dead, desperately honest Cunningham he swore that no personal profit or convenience or safety should be allowed to stand between him and what was honorable and right. Mahommed Gunga had no secrets from himself, nor lack of imagination. He knew that he was riding—not to preserve the peace of India, for that was as good as gone—but to make possible the winning back of it. And he rode with a smile on his thin lips, as the crusaders once rode on a less self-advertising errand.

CHAPTER IV

"You have failed!" whispered Fate, and a weary civilian
Threw up his task as a matter of course.
"Failed?" said the soldier. He knew a million
Chances untackled yet. "Get me a horse!"

THAT was a strange ride of Mahommed Gunga's, and a fateful one—more full of portent for the British Raj in India than he, or the British, or the men amid whose homes he rode could ever have anticipated. He averaged a little less than twenty miles a day, and through an Indian hot-weather, and with no spare horse, none but a born horseman —a man of light weight and absolute control of temper—could have accomplished that for thirty days on end.

Wherever he rode there was the same unrest. Here and there were new complaints he had not yet heard of, imaginary some of them, and some only too well founded. Wherever there were Rajputs—and that race of fighting men is scattered all about the north—there was ill-suppressed impatience for the bursting of the wrath to come. They bore no grudge against the English, but they did bear more than grudge against the money-lenders and the fat, litigious traders who had fattened under British rule. At least at the beginning it was evi-

dent that all the interest of all the Rajputs lay in
letting the British get the worst of it; even should
the British suddenly wake up and look about them
and take steps—or should the British hold their
own with native aid, and so save India from anarchy, and afterward reward the men who helped—
the Rajputs would stand to gain less individually,
or even collectively, than if they let the English be
driven to the sea, and then reverted to the age-old
state of feudal lawlessness that once had made them
rich.

Many of the Hindoo element among them were
almost openly disloyal. The ryots—the little one
and two acre farmers—were the least unsettled;
they, when he asked them—and he asked often—
disclaimed the least desire to change a rule that
gave them safe holdings and but one tax-collection a
year; they were frankly for their individual selves—
not even for one another, for the ryots as a class.

Nobody seemed to be for India, except Mahommed
Gunga; and he said little, but asked ever-repeated
questions as he rode. There were men who would
like to weld Rajputana into one again, and override the rest of India; and there were other men who
planned to do the same for the Punjaub; there
were plots within plots, not many of which he
learned in anything like detail, but none of which
were more than skin-deep below the surface. All
men looked to the sudden, swift, easy whelming
of the British Raj, and then to the plundering of
India; each man expected to be rich when the

whelming came, and each man waited with ill-controlled impatience for the priests' word that would let loose the hundred-million flood of anarchy.

"And one man—one real man whom they trusted —one leader—one man who had one thousand at his back—could change the whole face of things!" he muttered to himself. "Would God there were a Cunnigan! But there is no Cunnigan. And who would follow me? They would pull my beard, and tell me I was scheming for my own ends!—I, who was taught by Cunnigan, and would serve only India!"

He would ride before dawn and when the evening breeze had come to cool the hot earth a little; through the blazing afternoons he would lie in the place of honor by some open window, where he could watch a hireling flick the flies off his lean, road-hardened horse, and listen to the plotting and the carried tales of plots, pretending always to be sympathetic or else open to conviction.

"A soldier? Hah! A soldier fights for the side that can best reward him!" he would grin. "And, when there is no side, perhaps he makes one! I am a soldier!"

If they pressed him, he would point to his medal ribbons, that he always wore. "The British gave me those for fighting against the northern tribes beyond the Himalayas," he would tell them. "The southern tribes—Bengalis of the south and east —would give better picking than mere medal ribbons!"

They were not all sure of him. They were not all satisfied why he should ride on to Peshawur, and decline to stay with them and talk good sedition.

"I would see how the British are!" he told them. And he told the truth. But they were not quite satisfied; he would have made a splendid leader to have kept among them, until he—too—became too powerful and would have to be deposed in turn.

His own holding was a long way from Peshawur, and he was no rich man who could afford at a mere whim to ride two long days' march beyond his goal. Nor was he, as he had explained to Miss McClean, a letter-carrier; he would get no more than the merest thanks for delivering her letters to where they could be included in the Government mail-bag. Yet he left the road that would have led him homeward to his left, and carried on—quickening his pace as he neared the frontier garrison town, and wasting, then, no time at all on seeking information. Nobody supposed that the Pathans and the other frontier tribes were anything but openly rebellious, and he would have been an idiot to ask questions about their loyalty.

Because of their disloyalty, and the ever-present danger that they were, the biggest British garrison in India had to be kept cooped up in Peshawur, to rot with fever and ague and the other ninety Indian plagues.

He wanted to see that garrison again, and estimate it, and make up his mind what exactly, or probably, the garrison would do in the event of the rebellion blazing out. And he wanted to try once more to warn some one in authority, and make him see the smouldering fire beneath the outer covering of sullen silence.

He received thanks for the letters. He received an invitation to take tea on the veranda of an officer so high in the British service that many a staff major would have given a month's pay for a like opportunity. But he was laughed at for the advice he had to give.

"Mahommed Gunga, you're like me, you're getting old!" said the high official.

"Not so very old, sahib. I was a young man when Cunnigan-bahadur raised a regiment and licked the half of Rajputana into shape with it. Not too old, sahib, to wish there were another Cunnigan to ride with!"

"Well, Mahommed Gunga, you're closer to your wish than you suppose!. Young Cunningham's gazetted, and probably just about starting on his way out here via the Cape of Good Hope. He should be here in three or four months at the outside."

"You mean that, sahib?"

"Wish I didn't! The puppy will arrive here with altogether swollen notions of his own importance and what is due his father's son. He's been captain of his college at home, and that won't lessen his sense of self-esteem either. I can foresee trouble with that boy!"

"Sahib, there is a service I could render!"

The Rajput spoke with a strangely constrained

voice all of a sudden, but the Commissioner did
not notice it; he was too busy pulling on a wool-
lined jacket to ward off the evening chill.

"Well, risaldar—what then?"

"I think that I could teach the son of Cunnigan-
bahadur to be worth his salt."

"If you'll teach him to be properly respectful
to his betters I'll be grateful to you, Mahommed
Gunga."

"Then, sahib, I shall have certain license allowed
me in the matter?"

"Do anything you like, in reason, risaldar! Only
keep the pup from cutting his eye-teeth on his
seniors' convenience, that's all!"

Mahommed Gunga wasted no time after that on
talking, nor did he wait to specify the nature of
the latitude he would expect to be allowed him;
he knew better. And he knew now that the one
chance that he sought had been given him.

Like all observant natives, he was perfectly aware
that the British weakness mostly lay in the age of
the senior officers and the slowness of promotion.
There were majors of over fifty years of age, and if
a man were a general at seventy he was considered
fortunate and young. The jealousy with which
younger men were regarded would have been hu-
morous had it not come already so near to plunging
India into anarchy.

He did not even trouble to overlook the garrison.
He took his leave, and rode away the long two-day
ride to his own place, where a sadly attenuated rent-

roll and a very sadly thinned-down company of servants waited his coming. There, through fourteen hurried, excited days, he made certain arrangements about the disposition of his affairs during an even longer absence; he made certain sales—pledged the rent of fifty acres for ten years, in return for an advance—and on the fifteenth day rode southward, at the head of a five-man escort that, for quality, was worthy of a prince.

A little less than three months later he arrived at Bombay, and by dint of much hard bargaining and economy fitted out himself and his escort, so that each man looked as though he were the owner of an escort of his own. Then, fretful at every added day that strained his fast-diminishing resources, he settled down to wait until the ship should come that brought young Cunningham.

CHAPTER V

Lies home beneath a sickly sun,
Where humbleness was taught me?
Or here, where spurs my father won
On bended knee are brought me?

HE landed, together with about a dozen other newly gazetted subalterns and civil officers, cramped, storm-tossed, snubbed, and then disgorged from a sailing-ship into a port that made no secret of its absolute contempt for new arrivals.

There were liners of a kind on the Red Sea route, and the only seniors who chose the long passage round the Cape were men returning after sick-leave—none too sweet-tempered individuals, and none too prone to give the young idea a good conceit of himself. He and the other youngsters landed with a crushed-in notion that India would treat them very cavalierly before she took them to herself. And all, save Cunningham, were right.

The other men, all homesick and lonely and bewildered, were met by bankers' agents, or, in cases, only by a hotel servant armed with a letter of instructions. Here and there a bored, tired-eyed European had found time, for somebody-or-other's sake, to pounce on a new arrival and bear him away to breakfast and a tawdry imitation of the real hos-

pitality of northern India; but for the most part
the beardless boys lounged in the red-hot customs
shed (where they were to be mulcted for the privilege of serving their country) and envied young
Cunningham.

He—as pale as they, as unexpectant as they were
of anything approaching welcome—was first amazed,
then suspicious, then pleased, then proud, in turn.
The different emotions followed one another across
his clean-lined face as plainly as a dawn vista changes;
then, as the dawn leaves a landscape finally, true
and what it is for all to see, true dignity was left
and the look of a man who stands in armor.

"His father's son!" growled Mahommed Gunga;
and the big, black-bearded warriors who stood behind him echoed, "Ay!"

But for four or five inches of straight stature,
and a foot, perhaps, of chest-girth, he was a second
edition of the Cunnigan-bahadur who had raised
and led a regiment and licked peace into a warring
countryside; and though he was that much bigger
than his father had been, they dubbed him "Chota"
Cunnigan on the instant. And that means "Little
Cunningham."

He had yet to learn that a Rajput, be he poorest
of the poor, admits no superior on earth. He did
not know yet that these men had come, at one
man's private cost, all down the length of India
to meet him. Nobody had told him that the feudal
spirit dies harder in northern Hindustan than it
ever did in England, or that the Rajput clans cohere

more tightly than the Scots. The Rajput belief that honest service—unselfishly given—is the greatest gift that any man may bring—that one who has received what he considers favors will serve the giver's son—was an unknown creed to him as yet.

But he stood and looked those six men in the eye, and liked them. And they, before they had as much as heard him speak, knew him for a soldier and loved him as he stood.

They hung sickly scented garlands round his neck, and kissed his hand in turn, and spoke to him thereafter as man to man. They had found their goal worth while, and they bore him off to his hotel in clattering glee, riding before him as men who have no doubt of the honor that they pay themselves. No other of the homesick subalterns drove away with a six-man escort to clear the way and scatter sparks!

They careered round through the narrow gate of the hotel courtyard as though a Viceroy at least were in the trap behind them; and Mahommed Gunga —six medalled, strapping feet of him—dismounted and held out an arm for him to take when he alighted. The hotel people understood at once that Somebody from Somewhere had arrived.

Young Cunningham had never yet been somebody. The men who give their lives for India are nothing much at home, and their sons are even less. Scarcely even at school, when they had made him captain of the team, had he felt the feel of homage and the subtle flattery that undermines a bad man's character; at schools in England they confer honors but take simultaneous precautions. He was green to the dangerous influence of feudal loyalty, but he quitted himself well, with reserve and dignity.

"He is good! He will do!" swore Mahommed Gunga fiercely, for the other emotions are meant for women only.

"He is better than the best!"

"We will make a man of this one!"

"Did you mark how he handed me his purse to defray expenses?" asked a black-bearded soldier of the five.

"He is a man who knows by instinct!" said Mahommed Gunga. "See to it that thy accounting is correct, and overpay no man!"

Deep-throated as a bull, erect as a lance, and pleased as a little child, Mahommed Gunga came to him alone that evening to talk, and to hear him talk, and to tell him of the plans that had been made.

"Thy father gave me this," he told him, producing a gold watch and chain of the hundred-guinea kind that nowadays are only found among the heirlooms. Young Cunningham looked at it, and recognized the heavy old-gold case that he had been allowed to "blow open" when a little boy. On the outside, deep-chiselled in the gold, was his father's crest, and on the inside a portrait of his mother.

"Thy father died in these two arms, bahadur! Thy father said: 'Look after him, Mahommed Gunga, when the time is ripe for him to be a soldier.'

And I said: 'Ha, huzoor!' So! Then. here is India!"

He waved one hand grandiloquently, as though he were presenting the throne of India to his protégé!

"Here, sahib, is a servant—blood of my own blood."

He clapped his hands, and a man who looked like the big, black-ended spirit of Aladdin's lamp stood silent, instant, in the doorway.

"He speaks no English, but he may help to teach thee the Rajput tongue, and he will serve thee well —on *my* honor. His throat shall answer for it! Feed him and clothe him, sahib, but pay him very little—to serve well is sufficient recompense."

Young Cunningham gave his keys at once to the silent servant, as a tacit sign that from that moment he was trusted utterly; and Mahommed Gunga nodded grim approval.

"Thy father saw fit to bequeath me much in the hour when death came on him, sahib. I am no boaster, as *he* knew. Remember, then, to tell me if I fail at any time in what is due. I am at thy service!"

Tact was inborn in Cunningham, as it had been in his father. He realized that he ought at once to show his appreciation of the high plane of the service offered.

"There is one way in which you could help me almost at once, Mahommed Gunga," he answered.

"Command me, sahib."

"I need your advice—the advice of a man who

really knows. I need horses, and—at first at least
—I would rather trust your judgment than my own.
Will you help me buy them?"

The Rajput's eyes blazed pleasure. On war, and
wine, and women, and a horse are the four points to
ask a man's advice and win his approval by the
asking.

"Nay, sahib; why buy horses here? These Bombay traders have only crows' meat to sell to the ill-
advised. I have horses, and spare horses for the
journey; and in Rajputana I have horses waiting
for thee—seven, all told—sufficient for a young
officer. Six of them are country-bred—sand-weaned
—a little wild perhaps, but strong, and up to thy
weight. The seventh is a mare, got by thy father's
stallion Aga Khan (him that made more than a
hundred miles within a day under a fifteen-stone
burden, with neither food nor water, and survived!).
A good mare, sahib—indeed a mare of mares—fit for
thy father's son. That mare I give thee. It is little,
sahib, but my best; I am a poor man. The other
six I bought—there is the account. I bought them
cheaply, paying less than half the price demanded in
each case—but I had to borrow and must pay back."

Young Cunningham was hard put to it to keep
his voice steady as he answered. This man was a
stranger to him. He had a hazy recollection of a
dozen or more bearded giants who formed a moving
background to his dreams of infancy, and he had
expected some sort of welcome from one or two,
perhaps, of his father's men when he reached the

north. But to have men borrow money that they might serve him, and have horses ready for him, and to be met like this at the gate of India by a man who admitted he was poor, was a little more than his self-control had been trained as yet to stand.

"I won't waste words, Mahommed Gunga," he said, half-choking. "I'll—er—I'll try to prove how I feel about it."

"Ha! How said I? Thy father's son, I said! He, too, was no believer in much promising! I was his servant, and will serve him still by serving thee. The honor is mine, sahib, and the advantage shall be where thy father wished it."

"My father would never have had me——"

"Sahib, forgive the interruption, but a mistake is better checked. Thy father would have flung thee, ungrudged, into a hell of bayonets, me, too, and would have followed after, if by so doing he could have served the cause he held in trust. He bred thee, fed thee, and sent thee oversea to grow, that in the end India might gain! Thou and I are but servants of the peace, as he was. If I serve thee, and thou the Raj—though the two of us were weaned on the milk of war and get our bread by war—we will none the less serve peace! Aie! For what is honor if a soldier lets it rust? Of what use is service, mouthed and ready, but ungiven? It is good, Chota-Cunnigan-bahadur, that thou art come at last!"

He saluted and backed out through the swinging door. He had come in his uniform of risaldar of

the elder Cunningham's now disbanded regiment, so
he had not removed his boots as another native—
and he himself if in mufti—would have done. Young
Cunningham heard him go swaggering and clank-
ing and spur-jingling down the corridor as though
he had half a troop of horse behind him and wanted
Asia to know it!

It was something of a brave beginning, that, for
a twenty-one-year-old! Something likely—and ex-
pressly calculated by Mahommed Gunga—to bring
the real man to the surface. He had been no Cunningham unless his sense of duty had been very
near the surface; no Englishman, had he not been
proud that men of a foreign, conquered race should
think him worthy of all that honor; and no man at
all if his eye had been quite dry when the veteran
light-horseman swaggered out at last and left him
to his own reflections.

He had not been human if he had not felt a little
homesick still, although home to him had been a
place where a man stayed with distant relatives
between the intervals of school. He felt lonely, in
spite of his reception—a little like a baby on the
edge of all things new and wonderful. He would
have been no European if he had not felt the heat;
the hotel was like a vapor-bath.

But the leaping red blood of youth ran strong
in him. He had imagination. He could dream.
The good things he was tasting were a presage
only of the better things to come, and that is a
wholesome point of view. He was proud—as who

would not be?—to step straight into the tracks of
such a father; and with that thought came another
—just as good for him, and for India, that made
him feel as though he were a robber yet, a thief in
another's corn-field, gathering what he did not sow.
It came over him in a flood that he must pay the
price of all this homage.

Some men pay in advance, some at the time, and
some pay afterward. All men, he knew, must pay.
It would be his task soon to satisfy these gentlemen, who took him at his face value, by proving to
them that they had made no very great mistake. The
thought thrilled him instead of frightening—brought
out every generous instinct that he had and made
him thank the God of All Good Soldiers that at
least he would have a chance to die in the attempt.
There was nothing much the matter with young
Cunningham.

CHAPTER VI

I take no man at rumor's price,
  Nor as the gossips cry him.
A son may ride, and stride, and stand;
  His father's eye—his father's hand—
His father's tongue may give command;
  But ere I trust I'll try him!

BUT before young Cunningham was called upon
to pay even a portion of the price of fealty there
was more of the receiving of it still in store for him,
and he found himself very hard put to it, indeed, to
keep overboiling spirits from becoming exultation
of the type that nauseates.

None of the other subalterns had influence, nor
had they hereditary anchors in the far northwest
that would be likely to draw them on to active service early in their career. They had already been
made to surrender their boyhood dreams of quick
promotion; now, standing in little groups and asking hesitating questions, they discovered that their
destination—Fort William—was about the least de-
sirable of all the awful holes in India.

They were told that a subaltern was lucky who
could mount one step of the promotion ladder in his
first ten years; that a major at fifty, a colonel at
sixty, and a general at seventy were quite the usual
thing. And they realized that the pay they would

receive would be a mere beggar's pittance in a neighborhood so expensive as Calcutta, and that their
little private means would be eaten up by the mere
necessities of life. They showed their chagrin,
and it was not very easy for young Cunningham,
watching Mahommed Gunga's lordly preparations
for the long up-country journey, to strike just the
right attitude of pleasure at the prospect without
seeming to flaunt his better fortune.

Mahommed Gunga interlarded his hoarse orders
to the mule-drivers with descriptions in stateliest
English, thrown out at random to the world at
large, of the glories of the manlier north—of the
plains, where a man might gallop while a horse
could last, and of the mountains up beyond the
plains. He sniffed at the fetid Bombay reek, and
spoke of the clean air sweeping from the snow-topped
Himalayas, that put life and courage into the lungs
of men who rode like centaurs! And the other subalterns looked wistful, eying the bullock-carts that
would take their baggage by another route.

Fully the half of what Mahommed Gunga said
was due to pride of race and country. But the rest
was all deliberately calculated to rouse the wicked
envy of those who listened. He meant to make this
son of "Pukka" Cunnigan feel, before he reached
his heritage, that he was going up to something
worth his while. To quote his own north-country
metaphor, he meant to "make the colt come up to
the bit." He meant that "Chota" Cunnigan should
have a proper sense of his own importance, and

should chafe at restraint, to the end that when his chance did come to prove himself he would jump at it. Envy, he calculated—the unrighteous envy of men less fortunately placed—would make a good beginning. And it did, though hardly in the way he calculated.

Young Cunningham, tight-lipped to keep himself from grinning like a child, determined to prove himself worthy of the better fortune; and Mahommed Gunga would have cursed into his black beard in disgust had he known of the private resolutions being formed to obey orders to the letter and obtain the good will of his seniors. The one thing that the grim old Rajput wished for his protégé was jealousy! He wanted him so well hated by the "nabobs" who had grown crusty and incompetent in high command that life for him in any northern garrison would be impossible.

Throughout the two months' journey to the north Mahommed Gunga never left a stone unturned to make Cunningham believe himself much more than ordinary clay. All along the trunk road, that trails by many thousand towns and listens to a hundred languages, whatever good there was was Cunningham's. Whichever room was best in each dak-bungalow, whichever chicken the kansamah least desired to kill, whoever were the stoutest dhoolee-bearers in the village, whichever horse had the easiest paces—all were Cunningham's. Respect were his, and homage and obeisance, for the Rajput saw to it.

Of evenings, while they rested, but before the sun went down, the old risaldar would come with his naked sabre and defy "Chota" Cunnigan to try to touch him. For five long weeks he tried each evening, the Rajput never doing anything but parry,— changing his sabre often to the other hand and grinning at the schoolboy swordsmanship—until one evening, at the end of a more than usually hard-fought bout, the youngster pricked him, lunged, and missed slitting his jugular by the merest fraction of an inch.

"Ho!" laughed Mahommed Gunga later, as he sluiced out the cut while his own adherents stood near by and chaffed him. "The cub cuts his teeth, then! Soon it will be time to try his pluck."

"Be gentle with him, risaldar-sahib; a good cub dies as easily as a poor one, until he knows the way."

"Leave him to me! I will show him the way, and we will see what we will see. If he is to disgrace his father's memory and us, he shall do it where there are few to see and none to talk of it. When Alwa and the others ask me, as they will ask, 'Is he a man?' I will give them a true answer! I think he is a man, but I need to test him in all ways possible before I pledge my word on it."

But after that little accident the old risaldar had sword-sticks fashioned at a village near the road, and ran no more risks of being killed by the stripling he would teach; and before many more days of the road had ribboned out, young Cunningham—bareback or from the saddle—could beat him to the ground, and could hold his own on foot afterward with either hand.

"The hand and eye are good!" said Mahommed Gunga. "It is time now for another test."

So he made a plausible excuse about the horses, and they halted for four days at a roadside dak-bungalow about a mile from where a foul-mouthed fakir sat and took tribute at a crossroads. It was a strangely chosen place to rest at.

Deep down in a hollow, where the trunk road took advantage of a winding gorge between the hills —screened on nearly all sides by green jungle whose brown edges wilted in the heat which the inner steam defied—stuffy, smelly, comfortless, it stood like a last left rear-guard of a white-man's city, swamped by the deathless, ceaselessly advancing tide of green. It was tucked between mammoth trees that had been left there when the space for it was cleared a hundred years before, and that now stood like grim giant guardians with arms out-stretched to hold the verdure back.

The little tribe of camp-followers chased at least a dozen snakes out of corners, and slew them in the open, as a preliminary to further investigation. There were kas-kas mats on the foursquare floors, and each of these, when lifted, disclosed a swarm of scorpions that had to be exterminated before a man dared move his possessions in. The once white calico ceilings moved suggestively where rats and snakes chased one another, or else hunted some third species of vermin; and there was a smell and a many-voiced weird whispering that hinted at corruption and war to the death behind skirting boards and underneath the floor.

It had evidently not been occupied for many years; the kansamah looked like a gray-bearded skeleton compressed within a tightened shroud of parchment skin that shone where a coffin or a tomb had touched it. He seemed to have forgotten what the bungalow was for, or that a sahib needed things to eat, until the ex-risaldar enlightened him, and then he complained wheezily.

The stables—rather the patch-and-hole-covered desolation that once had been stables—were altogether too snake-defiled and smelly to be worth repairing; the string of horses was quartered cleanly and snugly under tents, and Mahommed Gunga went to enormous trouble in arranging a ring of watch-fires at even distances.

"Are there thieves here, then?" asked Cunningham, and the Rajput nodded but said nothing. He seemed satisfied, though, that the man he had brought safely thus far at so much trouble would be well enough housed in the creaky wreck of the bungalow, and he took no precautions of any kind as to guarding its approaches.

Cunningham watched the preparations for his supper with ill-concealed disgust—saw the customary chase of a rubber-muscled chicken, heard its death gurgles, saw the guts removed, to make sure that the kansamah did not cook it with that part of its anatomy intact, as he surely would do unless watched—and then strolled ahead a little way along the road.

The fakir was squatting in the distance, on a big white stone, and in the quiet of the gloaming Cunningham could hear his coarse, lewd voice tossing crumbs of abuse and mockery to the seven or eight villagers who squatted near him—half-amused, half-frightened, and altogether credulous.

Even as he drew nearer Cunningham could not understand a word of what the fakir said, but the pantomime was obvious. His was the voice and the manner of the professional beggar who has no more need to whine but still would ingratiate. It was the bullying, brazen swagger and the voice that traffics in filth and impudence instead of wit; and, in payment for his evening bellyful he was pouring out abuse of Cunningham that grew viler and yet viler as Cunningham came nearer and the fakir realized that his subject could not understand a word of it.

The villagers looked leery and eyed Cunningham sideways at each fresh sally. The fakir grew bolder, until one of his listeners smothered an open laugh in both hands and rolled over sideways. Cunningham came closer yet, half-enamoured of the weird scene, half-curious to discover what the stone could be on which the fakir sat.

The fakir grew nervous. Perhaps, after all, this was one of those hatefully clever sahibs who know enough to pretend they do not know! The abuse and vile innuendo changed to more obsequious, less

obviously filthy references to other things than
Cunningham's religion, likes, and pedigree, and the
little crowd of men who had tacitly encouraged him
before got ready now to stand at a distance and
take sides against him should the white man turn
out to have understood.

But Cunningham happened to catch sight of a
cloud of paroquets that swept in a screaming ellipse
for a better branch to nest in and added the one
touch of gorgeous color needed to make the whole
scene utterly unearthly and unlike anything he had
ever dreamed of, or had seen in pictures, or had had
described to him. He stood at gaze—forgetful of
the stone that had attracted him and of the fakir
—spellbound by the wonder-blend of hues branch-
backed, and framed in gloom as the birds' scream
was framed in silence.

And, seeing him at gaze, the fakir recovered
confidence and jeered new ribaldry, until some one
suddenly shot out from behind Cunningham, and
before he had recovered from his surprise he saw
the fakir sprawling on his back, howling for mercy,
while Mahommed Gunga beat the blood out of him
with a whalebone riding-whip.

The sun went down with Indian suddenness and
shut off the scene of upraised lash and squirming,
naked, ash-smeared devil, as a magic-lantern picture
disappears. Only the creature's screams reverber-
ated through the jungle, like a belated echo to the
restless paroquets.

"He will sleep less easily for a week or two!"

hazarded Mahommed Gunga, stepping back toward Cunningham. In the sudden darkness the white breeches showed and the whites of his eyes, but little else; his voice growled like a rumble from the underworld.

"Why did you do it, risaldar? What did he say?"

"It was enough, bahadur, that he sat on that stone; for that alone he had been beaten! What he said was but the babbling of priests. All priests are alike. They have a common jargon—a common disrespect for what they dare not openly defy. These temple rats of fakirs mimic them. That is all, sahib. A whipping meets the case."

"But the stone? Why shouldn't he sit on it?"

"Wait one minute, sahib, and then see." He formed his hands into a trumpet and bellowed through them in a high-pitched, nasal, ululating order to somebody behind:

"Oh-h-h—Battee—lao!"

The black, dark roadside echoed it, and a dot of light leapt up as a man came running with what gradually grew into a lamp.

Mahommed Gunga seized the lamp, bent for a few seconds over the still sprawling fakir, whipped him again twice, cursed him and kicked him, until he got up and ran like a spectre for the gloom beyond the trees. Then, with a rather stately sweep of the lamp, and a tremble in his voice that was probably intentional—designed to make Cunningham at least aware of the existence of emotion before he looked—he let the light fall on the slab on which the fakir had been squatting.

"Look, Cunnigan-sahib!"

The youngster bent down above the slab and tried, in the fitful light, to make out what the markings were that ran almost from side to side, in curves, across the stone; but it was too dark; the light was too fitful; the marks themselves were too faint from the constant squatting of roadside wanderers.

Mahommed Gunga set the lamp down on the stone, and he and the attendant took little sticks, sharp-pointed, with which they began to dig hurriedly, scratching and scraping at what presently showed, even in that rising and falling light, as Roman lettering. Soon Cunningham himself began to lend a hand. He made out a date first, and he could feel it with his fingers before his eyes deciphered it. Gradually, letter by letter—word by word—he read it off, feeling a strange new thrill run through him, as each line followed, like a voice from the haunted past.

A. D. 1823. A. D.

SACRED TO THE MEMORY OF

General Robert Francis

CUNNINGHAM

WHO DIED ON THIS SPOT

ÆTAT 81

FROM

WOUNDS INFLICTED BY A

TIGER

There was no sound audible except the purring of the lamp flame and the heavy breathing of the three as Cunningham gazed down at the very crudely carved, stained, often-desecrated slab below which lay the first of the Anglo-Indian Cunninghams.

This man—these crumbled bones that lay under a forgotten piece of rock—had made all of their share of history. They had begotten "Pukka" Cunningham, who had hacked the name deeper yet in the crisscrossed annals of a land of war. It was strange—it was queer—uncanny—for the third of the Cunninghams to be sitting on the stone. It was unexpected, yet it seemed to have a place in the scheme of things, for he caught himself searching his memory backward.

He received an impression that something was expected of him. He knew, by instinct and reasoning he could not have explained, that neither Mahommed Gunga nor the other men would say a word until he spoke. They were waiting—he knew they were—for a word, or a sign, or an order (he did not know which), on which would hang the future of all three of them.

Yet there was no hurry—no earthly hurry. He felt sure of it. In the silence and the blackness— in the tense, steamy atmosphere of expectancy— he felt perfectly at ease, although he knew, too, that there was superstition to be reckoned with; and that is something which a white man finds it hard to weigh and cope with, as a rule.

The sweat ran down his face in little streams, and the prickly heat began to move across his skin, like a fiery-footed centiped beneath his undershirt, but he noticed neither. He began to be unconscious of anything except the knowledge that the bones of his grandsire lay underneath him and that Mahommed Gunga waited for the word that would fit into the scheme and solve a problem.

"Are there any tigers here now?" he asked presently, in a perfectly normal voice. He spoke as he had done when his servant asked him which suit he would wear.

"Ha, sahib! Many."

"Man-eaters, by any chance?"

Mahommed Gunga and the other man exchanged quick glances, but Cunningham did not look up. He did not see the quick-flashed whites as their eyes met and looked down again.

"There is one, sahib—so say the kansamah and the head man—a full-grown tiger, in his prime."

"I will shoot him." Four words, said quietly—not "Do you think," or "I would like to," or "Perhaps." They were perfectly definite and spoken without a trace of excitement; yet this man had never seen a tiger.

"Very good, sahib." That, too, was spoken in a level voice, but Mahommed Gunga's eyes and the other man's met once again above his head. "We will stay here four days; by the third day there will be time enough to have brought an elephant and——"

"I will go on foot," said Cunningham, quite quietly. "To-morrow, at dawn, risaldar-sahib. Will you be good enough to make arrangements? All we need to know is where he is and how to get there—will you attend to that?"

"Ha, sahib."

"Thanks. I wonder if my supper's ready."

He turned and walked away, with a little salute-like movement of his hand that was reminiscent of his father. The two Rajputs watched him in heavy-breathing silence until the little group of lights, where the horse-tents faced the old dak-bungalow, swallowed him. Then:

"He is good. He will do!" said the black-beard who had brought the lamp.

"He is good. But many sahibs would have acted coolly, thus. There must be a greater test. There must be no doubt—no littlest doubt. Alwa and the others will ask me on my honor, and I will answer on my honor, yes or no."

It was an hour before the two of them returned, and looked the horses over, and strolled up to bid Cunningham good night; and in the meanwhile they had seen about the morrow's tiger, and another matter.

CHAPTER VII

What found ye, then?   Why heated ye the pot?
What useful metal down the channels ran?
Gold?   Steel for making weapons?   Iron?   What?
Nay.   Out from the fire we kindled strode a man!

THEY set the legs of Cunningham's string-woven
bed into pans of water, to keep the scorpions and
ants and snakes at bay, and then left him in pitch
darkness to his own devices, with a parting admo-
nition to keep his slippers on—for the floor, in the
dark, would be the prowling-place of venomed death.

It was he who set the lamp on the little table
by his bedside, for his servant—for the first time
on that journey—was not at hand to execute his
thoughts almost before he had spoken them. Mahommed Gunga had explained that the man was
sick; and that seemed strange, for he had been well
enough, and more than usually efficient, but an hour
before.

But there were stranger things and far more
irritating ones to interfere with the peaceful passage
of the night. There were sounds that were unac-
countable; there was the memory of the wayside
tombstone and the train of thought that it engen-
dered. Added to the hell-hot, baking stuffiness that
radiated from the walls, there came the squeaking

of a punka rope pulled out of time—the piece of
piping in the mud-brick wall through which the
rope passed had become clogged and rusted, and
the villager pressed into service had forgotten how
to pull; he jerked at the cord between nods as the
heat of the veranda and the unaccustomed night
duty combined to make him sleepy.

Soon the squeaking became intolerable, and Cunningham swore at him—in English, because he spoke
little of any native language yet, and had not the
least idea in any case what the punka-wallah's
tongue might be. For a while after that the pulling
was more even; he lay on one elbow, letting the
swinging mat fan just miss his ear, and examining
his rifle and pistols for lack of anything better to
keep him from going mad. Then, suddenly, the
pulling ceased altogether. Silence and hell heat
shut down on him like a coffin lid. Even the lamp
flame close beside him seemed to grow dim; the
weight of black night that was suffocating him
seemed to crush light out of the flame as well.

No living mortal could endure that, he imagined.
He swore aloud, but there was no answer, so he got
up, after crashing his rifle-butt down on the floor
to scare away anything that crawled. For a moment he stood, undecided whether to take the lamp
or rifle with him—then decided on the rifle, for the
lamp might blow out in some unexpected night
gust, whereas if he left it where it was it would go
on burning and show him the way back to bed again.
Besides, he was too unaccustomed to the joy of

owning the last new thing in sporting rifles to hesitate for long about what to keep within his grasp.

Through the open door he could see nothing but
pitch-blackness, unpunctuated even by a single star.
There were no lights where the tents stood, so he
judged that even the accustomed natives had found
the added heat of Mahommed Gunga's watch-fires
intolerable and had raked them out; but from where
he imagined that the village must be came the dum-
tu-dum-tu-dum of tom-toms, like fever blood pul-
sating in the veins of devils of the night.

The punka-wallah slept. He could just make
out the man's blurred shape—a shadow in the shadows—dog-curled, with the punkah rope looped round
his foot. He kicked him gently, and the man
stirred, but fell asleep again. He kicked him
harder. The man sat up and stared, terrified; the
whites of his eyes were distinctly visible. He
seemed to have forgotten why he was there, and to
imagine that he saw a ghost.

Cunningham spoke to him—the first words that
came into his head.

"Go on pulling," he said in English, quite kindly.

But if he had loosed his rifle off, the effect could
not have been more instantaneous. Clutching his
twisted rag of a turban in one hand, and kicking
his leg free, he ran for it—leaped the veranda rail,
and vanished—a night shadow, swallowed by its
mother night.

"Come back!" called Cunningham. "Iderao!
I won't hurt you!"

But there was no answer, save the tom-toms'
thunder, swelling now into a devil's chorus—coming
nearer. It seemed to be coming from the forest,
but he reasoned that it could not be; it must be
some village marriage feast, or perhaps an orgy;
he had paid out what would seem to the villagers a
lot of money, and it might be that they were cele-
brating the occasion. It was strange, though, that
he could see no lights where the village ought to be.

For a moment he had a half-formed intention to
shout for Mahommed Gunga; but he checked that,
reasoning that the Rajput might think he was
afraid. Then his eye caught sight of something
blacker than the shadows—something long and thin
and creepy that moved, and he remembered that
bed, where the pans of water would protect him,
was the only safe place.

So he returned into the hot, black silence where
the tiny lamp-flame guttered and threw shadows.
He wondered why it guttered. It seemed to be
actually short of air. There were four rooms, he
remembered, to the bungalow, all connected and
each opening outward by a door that faced one of
the four sides; he wondered whether the outer
doors were opened to admit a draught, and started
to investigate.

Two of them were shut tight, and he could not
kick them open; the dried-out teak and the heavy
iron bolts held as though they had been built to
resist a siege; the noise that he made as he rattled
at them frightened a swarm of unseen things—

unguessed-at shapes—that scurried away. He
thought he could see beady little eyes that looked
and disappeared and circled round and stopped to
look again. He could hear creepy movements in the
stillness. It seemed better to leave those doors alone.

One other door, which faced that of his own room,
was open wide, and he could feel the forest through
it; there was nothing to be seen, but the stillness
moved. The velvet blackness was deeper by a
shade, and the heat, uprising to get even with the
sky, bore up a stench with it. There was no draught,
no movement except upward. Earth was panting—
in time, it seemed, to the hellish thunder of the tom-
toms.

He went back and lay on the bed again, leaning
the rifle against the cot-frame, and trying by sheer
will-power to prevent the blood from bursting his
veins. He realized before long that he was parched
with thirst, and reached out for the water-jar that
stood beside the lamp; but as he started to drink he
realized that a crawling evil was swimming round
and round in rings in the water. In a fit of horror
he threw the thing away and smashed it into a
dozen fragments in a corner. He saw a dozen rats,
at least, scamper to drink before the water could
evaporate or filter through the floor; and when
they were gone there was no half-drowned crawling
thing either. They had eaten it.

He clutched his rifle to him. The barrel was hot,
but the feel of it gave him a sense of companionship.
And then, as he lay back on the bed again, the lamp

went out. He groped for it and shook it. There was no oil.

Now, what had been hot horror turned to fear that passed all understanding—to the hate that does not reason—to the cold sweat breaking on the roasted skin. Where the four walls had been there was blackness of immeasurable space. He could hear the thousand-footed cannibals of night creep nearer—driven in toward him by the dinning of the tom-toms. He felt that his bed was up above a scrambling swarm of black-legged things that fought.

He had no idea how long he lay stock-still, for fear of calling attention to himself, and hated his servant and Mahommed Gunga and all India. Once—twice—he thought he heard another sound, almost like the footfall of a man on the veranda near him. Once he thought that a man breathed within ten paces of him, and for a moment there was a distinct sensation of not being alone. He hoped it was true; he could deal with an assassin. That would be something tangible to hate and hit. Manhood came to his assistance—the spirit of the soldier that will bow to nothing that has shape; but it died away again as the creeping silence once more shut down on him.

And then the thunder of the tom-toms ceased. Then even the venomed crawlers that he knew were near him faded into nothing that really mattered, compared to the greater, stealthy horror that he knew was coming, born of the shuddersome, shut silence that ensued. There was neither air nor view—no sense of time or space—nothing but the coal-black pit of terror yawning—cold sweat in the heat, and a footfall—an undoubted footfall—followed by another one, too heavy for a man's.

Where heavy feet were there was something tangible. His veins tingled and the cold sweat dried. Excitement began to reawaken all his soldier senses, and the wish to challenge seized him—the soldierly intent to warn the unaware, which is the actual opposite of cowardice.

"Halt! Who comes there?"

He lipped the words, but his dry throat would not voice them. Before he could clear his throat or wet his lips his eye caught something lighter than the night—two things—ten—twelve paces off—two things that glowed or sheened as though there were light inside them—too big and too far apart to be owl's eyes, but singularly like them. They moved, a little sideways and toward him; and again he heard the heavy, stealthy footfall.

They stayed still then for what may have been half a minute, and another sense—smell—warned him and stirred up the man in him. He had never smelled it in his life; it must have been instinct that assured him of an enemy behind the strange, unpleasant, rather musky reek that filled the room. His right hand brought the rifle to his shoulder without sound, and almost without conscious effort on his part.

He forgot the heat now and the silence and discomfort. He lay still on his side, squinting down the rifle barrel at a spot he judged was midway between a pair of eyes that glowed, and wondering where his foresight might be. It struck him all at once that it was quite impossible to see the foresight—that he must actually touch what he would hit, if he would be at all sure of hitting it. He remembered, too, in that instant—as a born soldier does remember things—that in the dark an attacking enemy is probably more frightened than his foe. His father had told it him when he was a little lad afraid of bogies; he in turn had told it to the other boys at school, and they had passed it on until in that school it had become rule number one of schoolboy lore—just as rule number two in all schools where the sons of soldiers go is "Take the fight to him."

He leaped from the bed, with his rifle out in front of him—white-nightshirted and unexpected—sudden enough to scare the wits out of anything that had them. He was met by a snarl. The two eyes narrowed, and then blazed. They lowered, as though their owner gathered up his weight to spring. He fired between them. The flash and the smoke blinded him; the burst of the discharge within four echoing walls deadened his ears, and he was aware of nothing but a voice beside him that said quietly: "Well done, bahadur! Thou art thy father's son!"

He dropped his rifle butt to the floor, and some one struck a light. Even then it was thirty seconds before his strained eyes grew accustomed to the flare and he could see the tiger at his feet, less than a yard away—dead, bleeding, wide-eyed, obviously taken by surprise and shot as he prepared to spring. Beside him, within a yard, Mahommed Gunga stood, with a drawn sabre in his right hand and a pistol in his left, and there were three other men standing like statues by the walls.

"How long have you been here?" demanded Cunningham.

"A half-hour, sahib."

"Why?"

"In case of need, sahib. That tiger killed a woman yesterday at dawn and was driven off his kill; he was not likely to be an easy mark for an untried hunter."

"Why did you enter without knocking?"

The ex-risaldar said nothing.

"I see that you have shoes on."

"The scorpions, sahib——"

"Would you be pleased, Mahommed Gunga, if I entered your house with my hat on and without knocking or without permission?"

"Sahib, I——"

"Be good enough to have that brute's carcass dragged out and skinned, and—ah—leave me to sleep, will you?"

Mahommed Gunga bowed, and growled an order; another man passed the order on, and the tom-tom thundering began again as a dozen villagers pattered in to take away the tiger.

"Tell them, please," commanded Cunningham, "that that racket is to cease. I want to sleep."

Again Mahommed Gunga bowed, without a smile or a tremor on his face; again a growled order was echoed and re-echoed through the dark. The drumming stopped.

"Is there oil in the bahadur's lamp?" asked Mahommed Gunga.

"Probably not," said Cunningham.

"I will command that——"

"You needn't trouble, thank you, risaldar-sahib. I sleep better in the dark. I'll be glad to see you after breakfast as usual—ah—without your shoes, unless you come in uniform. Good night."

The Rajput signed to the others and withdrew with dignity. Cunningham reloaded his rifle in the dark and lay down. Within five minutes the swinging of the punka and the squeaking of the rope resumed, but regularly this time; Mahommed Gunga had apparently unearthed a man who understood the business. Reaction, the intermittent coolth, as the mat fan swung above his face, the steady, evenly timed squeak and movement—not least, the calm of well-asserted dignity—all joined to have one way, and Chota-Cunnigan-bahadur slept, to dream of fire-eyed tigers dancing on tombstones laid on the roof of hell, and of a grandfather in full general's uniform, who said: "Well done, bahadur!"

But outside, by a remade camp-fire, Mahommed Gunga sat and chuckled to himself, and every now and then grew eloquent to the bearded men who sat beside him.

"Aie! Did you hear him reprimand me? By the beard of God's prophet, that is a man of men! So was his father! Now I will tell Alwa and the others that I bring a man to them! By the teeth of God and my own honor I will swear to it! His first tiger—he had never seen a tiger!—in the dark, and unexpected—caught by it, to all seeming, like a trapped man in a cage—no lamp—no help at hand, or so *he* thought until it was all over. And he ran *at* the tiger! And then, 'you come with your shoes on, Mahommed Gunga—why, forsooth?' Did you hear him? By the blood of Allah, we have a man to lead us!"

CHAPTER VIII

Now, the gist of the thing is—Be silent. Be calm.
Be awake. Be on hand on the day.
Be instant to heed the first note of alarm.
And—precisely—exactly—Obey.

AT Howrah, while Mahommed Gunga was employing each chance circumstance to test the pluck and decision and reliability of Cunningham at almost every resting-place along the Grand Trunk Road, the armed squire he had left behind with a little handful of gold mohurs and three horses was finding time heavy on his hands.

Like his master, Ali Partab was a man of action, to whom the purlieus of a caravansary were well enough on rare occasions. He could ruffle it with the best of them; like any of his race, he could lounge with dignity and listen to the tales that hum wherever many horsemen congregate; and he was no mean raconteur—he had a tale or two to tell himself, of women and the chase and of the laugh that he, too, had flung in the teeth of fear when opportunity arose.

But each new story of the paid taletellers, who squat and drone and reach a climax, and then pass the begging bowl before they finish it—each merrily related jest brought in by members of the constantly arriving trading parties—each neigh of his three chargers—every new phase of the kaleidoscopic life he watched stirred new ambition in him to be up, and away, and doing. Many a dozen times he had to remind himself that "there had been a trust imposed."

He exercised the horses daily, riding each in turn until he was as lean and lithe and hard beneath the skin as they were. They were Mahommed Gunga's horses—he Mahommed Gunga's man; therefore, his honor was involved. He reasoned, when he took the trouble to, along the good clean feudal line that lays down clearly what service is: there is no honor, says that argument, in serving any one who is content with half a service, and the honor is the only thing that counts.

As day succeeded ever sultrier, ever longer-drawn-out day—as each night came that saw him peg the horses out wherever what little breezes moved might fan them—as he sat among the courtyard groups and listened in the heavy heat, the fact grew more apparent to him that this trust of his was something after all which a man of worth might shoulder proudly. There was danger in it.

The talk among the traders—darkly hinted, most of it, and couched in metaphor—was all of blood, and what would follow on the letting of it. Now and then a loud-mouthed boaster would throw caution to the winds and speak openly of a grim day coming for the British; he would be checked

instantly by wiser men, but not before Ali Partab
had heard enough to add to his private store of information.

Priests came from a dozen cities to the eastward,
all nominally after pilgrims for the sacred places,
but all strangely indifferent to their quest. They
preferred, it would seem, to sit in rings with chance-
met ruffians—with believers and unbelievers alike—
even with men of no caste at all—and talk of other
things than pilgrimages.

"Next year, one hundred years ago the English
conquered India. Remember ye the prophecy?
One hundred years they had! This, then, is the
last year. Whom the gods would whelm they first
deprive of reason; mark ye this! The cartridges
they serve out to the sepoys now are smeared with
the blended fat of cows and pigs. Knowing that
we Hindoos hold the cow a sacred beast, they do this
sacrilege—and why? They would make us bite
the cartridges and lose our caste. And why again?
Because they would make us Christians! That is
the truth! Else why are the Christian missionaries
here in Howrah?"

The listeners would nod while the little red fires
glowed and purred above the pipes, and others not
included in the circle strained forward through the
dark to listen.

"The gods get ready now! Are ye ready?"

Elsewhere, a hadji—green-turbaned from the pil-
grimage to Mecca—would hold out to a throng of
true believers.

"Ay! Pig's fat on the cartridges! The new drill is that the sepoy bites the cartridge first, to spill a little powder and make priming. Which true believer wishes to defile himself with pig's fat? Why do they this? Why are the Christian missionaries here? Ask both riddles with one breath, for both two are one!"

"Slay, then!"

"Up now, and slay!"

There would be an instant, eager restlessness, while Ali Partab would glance over to where the horses stood, and would wonder why the word that loosed him was so long in coming. The hadji would calm his listeners and tell them to get ready, but be still and await the sign.

"There were to be one hundred years, ran the prophecy; but ninety-nine and a portion have yet run. Wait for the hour!"

Then, for perhaps the hundredth time, Ali Partab would pretend that movement alone could save one or other of his horses from heat apoplexy. He would mount, and ride at a walking pace through the streets that seemed like a night view of a stricken battle-field, turn down by the palace wall, and then canter to the schoolhouse, where the hag—wiser than her mistress—would be sleeping in the open.

"Thou! Mother of a murrain! Toothless one! Is there no word yet?"

The hag would leer up through the heavy darkness—make certain that he had no lance with him

with which to prod her in the ribs—scratch herself
a time or two like a stray dog half awakened—and
then leer knowingly.

"Hast thou the gold mohurs?" she would demand.

"Am I a sieve?"

"Let my old eyes see them, sahib."

He would take out two gold coins and hold them
out in such a way that she could look at them without the opportunity to snatch.

"There is no word yet," she would answer, when
her eyes had feasted on them as long as his patience
would allow.

"Have they no fear then?"

"None. Only madness!"

"See that they bite thee not! Keep thy wits
with thee, and be ready to bring me word in time,
else——"

"Patience, sahib! Show me the coins again—
one little look—again once!"

But Ali Partab would wheel and ride away, leaving her to mumble and gibber in the road and curl
again on to her blanket in the blackest corner by
the door.

Once, on an expedition of that kind, he encoun-
tered Duncan McClean himself. The lean, tall
Scotsman, gray-headed from the cares he had taken
on himself, a little bowed from heat and hopeless-
ness, but showing no least symptom of surrender in
the kind, strong lines of a rugged face, stood, eyes
upward, in the moonlight. The moon, at least,
looked cool. It was at the full, like a disk of silver,

and he seemed to drink in the beams that bathed him.

"Does he worship it?" wondered Ali Partab, reining from an amble to a walk and watching half-reverently. The followers of Mohammed are mostly superstitious about the moon. The feeling that he had for this man of peace who could so gaze up at it was something very like respect, and, with the twenty-second sense that soldiers have, he knew, without a word spoken or a deed seen done, that this would be a wielder of cold steel to be reckoned with should he ever slough the robes of peace and take it into his silvered head to fight. The Rajput, that respects decision above all other virtues, perhaps because it is the one that he most lacks, could sense firm, unshakable, quick-seized determination on the instant.

Duncan McClean acknowledged the fierce-seeming stare with a salute, and Ali Partab dismounted instantly. He who holds a trust from such as Mahommed Gunga is polite in recognition of the trust. He leaned, then, against the horse's withers, wondering how far he ought to let politeness go and whether his honor bade him show contempt for the Christian's creed.

"Is there any way, I wonder," asked the Scotsman, the clean-clipped suspicion of Scots dialect betraying itself even through the Hindustanee that he used, "of getting letters through to some mail station?"

"I know not," said the Rajput.

"You are a Mohammedan?" The Scotsman peered at him, adjusting his view-point to the moon's rays. "I see you are. A Rajput, too, I think."

"Ha, sahib."

"There was a Rangar here not very long ago" this man evidently knew the proper title to give a true believer of the proudest race there is. Ali Partab's heart began to go out to him—"an officer, I think, once of the Rajput Horse, who very kindly carried letters for me. Perhaps you know of some other gentleman of your race about to travel northward? He could earn, at least, gratitude."

"So-ho!" thought Ali Partab to himself. "I have known men of his race who would have offered money, to be spat on!—Not now, sahib," he answered aloud.

"Mahommed Gunga was the officer's name. Do you know him, or know of him, by any chance?"

"Ha, sahib, I know him well. It is an honor."

The Scotsman smiled. "He must be very far away by this time. How many are there, I wonder, in India who have such things said of them when their backs are turned?"

"More than a few, sahib! I would draw steel for the good name of more than a hundred men whom I know, and there be many others!"

"Men of your own race?"

"And yours, sahib."

There was no bombast in the man's voice; it was said good-naturedly, as a man might say, "There

are some friends to whom I would lend money."
No man with any insight could mistake the truth
that underlay the boast. The Scotsman bowed.

"I am glad, indeed, to have met you. Will you
sit down a little while?"

"Nay, sahib. The hour is late. I was but keeping the blood moving in this horse of mine."

"Well, tell me, since you won't stay, have you
any notion who the man was whom Mahommed
Gunga sent to get my letters? My daughter handed
them to him one evening, late, at this door."

"I am he, sahib."

"Then—I understood—perhaps I was mistaken—
I thought it was his man who came?"

"Praised be Allah, I am his man, sahib!"

"Oh! I wonder whether my servants praise God
for the privilege!" McClean made the remark
only half-aloud and in English. Ali Partab could
not have understood the words, but he may have
caught their meaning, for he glanced sideways at the
old hag mumbling in the shadow and grinned into
his beard. "Are you in communication with him?
Could you get a letter to him?"

"I have no slightest notion where he is, sahib."

"If my letters could once reach him, wherever he
might be, I would feel confident of their arriving at
their destination."

"I, too, sahib!"

"I sent one letter—to a government official. It
cannot have reached him, for there should have been
an answer and none has come. It had reference to

this terrible suttee business. Suttee is against the law as well as against all dictates of reason and humanity; yet the Hindoos make a constant practice of it here under our very eyes. These native states are under treaty to observe the law. I intend to do all in my power to put a stop to their ghoulish practices, and Maharajah Howrah knows what my intentions are. It must be a Mohammedan, this time, to whom I intrust my correspondence on suttee!"

Now, a Rangar is a man whose ancestors were Hindoos but who became converts to Islam. Like all proselytes, they adhere more enthusiastically to their religion than do the men whose mother creed it is; and the fact that the Rangars originally became converts under duress is often thrown in their teeth by the Hindoos, who gain nothing in the way of brotherly regard in the process. A Rangar hates a Hindoo as enthusiastically as he loves a fight. Ali Partab began to drum his fingers on his teeth and to exhibit less impatience to be off.

"There is no knowing, sahib. I, too, am no advocate of superstitious practices involving cruelty. I might get a letter through. My commission from the risaldar-sahib would include all honorable matters not obstructive to the main issue. I have certain funds——"

"I, too, have funds," smiled the missionary.

"I am not allowed, sahib, to involve myself in any brawl until after my business is accomplished. It would be necessary first to assure me on that point. My honor is involved in that matter. To whom, and of what nature, would the letter be?"

"A letter to the Company's Resident at Abu, reporting to him that Hindoo widows are still compelled in this city to burn themselves to death above their husbands' funeral pyres."

The Rajput grinned. "Does the Resident sahib not know it, then?"

"There will be no chance of his not knowing should my report reach him!"

"I will see, sahib, what can be done, then, in the matter. If I can find a man, I will bring him to you."

The missionary thanked him and stood watching as the Rajput rode away. When the horseman's free, lean back had vanished in the inky darkness his eyes wandered over to a point where tongues of flame licked upward, casting a dull, dancing, crimson glow on the hot sky. Here and there, silhouetted in the firelight, he could see the pugrees and occasional long poles of men who prodded at the embers. Ululating through the din of tom-toms he could catch the wails of women. He shuddered, prayed a little, and went in.

That day even the little bazaar fosterlings, whom he had begged, and coaxed, and taught, had all deserted to be present at the burning of three widows. Even the lepers in the tiny hospital that he had started had limped out for a distant view. He had watched a year's work all disintegrating in a minute at the call of bestial, loathsome, blood-hungry superstition.

And he was a man of iron, as Christian missionaries go. He had been hard-bitten in his youth and trained in a hard, grim school. In the Isle of Skye he had seen the little cabin where his mother lived pulled down to make more room for a fifty-thousand-acre deer-forest. He had seen his mother beg.

He had worked his way to Edinburgh, toiled at starvation wages for the sake of leave to learn at night, burned midnight oil, and failed at the end of it, through ill health, to pass for his degree.

He had loved as only hard-hammered men can love, and had married after a struggle the very thought of which would have melted the courage of an ordinary man, only to see his wife die when her child was born. And even then, in that awful hour, he had not felt the utterness of misery such as came to him when he saw that his work in Howrah was undone. He had given of his best, and all his best, and it seemed that he had given it for nothing.

"Who was that man, father?" asked a very weary voice through which courage seemed to live yet, as the tiniest suspicion of a sweet refrain still lives through melancholy bars.

"The man who took your home letters to Mahommed Gunga."

"And——?"

"He has promised to try to find a man for me who will take my report on this awful business to the Resident at Abu."

"Father, listen! Listen, please!" Rosemary

McClean drew a chair for him and knelt beside him. Youth saved her face from being drawn as his, but the heat and horror had begun to undermine youth's powers of resistance. She looked more beautiful than ever, but no law lays down that a wraith shall be unlovely. She had tried the personal appeal with him a hundred times, and argument a thousand; now, she used both in a concentrated, earnest effort to prevail over his stubborn will. Her will was as strong as his, and yielded place to nothing but her sense of loyalty. There were not only Rajputs, as the Rajputs knew, who could be true to a high ideal. "I am sure that whoever that man is he must be the link between us and the safety Mahommed Gunga spoke of. Otherwise, why does he stay behind? Native officers who have servants take their servants with them, as a rule."

"Well?"

"Give the word! Let us at least get in touch with safety!"

"For myself, no. For you, yes! I have been weak with you, dear. I have let my selfish pleasure in having you near me overcome my sense of duty —that, and my faithless fear that you would not be properly provided for. I think, too, that I have never quite induced myself to trust natives sufficiently—even native gentlemen. You shall go, Rosemary. You shall go as soon as I can get word to Mahommed Gunga's man. Call that old woman in."

"Father, I will *not* go without you, and you know it! My place is with you, and I have quite made up my mind. If you stay, I stay! My presence here has saved your life a hundred times over. No, I don't mean just when you were ill; I mean that they dare not lay a finger on me! They know that a nation which respects their women would strike hard and swiftly to avenge a woman of its own! If I were to go away and leave you they would poison you or stab you within a day, and then hold a mock trial and hang some innocent or other to blind the British Government. I would be a murderess if I left you here alone! Come! Come away!"

He shook his head. "It was wrong of me to ever bring you here," he said sadly. "But I did not know—I would never have believed." Then wrath took hold of him—the awful, cold anger of the Puritan that hates evil as a concrete thing, to be ripped apart with steel. "God's wrath shall burst on Howrah!" he declared. "Sodom and Gomorrah were no worse! Remember what befell them!"

"Remember Lot!" said Rosemary. "Come away!"

"Lot stayed on to the last, and tried to warn them! I will warn the Resident! Here, give me my writing things—where are they?"

He pushed her aside, none too gently, for the fire of a Covenanter's anger was blazing in his eyes.

"There are forty thousand British soldiers standing still, and wrong—black, shameful wrong—is

being done! For a matter of gold—for fear of the
cost in filthy lucre—they refrain from hurling wrong-
doers in the dust! For the sake of dishonorable
peace they leave these native states to misgovern
themselves and stink to high heaven! Will God
allow what they do? The shame and the sin is on
England's head! Her statesmen shut their eyes
and cry 'Peace, peace!' where there is no peace.
Her queen sits idle on the throne while widows burn,
screaming, in the flames of superstitious priests.
Men tell her, 'All is well; there is British rule in
India!' They are too busy robbing widows in the
Isle of Skye to lend an ear to the cries of India's
widows! Corruption — superstition — murder — lies
—black wrong—black selfishness—all growing rank
beneath the shadow of the British rule—how long
will God let that last?"

He was pacing up and down like a caged lion, not
looking at Rosemary, not speaking to her—speaking to himself, and giving rein to all the rankling
rage at wrong that wrong had nurtured in him since
his boyhood. She knelt still by the chair, her eyes
following him as he raged up and down the matted
floor. She pitied him more than she did India.

When he took the one lamp at last and set it
where the light would fall above his writing pad,
she left the room and went to stand at the street-
door, where the sluggish night air was a degree less
stifling than in the mud-plastered, low-ceilinged
room. As she stood there, one hand on either door-
post to remind her she was living in a concrete

world, not a charred whisp swaying in the heat, a black thing rose out of the blackness, and the toothless hag held out a bony hand and touched her.

"Is it not time yet for the word to go?" she asked.

"No. No word yet, Joanna."

CHAPTER IX

Now, God give good going to master o' mine,
 God speed him, and lead him, and nerve him;
God give him a lead of a length in the line,
 And,—God let him boast that I serve him!

THE dawn was barely breaking yet when things
stirred in the little mission house. The flea-bitten
gray pony was saddled by a sleepy saice, and brought
round from his open-sided thatch stable in the rear.
The violet and mauve, that precede the aching yellow glare of day were fading; a coppersmith began
his everlasting *bong-bong-bong*, apparently reverberating from every direction; the last, almost in-
detectable, warm whiff of night wind moved and
died away, and the monkeys in the near-by baobab
chattered it a requiem. Almost on the stroke of
sunrise Rosemary McClean stepped out—settled her
sun-helmet, with a moue above the chin-strap that
was wasted on flat-bosomed, black grandmotherdom
and sulky groom—and mounted.

She needed no help. The pony stood as though
he knew that the hot wind would soon dry the life
out of him; and, though dark rings beneath dark
eyes betrayed the work of heat and sleepless worry
on a girl who should have graced the cool, sweet,

rain-swept hills of Scotland, she had spirit left yet and an unspent store of youth. The saice seemed more weathered than the twenty-year-old girl, for he limped back into the smelly shelter of the servants' quarters to cook his breakfast and mumble about dogs and sahibs who prefer the sun.

She looked shrunk inside the riding-habit—not shrivelled, for she sat too straight, but as though the cotton jacket had been made for a larger woman. If she seemed tired, and if a stranger might have guessed that her head ached until the chestnut curls were too heavy for it, she was still supple. And, as she whipped the pony into an unwilling trot and old mission-named Joanna broke into a jog behind, revolt—no longer impatience, or discontent, or sorrow, but reckless rebellion—rode with her.

It was there, plain for the world to see, in the firm lines of a little Puritan mouth, in the angle of a high-held chin, in the set of a gallant little pair of shoulders. The pony felt it, and leaned forward to a canter. Joanna scented, smelt, or sensed in some manner known to Eastern old age, that purpose was afoot; this was to be no early-morning canter, merely out and home again; there was no time, now, for the customary tricks of corner-cutting and rest-snatching under eaves; she tucked her head down and jogged forward in the dust, more like a dog than ever. It was a dog's silent, striving determination to be there when the finish came—a dog's disregard of all object or objective but his master's—but a long-thrown stride, and a crafty, beady eye that promised more usefulness than a dog's when called on.

The first word spoken was when Rosemary drew rein a little more than half-way along the palace wall.

"Are you tired yet, Joanna?"

"Uh-uh!" the woman answered, shaking her head violently and pointing at the sun that mounted every minute higher. The argument was obvious; in less than twenty minutes the whole horizon would be shimmering again like shaken plates of brass; wherever the other end might be, a rest would be better there than here! Her mistress nodded, and rode on again, faster yet; she had learned long ago that Joanna could show a dusty pair of heels to almost anything that ran, and she had never yet known distance tire her; it had been the thought of distance and speed combined that made her pause and ask.

She did not stop again until they had cantered up through the awakening bazaar, where unclean-looking merchants and their underlings rinsed out their teeth noisily above the gutters, and the pariah dogs had started nosing in among the muck for things unthinkable to eat. The sun had shortened up the shadows and begun to beat down through the gaps; the advance-guard of the shrivelling hot wind had raised foul dust eddies, and the city was ahum when she halted at last beside the big brick arch of the caravansary, where Mahommed Gunga's boots and spurs had caught her eye once.

"Now, Joanna!" She leaned back from the saddle and spoke low, but with a certain thrill. "Go in there, find me Mahommed Gunga-sahib's man, and bring him out here!"

"And if he will not come?" The old woman seemed half-afraid to enter.

"Go in, and don't come out without him—unless you want to see me go in by myself!"

The old woman looked at her piercingly with eyes that gleamed from amid a bunch of wrinkles, then motioned with a skinny arm in the direction of an awning where shade was to be had from the dangerous early sun-rays. She made no move to enter through the arch until her mistress had taken shelter.

Fifteen minutes later she emerged with Ali Partab, who looked sleepy, but still more ashamed of his unmilitary dishabille. Rosemary McClean glanced left and right—forgot about the awning and the custom which decrees aloofness—ignored the old woman's waving arm and Ali Partab's frown, and rode toward him eagerly.

"Did Mahommed Gunga-sahib leave you here with any orders relative to me?" she asked.

The Rajput bowed.

"Before he went away, he spoke to me of safety, and told me he would leave a link between me and men whom I may trust."

The Rajput bowed again. Neither of them saw an elbow laid on the window-ledge of a room above the arch; it disappeared, and very gingerly a bared

black head replaced it. Then the head too disappeared.

The girl's eyes sparkled as the reassurance came
that at least one good fighting man was waiting to
do nothing but assist her. For the moment she
threw caution to the winds and remembered nothing
but her plight and her father's stubbornness.

"My father will not come away, but——"

Ali Partab's eyes betrayed no trace of concern.

"But—I thought— Are you all alone?"

"All alone, Miss-sahib, but your servant."

"Oh! I thought—perhaps that"—she checked
herself, then rushed the words out as though
ashamed of them—"that, if you had men to help
you, you might carry him away against his will!
Where are these others who are to be trusted?"

Ali Partab grinned and then drew himself up with
a movement of polite dissent. It was not for him
to question the suggestions of a Miss-sahib; he con-
veyed that much with an inimitable air. But it
was his business to keep strictly to the letter of his
orders.

"Miss-sahib, I cannot do that. So said Mahommed Gunga: 'When the hag brings word, then take
three horses and bear the Miss-sahib and her father
to my cousin Alwa's place.' I stand ready to obey,
but the padre-sahib comes not against his will."

"To whose place?"

"Alwa's, Miss-sahib."

"And who is he?" She seemed bewildered. "I
had hoped to be escorted to some British residency."

"That would be for Alwa, should he see fit. He has men and horses, and a fort that is impregnable. The Miss-sahib would be safe there under all circumstances."

"But—but, supposing I declined to accept that invitation? Supposing I preferred not to be carried off to a—er—a Mohammedan gentleman's fort. What then?"

"I could but wait here, Miss-sahib, until the hour came when you changed your mind, or until Mahommed Gunga by letter or by word of mouth relieved me of my trust."

"Oh! Then you will wait here until I ask?"

"Surely, Miss-sahib."

The head again peered through the window up above them, but disappeared below the ledge furtively, and none of the three were aware of it. For that matter, the old woman was gazing intently at Ali Partab and listening eagerly; he stood almost underneath the arch, and Miss McClean was staring at him, frowning with the effort to translate her thoughts into a language that is very far from easy. They would none of them have seen the roof descending on them.

"And—and won't you under any circumstances take us, say, to the Resident at Abu instead?"

"I may not, Miss-sahib."

"But why?"

"Of a truth I know not. I never yet knew Mahommed Gunga to give an order without good reason for it; but beyond that he chose me, because he said the task might prove difficult and he trusted me, I know nothing."

"Have you no idea of the reason?"

"Miss-sahib, I am a soldier. To me an order is an order to be carried out; suspicions, fears are nothing unless they stand in the way of accomplishment. I await your word. I am ready. The horses are here—good horses—lean and hard. The order is that you must ask me."

"Thank you—er—Ali what?—thank you, Ali Partab." The disappointment in her voice was scarcely more noticeable than the despondency her drooping figure showed. The little shoulders that had sat so square and gallantly seemed to have lost their strength, and there was none of the determined ring left in the words she hesitated for. "I—hope you will understand that I am grateful—but—I cannot—er—see my way just yet to——"

"In your good time, Miss-sahib. I was ordered to have patience!"

"At least I will have more confidence, knowing that you are always close at hand."

The Rajput bowed. She reined back. He saluted, and she bowed again; then, with a glance to make sure that Joanna followed, she started back at little more than a walking pace—a dejected wraith of a girl on a dejected-looking pony, too overcome by the upsetting of her rebellious scheme to care or even think whether Joanna dropped out of sight or not.

Ali Partab watched her down the street with a

face that betrayed no emotion and no suspicion of
what his thoughts might be. When she was out of
sight he went back under the arch to attend to his
three horses; and the moment that he did so a fat
but very furtive Hindoo took his place—glanced
down the street once in the direction that Rosemary had taken—and then darted up-street as fast
as his shaking paunch would let him. He had been
gone at the least ten minutes, when Joanna, also
furtive, also in a hurry, dodged here and there among
the commencing surge of traffic and approached the
arch again.

It would be useless to try to read her mind, or to
translate the glitter of her beady eyes into thoughts
intelligible to any but an Oriental. It was quite
clear, though, that she wished not to be noticed,
that she feared the occupants of the caravansary,
and that she had returned for word with Ali Partab. He, least of all, would have doubted her intention of demanding the two gold mohurs, for it
was she who had brought the word that Miss Mc-
Clean wanted him. But what relation that intention had to her loyalty or treachery, or whether she
were capable of either—capable of anything except
greed, and obedience for the sake of pay—were
problems no man living could have guessed.

She asked the lounging sweeper by the arch
whether Ali Partab had ridden out as yet. He
jeered back outrageous improprieties, suggestive of
impossible ambition on the hag's part. She called
him "sahib," dubbed him "father of a dozen stal-

wart sons," returned a few of his immodest compliments with a flattering laugh, and learned that Ali Partab was still busy in the caravansary. Then she proceeded to make herself very inconspicuous beside a two-wheeled wagon, up-ended in the gutter opposite the arch, and waited with eastern patience for the horseman to ride out.

She saw the fat Hindoo come back, in no particular hurry now, and seat himself not far from her. Later she saw eight horsemen ride down the street, pass the arch, wheel, and halt. She noticed that they were not Maharajah Howrah's men but a portion of his brother Jaimihr's body-guard, then took no further notice of them. If they chose to wait there, it was no affair of hers, and to appear inquisitive would be to invite a lance-butt, very shrewdly thrust where it would hurt.

It was an hour at least before Ali Partab rode out through the arch, looking down anxiously at his horse's off-hind that had been showing symptoms of "brushing" lately. Joanna rose instantly to cross the street and intercept him; and she recoiled in the nick of time to save herself from being ridden down.

At a sign from the fat Hindoo the eight horsemen spurred, and swooped up-street with the speed and certainty of sparrow-hawks and the noise of devastation. They rode down Ali Partab—unhorsed him —bound him—threw him on his horse again—and galloped off before any but the Hindoo had time to realize that he was their objective. He was gone—

snatched like a chicken from the coop. Noise and dust were all the trace or explanation that he left. The mazy streets swallowed him; the Hindoo waddled over to the arch and disappeared without a smile on his face to show even interest. The interrupted trading and bartering went on again, and no one commented or made a move to follow but Joanna.

She watched the fat Hindoo, and made sure that she would recognize him anywhere again. Then, by a trail that no one would have guessed at and few could have followed, she made her way to Jaimihr's palace—three miles away from Howrah's —where a dozen sulky-looking sepoys lolled, dismounted, by the wooden gate. There was neither sight nor sound of mounted men, and the gate was shut; but in the middle of the roadway there was smoking dung, and there was a suspicion of overacting about the indifference of the guardians of the entrance.

There was no overacting, though, in what Joanna did. Nobody would have dreamed that she was playing any kind of part, or interested in anything at all except the coppers that she begged for. She squatted in the roadway, ink-black and clear-cut in the now blazing sunlight, alternately flattering them and pretending to a knowledge of unguessed-at witchcraft.

She was there still at midday when they changed the guard. She was there when night fell, still squatting in the roadway, still exchanging repartee

and hints at the supernatural with armed men who
shuddered now and then between their bursts of
mockery. The sore, suffering dogs that sniff through
the night for worse eyesores than themselves whim-
pered and watched her. The guard changed and
the moon paled, but she stayed on; and whatever
her purpose, or whatever information she obtained
in fragments amid the raillery, she did not return
to the mission house.

It was not until Rosemary McClean returned and
dismounted by the door that she realized Joanna
had not kept pace. Even then she thought little
of it; the old woman often lingered on the homeward way when the chance of her being needed was
remote. Two or three hours passed before the suspicion rose that anything might have happened to
Joanna, and even then she might not have been
remembered had not Duncan McClean asked for
her.

"I have changed my mind," he said, calling Rosemary into the long, low living-room. It was darkened to exclude the hot wind and the glare, and he
looked like a ghost as he rose to meet her. "I have
decided that my duty is to get away from this place
for your sake and for the sake of the cause I have
at heart. We are doing no good here. I can do
most by going to the Resident, or even to somebody higher up than he, and laying my case before
him personally. Send for Joanna, and tell her to
go and bring Mahommed Gunga's man."

It was then that they missed Joanna and began

to search for her. But no Joanna came. It was
then that Rosemary McClean rehearsed with her
father her former conversation with Mahommed
Gunga and part, at least, of her recent one with
Ali Partab, and the missionary started off himself
to find the horseman whom Mahommed Gunga had
so thoughtfully left behind.

But he very naturally found no Ali Partab. What
he did discover was that he was followed—that a
guard, unarmed but obvious, was placed around
the mission house—that his servants deserted one
by one—that no more children came to the mission
school.

He decided to take chances and ride off with his
daughter in the night. But the ponies went mysteriously lame, and nobody would lend or sell him
horses on any terms at all. He did his best to get
a letter through to anywhere where there were
British, but nobody would take it. And then
Jaimihr came, swaggering with his escort, to offer
him and his daughter the hospitality of his palace.

He declined that offer a little testily, for the insolence behind the offer was less than half con-
cealed. Jaimihr sneered as he rode away.

"Perhaps a month or two of undisturbed enjoyment will induce the padre-sahib to change his mind
about my invitation!" he said nastily. And he
made no secret then, as he ordered them about
before he went, that the men who lounged and
watched at every vantage-point were his.

CHAPTER X

They looked into my eyes and laughed,—
But, what when I was gone?
Have strong men made one of them?
Or do I ride alone?

On the morning after Mahommed Gunga's daring experiment with Cunningham's nervous system he was anxious to say the least of it; and that is only another way of saying that he was irritable. He watched the Englishman at breakfast, on the dak-bungalow veranda, with a sideways restless glance that gave the lie a dozen times over to his assumed air of irascible authority.

"We will see now what we will see," he muttered to himself. "These who know such a lot imagine that the test is made. They forget that there be many brave men of whom but a few are fit to lead. Now—*now*—we will see!" And he kept on repeating that assurance to himself, with the air of a man who would like to be assured, but is not, while he ostentatiously found fault with every single thing on which his eyes lit.

"One would think that the Risaldar-sahib were afraid of consequences!" whispered the youngest of his followers, stung to the quick by a quite unmerited

rebuke. "Does he fear that Chota-Cunnigan will
beat him?"

White men have been known—often—to do stu-
pider things than that, and particularly young white
men who have not yet learned to gauge proportions
accurately; so there was nothing really ridiculous
in the suggestion. A young white man who has
had his temper worked up to the boiling-point, his
nerves deliberately racked, and then has been sub-
jected to the visit of a driven tiger, may be confidently expected to exhibit all the faults of which
his character is capable.

To make the situation even more ticklish, Cunningham's servant, in his zeal for his master's comfort, had forgotten to sham sickness, and instead of
limping was in abominably active evidence. He
was even doing more than was expected of him.
Ralph Cunningham had said nothing to him—had
not needed to; every single thing that a pampered
sahib could imagine that he needed was done for
him in the proper order, without noise or awk-
wardness, and the Risaldar cursed as he watched
the clockwork-perfect service. He had hoped for a
lapse that might call forth some pointer, either by
way of irritation or amusement, as to how young
Cunningham was taking things.

But not a thing went wrong and not a sign of
any sort gave Cunningham. The youngster did not
smile—either to himself darkly or at his servant.
He lit his after-breakfast cigar and smoked it peace-
fully, as though he had spent an absolutely normal

night, without even a dream to worry him, and if he eyed Mahommed Gunga at all, he did it so naturally, and with so little interest, that no deductions could be drawn from it. He was neither more nor less than a sahib at his ease—which was disconcerting, very, to the Oriental mind.

He smoked the cigar to a finish, without a word or sign that he wished to give audience. Then his eyes lit for the first time on the tiger-skin that was pegged out tight, raw side upward, for the sun to sterilize; he threw the butt of his cigar away and strolled out to examine the skin without a sign to Mahommed Gunga, counted the claws one by one to make sure that no superstitious native had purloined any of them, and returned to his chair on the veranda without a word.

"Is he vindictive, then?" wondered Mahommed Gunga. "Is he a mean man? Will he bear malice and get even with me later on? If so——"

"Present my compliments to Mahommed Gunga-sahib, and ask him to be good enough to——"

The Risaldar heard the order, and was on his way to the veranda before the servant started to convey the message. He took no chances on a reprimand about his shoes, for he swaggered up in riding-boots, which no soldier can be asked to take off before he treads on a private floor; and he saluted as a soldier, all dignity. It was the only way by which he could be sure to keep the muscles of his face from telling tales.

"Huzoor?"

"Morning, Mahommed Gunga. Take a seat, won't you?"

A camp-chair creaked under the descending Rajput's weight, and creaked again as he remembered to settle himself less stiffly—less guiltily.

"I say, I'm going to ask you chaps to do me a favor. You don't mind obliging me now and then, do you?"

The youngster leaned forward confidentially, one elbow on his knee, and looked half-serious, as though what he had to ask were more important than the ordinary.

"Sahib, there is nothing that we will not do."

"Ah! Then you won't mind my mentioning this, I'm sure. Next time you want to kennel a tiger in my bedroom, d'you mind giving me notice in advance? It's not the stink I mind, nor being waked up; it's the deuced awful risk of hurting somebody. Besides—look how I spoilt that tiger's mask! The skins I've always admired at home had been shot where it didn't show so badly."

There was not even the symptom of a smile on Cunningham's face. He looked straight into Mahommed Gunga's eyes, and spoke as one man talking calm common sense to another. He raised his hand as the Rajput began to stammer an apology.

"No. Don't apologize. If you'll forgive me for shooting your pet tiger, I'll overlook the rest of it. If I'd known that you kept him in there o' nights, I'd have chosen another room, that's all—some room where I couldn't smell him, and where I shouldn't

run the risk of killing an inoffensive man. Why,
I might have shot *you!* Think how sorry I'd have
been!"

The Risaldar did not quite know what to say; so,
wiser than most, he said nothing.

"Oh, and one other matter. I don't speak much
of the language yet, so, would you mind translating
to my servant that the next time he goes sick without giving me notice, and without putting oil in my
lamp, I'll have him fed to the tiger before he's
brought into my room? Just tell him that quietly,
will you? Say it slowly so that it sinks in. Thanks."

Straight-faced as Cunningham himself, the Risaldar tongue-lashed the servant with harsh, tooth-
rasping words that brought him up to attention.
Whether he interpreted or not the exact meaning of
what Cunningham had said, he at least produced
the desired effect; the servant mumbled apologetic
nothings and slunk off the veranda backward—
to go away and hold his sides with laughter at
the back of the dak-bungalow. There Mahommed
Gunga found him afterward and administered a
thrashing—not, as he was careful to explain, for
disobedience, but for having dared to be amused at
the Risaldar's discomfiture.

But there was still one point that weighed heavily
on Mahommed Gunga's mind as the servant shuffled
off and left him alone face to face with Cunningham.
There is as a very general rule not more than one
man-eating tiger in a neighborhood, and not even
the greenest specimen of subaltern new brought

from home would be likely to mistake one for the other kind. The man-eater was dead, and there was an engagement to shoot one that very morning. He hesitated—said nothing for the moment—and wondered whether his best course would be to go ahead and pretend to beat out the jungle and tell some lie or other about the tiger having got away. But Ralph Cunningham, with serious gray eyes fixed full on his, saved him the trouble of deciding.

"If it's all one to you, Mahommed Gunga," he said, the corner of his mouth just flickering, "we'll move on from here at once. This is a beastly old bungalow to sleep in, and shooting tigers don't seem so terribly exciting to me. Besides, the climate here must be rotten for the horses."

"As you wish, sahib."

"Very well—if the choice rests with me, I wish it. It might—ah—save the villagers a lot of hard work beating through the jungle, mightn't it—besides, there'll be other tigers on the road."

"Innumerable tigers, sahib."

"Good. Will you order a start then?"

The Risaldar departed round the corner of the bungalow, and a minute or two later Cunningham's ears caught the sound of a riding-switch, lustily applied, and of muffled groans. He suspected readily enough what was going on, particularly since his servant was not in evidence, but he dared not laugh on the veranda. He went inside, and made believe to be busy with his bag before he relaxed the muscles of his face.

"Now, I wonder whether I handled that situation rightly?" he asked himself between chuckles. "One thing I know—if that old ruffian plays another trick on me—one more of any kind—I'll show my teeth. There's a thing known as the limit!"

He would not have wondered, though, if he could have overheard Mahommed Gunga less than an hour later. The Risaldar had stayed behind to make sure nothing had been forgotten, and one of his men remained with him.

"There be sahibs and then sahibs," said Mahommed Gunga. "Two kinds are the worst—those who strike readily in anger and use bad language when annoyed, and those whose lips are thin and who save their vengeance to be wreaked later on. They are worse, either of them, than the sahib who is usually drunk."

"And Cunnigan?"

"Is altogether otherwise. As his father was, and as a few other sahibs I have met, he understands what is not spoken—concedes dignity to him who is caught napping, as one who having disarmed his adversary, allows him to recover his weapon—and——"

"And?"

"Proves himself a man worth following! I myself will slit the throat of any man I catch disparaging the name of Chota-Cunnigan-bahadur! By the blood of God—by my medals, my own honor, and the good name of Pukka-Cunnigan, his father, I swear it!"

"Rung Ho!" grinned the six-foot son of war who rode beside him.

They rode on at a walk past the tombstone that —at Mahommed Gunga's orders—the villagers had decked with sickly scented forest flowers, and as they passed they both saluted it in silence. The fakir of the night before, sitting not very far away from it, mimicked them. He sprang on the stone as soon as they were out of sight, scattering the flowers all about him, and calling down the vengeance of a hundred gods on the heads of Christian and Mohammedan alike.

CHAPTER XI

From lone hunt came the yearling cub
And brought a grown kill back;
With fangs aglut "'Tis nothing but
Presumption!" growled the pack.

RALPH CUNNINGHAM reached Peshawur at last
with no less than nine tigers to his gun, and that in
itself would have been sufficient to damn him in the
eyes of more than half of the men who held commands there. Jealousy in those days of slow promotion and intrenched influence had eaten into the
very understanding of men whose only excuse for
rule over a conquered people ought to have been
understanding.

It was not considered decent for a boy of twenty-
one to do much more than dare to be alive. For
any man at all to offer advice or information to his
senior was rank presumption. Criticism was high
treason. Sport, such as tiger-shooting, was for
those whose age and apoplectic temper rendered
them least fitted for it. Conservatism reigned:
"High Toryism, sir, old port, and proud Preroga-
tive!"

Mahommed Gunga grinned into his beard at the
reception that awaited the youngster whom he had
trained for months now in the belief that India had

nothing much to do except reverence him. He laughed aloud, when he could get away to do it, at the flush of indignation on his protégé's face. Tall, clean-limbed, full of health and spirits, he had paid his duty call on a General of Division; with the boyish enthusiasm that says so plainly, "Laugh with me, for the world is mine!" he had boasted of his good luck on the road, only to be snubbed thoroughly and told that tiger-shooting was not what he came for.

He took the snub like a man and made no complaint to anybody; he did not even mention it to the other subalterns, who, most of them, made no secret of their dissatisfaction and its hundred causes. He listened, and it was not very long before it dawned on him that, had not Mahommed Gunga gone with him to pay a call as well, the General of Division would not have so much as interviewed him.

Mahommed Gunga soon became the bane of his existence. The veteran seemed in no hurry to get back to his estate that must have been in serious need of management by this time, but would ride off on mysterious errands and return with a dozen or more black-bearded horsemen each time. He would introduce them to Cunningham in public, whenever possible under the eyes of outraged seniors who would swear and fume and ride away disgusted at the reverence paid to "a mere boy, sir—a bally, ignorant young jackanapes!"

Had Cunningham been other than a born soldier,

with his soldier senses all on edge and sleepless, he
would have fallen foul of disgrace within a month.
He was unattached as yet, and that fact gave opportunity to the men who looked for it to try to
"take the conceit out of the cub, by gad."

"They"—everybody spoke of them as "they"
—conceived the brilliant idea of confronting the
youngster with conditions which he lacked experience to cope with. They set him to deal with circumstances which had long ago proved too difficult
for themselves, and awaited confidently the outcome—the crass mistake, or oversight, or mere mis-
fortune that, with the aid of a possible court martial,
would reduce him to a proper state of humbleness.

Peshawur, the greatest garrison in northern India, was there on sufferance, apparently. For lack
of energetic men in authority to deal with them,
the border robbers plundered while the troops remained cooped up within the unhealthiest station
on the list. The government itself, with several
thousand troops to back it up, was paying blackmail to the border thieves! There was not a government bungalow in all Peshawur that did not have
its "watchman," hired from over the border, well
paid to sleep on the veranda lest his friends should
come and take tribute in an even more unseemly
manner.

The younger men, whose sense of fitness had not
yet been rotted by climate and system and prerog-
ative, swore at the condition; there were one or
two men higher up, destined to make history, whose

voices, raised in emphatic protest, were drowned in the drone of "Peace! Peace is the thing to work for. Compromise, consideration, courtesy, these three are the keys of rule." They failed to realize that cowardice was their real key-note, and that the threefold method that they vaunted was quite useless without a stiffening of courage.

So brave men, who had more courtesy in each of their fingers than most of the seniors had all put together, had to bow to a scandalous condition that made England's rule a laughing-stock within a stone's throw of the city limits. And they had to submit to the indecency of seeing a new, inexperienced arrival picked for the task of commanding a body of irregulars, for no other reason than because it was considered wise to make an exhibition of him.

Cunningham became half policeman, half soldier, in charge of a small special force of mounted men engaged for the purpose of patrol. He had nothing to do with the selection of them; that business was attended to perfunctorily by a man very high up in departmental service, who considered Cunningham a nuisance. He was a gentleman who did not know Mahommed Gunga; another thing he did not know was the comfortable feel of work well done; so he was more than pleased when Mahommed Gunga dropped in from nowhere in particular—paid him scandalously untrue compliments without a blush or a smile—and offered to produce the required number of men at once.

Only fifty were required. Mahommed Gunga

brought three hundred to select from, and, when asked to do so in order to save time and trouble, picked out the fifty best.

"There are your men!" said the Personage off-handedly, when they had been sworn in in a group. "Be good enough to remember, Mr. Cunningham, that you are now responsible for their behavior, and for the proper night patrolling of the city limits."

That was a tall order, and in spite of all of youth's enthusiasm was enough to make any young fellow nervous. But Mahommed Gunga met him in the street, saluted him with almost sacrilegious cere-mony, and drew him to one side.

"Have courage, now, bahadur! I ride away to visit my estates (he spoke of them always in the plural, as though he owned a county or two). You have under you the best eyes and the keenest blades along the border, for I attended to it! Be ruth-less! Use them—work them—sweat them to death! Keep away from messes and parades; seek no praise, for you will get none in any case! Work! Work for what is coming!"

"You speak as though the fate of a continent were hanging in the balance," laughed Cunningham, shaking hands with him.

"I speak truth!" said Mahommed Gunga, riding off and leaving the youngster wondering.

Now, there was nothing much the matter with the men on either side, taken in the main, who hated one another on that far-pushed frontier. Even the

insufferable incompetents who held the rotting reins
of control were such because circumstance had
blinded them. There was not a man among the
highly placed ones even who would have deliberately placed his own importance or his own opinion
in the scale against India's welfare. There was not
a border thief but was ready to respect what he
could recognize as strong-armed justice.

The root of the trouble lay in centralization of
authority, and rigid adherence to the rule of se-
niority. Combined, these two processes had served
to bring about a state of things that is nearly unbe-
lievable when viewed in the light of modern love
for efficiency. Young men, with the fire of ambition
burning in them and a proper scorn for mere superficial ceremony, had to sweat their tempers and bow
down beneath the yoke of senile pompousness.

Strong, savage, powder-weaned Hill-tribesmen—
inheritors of egoistic independence and a love of loot
—laughed loud and long and openly at System that
prevented officers from taking arms against them
until authority could come by delegate from somebody who slept. By that time they would be across
the border, quarrelling among themselves about division of the plunder!

They had respect in plenty for the youth and
virile middle age that dealt with them on the rare
occasions when a timely blow was loosed. Then
they had proof that from that strange, mad country
overseas there came men who could lead men—
men who could strike, and who knew enough to

hold their hands when the sudden blow had told—
just men, who could keep their plighted word. No
border thief pretended that the British *could* not
rule him; to a man, they laughed because the possible was not imposed. And to the last bold, ruffianly iconoclast they stole when, where, and what
they dared.

Things altered strangely soon after Ralph Cunningham, with the diffidence of youth but the blood
of a line of soldiers leaping in him, took charge of
his tiny force of nondescripts. They were neither
soldiers nor police. Nominally, he was everybody's
dog, and so were they; actually he found himself
at the head of a tiny department of his own, because it was nobody's affair to give him orders.
They had deliberately turned him loose "to hang
himself," and their hope that he might get his head
into a noose of trouble as soon as possible—the
very liberty they gave him, on purpose for his quick
damnation—was the means of making reputation
for him.

Nobody advised him; so with singularly British
phlegm and not more than ordinary common sense
he devised a method of his own for scotching night-
prowlers. He stationed his men at well-considered
vantage-points, and trusted them. With a party
of ten, he patrolled the city ceaselessly himself and
whipped every "watchman" he caught sleeping.
One by one, the blackmailing brigade began to see
the discomfort of a job that called for real wakefulness, and deserted over the Hills to urge the resump-

tion of raids in force. One by one, the night-prowling fraternity were shot as they sneaked past sentries. One by one, the tale of robberies diminished. It was merely a question of one man, and he awake, having power to act without first submitting a request to somebody in triplicate on blue-form B.

The time came, after a month or two, when even natives dared to leave their houses after dark. The time came very soon, indeed, when the nearest tribes began to hold war councils and inveigh against the falling off of the supply of plunder. Cunningham was complimented openly. He was even praised by one of "Them." So it was perfectly natural, and quite in keeping with tradition, that he should shortly be relieved, and that a senior to him should be placed in charge of his little force, with orders to "organize" it.

The organization process lasted about twelve hours; at the end of that time every single man had deserted, horse and arms! Two nights later, the prowling and plundering was once more in full swing, and Cunningham was blamed for it; it was obvious to any man of curry-and-port-wine proclivities that his method, or lack of it, had completely undermined his men's loyalty!

A whole committee of gray-headed gentlemen took trouble to point out to him his utter failure; but a brigadier, who was not a member of that committee, and who was considered something of an upstart, asked that he might be appointed to a troop of irregular cavalry that had recently been raised.

With glee—with a sigh of relief so heartfelt and unanimous that it could be heard across the street —the committee leaped at the suggestion. The proper person was induced without difficulty to put his signature to the required paper, and Cunningham found himself transferred to irregular oblivion. Incidentally he found himself commanding few less than a hundred men, so many of whose first names were Mahommed or Mohammed that the muster-roll looked like a list of Allah's prophets.

Cunningham was more than a little bit astonished, on the day he joined, in camp, a long way from Peshawur, to find his friend Mahommed Gunga seated in a bell tent with the Brigadier. He caught sight of the long black military boot and silver spur, and half-recognized the up-and-down movement of the crossed leg long before he reached the tent. It was like father and son meeting, almost, as the Rajput rose to greet him and waited respectfully until he had paid his compliments to his new commander. Cunningham felt throat-bound, and could scarcely more than stammer his introduction of himself.

"I know who you are and all about you," said the Brigadier. "Used to know your father well. I applied to have you in my command partly for your father's sake, but principally because Risaldar Mahommed Gunga spoke so highly of you. He tells me he has had an eye on you from the start, and that you shape well. Remember, this is irregular cavalry, and in many respects quite unlike regulars.

You'll need tact and a firm hand combined, and you mustn't ever forget that the men whom you will lead are gentlemen."

Cunningham reported to his Colonel, only to discover that he, too, knew all about him. The Colonel was less inclined to be restricted as to topic, and less mindful of discretion than the Brigadier.

"I hear they couldn't stand you in Peshawur. That's hopeful! If you'd come with a recommendation from that quarter, I'd have packed you off back again. I never in my life would have believed that a dozen men could all shut their eyes so tightly to the signs—never!"

"The signs, sir?"

"Yes, the signs! Come and look your troop over."

Cunningham found that the troop, too, had heard about his coming. He did not look them over. When he reached the lines, they came out in a swarm—passed him one by one, eyed him, as traders eye a horse—and then saluted him a second time, with the greeting:

"Salaam, Chota-Cunnigan-bahadur!"

"Yes! You're in disgrace!" said his Colonel, noticing the color rising to the youngster's cheeks.

CHAPTER XII

Sons of the sons of war we be,
Sabred and horsed, and whole and free;
One is the caste, and one degree,—
        One law,—one code decreed us.
Who heads wolves in the dawning day?
Who leaps in when the bull's at bay?
He who dare is he who may!
        Now, rede ye who shall lead us!

THE check that Ralph Cunningham's management of his police had caused, and the subsequent resumption of night looting, served to whet the appetites of the hungry crowd beyond the border. Those closest to Peshawur, who had always done the looting, were not the ultimate consignees by any means; there were other tribes who bought from them—others yet to whom they paid tribute in the shape of stolen rifles. Cunningham's administration had upset the whole modus vivendi of the lower Himalayas!

Though it all began again the moment he was superseded, there had been, none the less, a three-month interregnum, and that had to be compensated for. The tribes at the rear were clamorous and would not listen to argument or explanation; they had collected in hundreds, led by the notorious Khumel Khan, preparatory to raiding in real earnest and with sufficient force to carry all before them at the first surprise attack.

They were disappointed when the pilfering resumed, for a tribal Hillman would generally rather fight than eat, and would always prefer his dinner from a dead enemy's cooking-pot. They sat about for a long time, considering whether there were not excuse enough for war in any case and listening to the intricately detailed information brought by the deserting watchmen. And as they discussed things, but before they had time to decide on any plan, the Brigadier commanding the Irregulars got wind of them

He was a man who did not worry about the feelings of senile heads of red-tape-bound departments; nor was he particularly hidebound by respect for the laws of evidence. When he knew a thing, he knew it; then he either acted or did not act, as the circumstances might dictate. And when the deed was done or left undone, and was quite beyond the reach of criticism, he would send in a verbose, voluminous report, written out in several colored inks, on all the special forms he could get hold of. The heads of departments would be too busy for the next twelvemonth trying to get the form of the report straightened out to be able to give any attention to the details of it; and then it would be too late. But he was a brigadier, and what he could do with impunity and quiet amusement would have brought down the whole Anglo-Indian Government in awful wrath on the head of a subordinate.

He heard of the tribesmen under **Khumel Khan**
one evening. At dawn his tents stood empty and
the horse-lines were long bands of brown on the
green grass. The pegs were up; only the burying
beetles labored where the stamping chargers had
neighed overnight.

The hunger-making wind that sweeps down, snow-
sweetened, from the Himalayas bore with it intermittent thunder from four thousand hoofs as, split
in three and swooping from three different directions, the squadrons viewed, gave tongue, and
launched themselves, roaring, at the half-awakened
plotters of the night before.

There was a battle, of a kind, in a bowlder-lined
valley where the early morning sun had not yet
reached to lift the chill. Long lances—devils' an-
tennæ—searched out the crevices where rock-bred
mountain-men sought cover; too suddenly for clumsy-
fingered Hillmen to reload, the re-formed troops
charged wedgewise into rallying detachments. In
an hour, or less, there were prisoners being herded
like cattle in the valley bottom, and a sting had
been drawn from the border wasp that would not
grow again for a year or two to come.

But Khumel Khan was missing. Khumel Khan,
the tulwar man—he whose boast it was that he
could hew through two men's necks at one whistling
sweep of his notched, curved cimeter—had broken
through with a dozen at his back. He had burst
through the half-troop guarding the upper end of
the defile, had left them red and reeling to count

their dead, and the overfolding hill-spurs swallowed him.

"Mr. Cunningham! Take your troop, please, and find their chief! Hunt him out, ride him down, and get him! Don't come back until you do!"

The real thing! The real red thing within a year! A lone command—and that is the only thing a subaltern of spunk may pray for!—eighty-and-eight hawk-eyed troopers asking only for the opportunity to show their worth—lean, hungry hills to hunt in, no commissariat, fair law to the quarry, and a fight—as sure as God made mountains, a fight at the other end! There are men here and there who think that the day when they pass down a crowded aisle with Her is the great one, to which other great days are all as gas-jets to the sun. And there are others. There are men, like Cunningham, who have heard the drumming of the hoofs behind them as they led their first un-apron-stringed unit out into the unknown. The one kind of man has tasted honey, but the other knows what fed, and feeds, the roaring sportsmen in Valhalla.

There were crisscross trails, where low-hung clouds swept curtainwise to make the compass seem like a lie-begotten trick. There were gorges, hewn when the Titans needed dirt to build the awful Himalayas—shadow-darkened—sheer as the edge of Nemesis. Long-reaching, pile on pile, the overlapping spurs leaned over them. The wind blew through them amid silence that swallowed and made nothing of the din which rides with armed men.

But, with eyes that were made for hunting, on horses that seemed part of them, they tracked and trailed—and viewed at last. Their shout gave Khumel Khan his notice that the price of a hundred murders was overdue, and he chose to make payment where a V-shaped cliff enclosed a small, flat plateau and not more than a dozen could ride at him at a time. His companions scattered much as a charge of shrapnel shrieks through the rocks, but Khumel Khan knew well enough that he was the quarry— his was the head that by no conceivable chance would be allowed to plan fresh villainies. He might have run yet a little way, but he saw the uselessness, and stood.

The troop, lined out knee to knee, could come within a hundred paces of him without breaking; it formed a base, then, to a triangle from which the man at bay could no more escape than a fire-ringed scorpion.

"Call on him to surrender!" ordered Cunningham.

A chevroned black-beard half a horse-length behind him translated the demand into stately Pashtu, and for answer the hill chieftain mounted his stolen horse and shook his tulwar. He had pistols at his belt, but he did not draw them; across his shoulder swung a five-foot-long jezail, but he loosed it and flung it to the ground.

"Is there any here dare take me single-handed?" he demanded with a grin.

Of the eight-and-eighty, there were eighty-eight

who dared; but there was an eighty-ninth, a lad of
not yet twenty-two, whom Indian chivalry desired
to honor. The troop had heard but the troop had
not yet seen.

"Ride in and take him!" ordered Cunningham,
and there was a thoroughly well acted make-believe
of fear, while every eye watched "Cunnigan-bahadur," and the horses, spurred and reined at once,
pranced at their bits for just so long as a good
man needs to make his mind up. And Cunningham
rode in.

He rode in as a Rajput rides, with a swoop and a
swinging sabre and a silent, tight-lipped vow that
he would prove himself. Green though he was yet,
he knew that the troop had found for him—had
rounded up for him—had made him his opportunity;
so he took it, right under their eyes, straight in
the teeth of the stoutest tulwar man of the lower
Himalayas.

He, too, had pistols at his belt, but there was no
shot fired. There was nothing but a spur-loosed
rush and a shock—a spark-lit, swirling, slashing,
stamping, snorting mêlée—a stallion and a mare
up-ended—two strips of lightning steel that slit the
wind—and a thud, as a lifeless border robber took
the turf.

There was silence then—the grim, good silence
of Mohammedan approval—while a native officer
closed up a sword-cut with his fingers and tore ten-
yard strips from his own turban to bind the youngster's head. They rode back without boast or noise

and camped without advertisement. There was no demonstration made; only—a colonel said, "I like things done that way, quickly, without fuss," and a brigadier remarked, "Hrrrumph! 'Gratulate you, Mr. Cunningham!"

Later, when they camped again outside Peshawur, a reward of three thousand rupees that had been offered on the border outlaw's head was paid to Cunningham in person—a very appreciable sum to a subaltern, whose pay is barely sufficient for his mess bills. So, although no public comment was made on the matter, it was considered "decent of him" to contribute the whole amount to a pension fund for the dependents of the regiment's dead.

"You know, that's your money," said his Colonel. "You can keep every anna of it if you choose."

"I suppose I needn't be an officer unless I choose?" suggested Cunningham.

"I don't know, youngster! I can't guess what your troop would do if you tried to desert it!"

That was, of course, merely a diplomatic recognition of the fact that Cunningham had done his duty in making his men like him, and was not intended seriously. Nobody—not even the Brigadier—had any notion that the troop would very shortly have to dispense with its leader's services whether it wanted to or not.

But it so happened that one troop at a time was requisitioned to be ornamental body-guard to such as were entitled to one in the frontier city; and the turn arrived when Cunningham was sent. None liked the duty. No soldier, and particularly no irregular, likes to consider himself a pipe-clayed ornament; but Cunningham would have "gone sick" had he had the least idea of what was in store for him.

It was bad enough to be obliged to act as bodyguard to men who had jockeyed him away because they were jealous of him. The white scar that ran now like a chin-strap mark from the corner of his eye to the angle of his jaw would blaze red often at some deliberately thought-out, not fancied, insult from men who should have been too big to more than notice him. And that, again, was nothing to the climax.

Mahommed Gunga chose to polish up his silver spurs and ride in from his "estates" on a protracted visit to Peshawur, and with an escort that must have included half the zemindars on the countryside as well as his own small retinue. Glittering on his own account like a regiment of horse, and with all but a regiment clattering behind him, he chose the occasion to meet Cunningham when the youngster was fuming with impatience opposite the club veranda, waiting to escort a general.

On the veranda sat a dozen men who had been at considerable pains to put and keep the officer of the escort in his place. If the jingle and glitter of the approaching cavalcade had not been sufficient to attract their notice, they could have stopped their ears and yet have been forced to hear the greeting.

"Aha! Salaam, sahib! Chota-Cunnigan-bahadur,

bohut salaam! Thy father's son! Sahib, I am much
honored!"

The white scar blazed, but Mahommed Gunga
affected not to notice the discomfort of his victim.
Many more than a hundred sabred gentlemen pressed
round to "do themselves the honor," as they expressed it, of paying Cunningham a compliment.
They rode up like knights in armor in the lists, and
saluted like heralds bringing tribute and allegiance.

"Salaam, Chota-Cunnigan!"

"Salaam, sahib!"

"Bohut salaam, bahadur!"

The Generals, the High-Court Judges, and Commis-
sioners on the club veranda sat unhonored, while
a boy of twenty-two received obeisance from men
whose respect a king might envy. No Rajput ever
lived who was not sure that his salute was worth
more than tribute; he can be polite on all occasions,
and what he thinks mere politeness would be considered overacting in the West, but his respect and
his salute he keeps for his equals or his betters—
and they must be men indeed.

The coterie of high officials sat indignation-bound
for ten palpitating minutes, until the General remembered that it was *his* escort that was waiting
for him. He had ordered it an hour too soon, for
the express sweet purpose of keeping Cunningham
waiting in the sun, but it dawned now on his apoplectic consciousness that his engagement was most
urgent. He descended in a pompous hurry, mounted
and demanded why—by all the gods of India—the

escort was not lined up to receive him. A minute later, after a loudly administered reprimand that was meant as much for the swarm of Rajputs as for the indignant Cunningham, he rode off with the escort clattering behind him.

But on the club veranda, when the Rajputs with Mahommed Gunga had dispersed, the big wigs sat and talked the matter over very thoroughly.

"It's no use blinking matters," said the senior man present, using a huge handkerchief to wave the flies away from the polished dome which rose between two side wisps of gray hair. "They're going to lionize him while he's here, so we'd better move him on."

"But where?"

"I've got it! There's a letter in from Everton at Abu, saying he needs a man badly to go to Howrah and act resident there—says he hasn't heard from the missionaries and isn't satisfied—wants a man without too much authority to go there and keep an eye on things in general. Howrah's a hell of a place from all accounts."

"But that 'ud be promotion!"

"Can't be helped. No excuse for reducing him, so far as I've heard. The trouble is the cub has done too dashed well. We've got to promote him if we want to be rid of him."

They talked it over for an hour, and at the end of it decided Cunningham should go to Howrah, provided a brigadier could be induced without too much argument to see reason.

"The Brigadier probably wants to keep him, and his Colonel will raise all the different kinds of Cain there are!" suggested the man who had begun the discussion.

"I've seen brigadiers before now reduced to a proper sense of their own unimportance!" remarked another man. And he was connected with the Treasury. He knew.

But a week later, when the papers were sent to the Brigadier for signature, he amazed everybody by consenting without the least objection. Nobody but he knew who his visitor had been the night before.

"How did you know about it, Mahommed Gunga?" he demanded, as the veteran sat and faced him over the tent candle, his one lean leg swaying up and down, as usual, above the other.

"Have club servants not got ears, sahib?"

"And you——?"

"I, too, have ears—good ones!"

The Brigadier drummed his fingers on the table, hesitating. No officer, however high up in the service, likes to lose even a subaltern from his command when that subaltern is worth his salt.

"Let him go, sahib! You have seen how we Rangars honor him—you may guess what difference he might make in a crisis. Sign, sahib—let him go!"

"But—where do you come in? What have you had to do with this?"

"First, sahib, I tested him thoroughly. I found him good. Second, I told tales about him, making him out better than even he is. Third, I made sure that all those in authority at Peshawur should hate him. That would have been impossible if he had been a fool, or a weak man, or an incompetent; but any good man can be hated easily. Fourth, sahib, I sent, by the hand of a man of mine, a message to Everton-sahib at Abu reporting to him that all was not in Howrah as it should be, and warning him that a sahib should be sent there. I knew that he would listen to a hint from me, and I knew that he had no one in his office whom he could send. Then, sahib, I brought matters to a head by bringing every man of merit whom I could raise to salute him and make an outrageous exhibition of him. That is what I have done!"

"One would think you were scheming for a throne, Mahommed Gunga!"

" Nay, sahib, I am scheming for the peace of India! But there will be war first."

"I know there will be war," said the Brigadier. "I only wish I could make the other sahibs realize it."

"Will you sign the paper, sahib?"

"Yes, I will sign the paper. But——"

"But what, sahib?"

"I'm not quite certain that I'm doing right."

"Brigadier-sahib, when the hour comes—and that is soon—it will be time to answer that! There lie the papers."

CHAPTER XIII

Even in darkness lime and sand
  Will blend to make up mortar.
Two by two would equal four
  Under a bucket of water.

Now it may seem unimaginable that two Europeans could be cooped in Howrah, not under physical restraint, and yet not able to communicate with any one who could render them assistance. It was the case, though, and not by any means an isolated case. The policy of the British Government, once established in India, was and always has been not to occupy an inch of extra territory until compelled by circumstances.

The native states, then, while forbidden to contract alliances with one another or the world outside, and obliged by the letter of written treaties to observe certain fundamental laws imposed on them by the Anglo-Indian Government, were left at liberty to govern themselves. And it was largely the fact that they could and did keep secret what was going on within their borders that enabled the so-called Sepoy Rebellion to get such a smouldering foothold before it burst into a blaze. The sepoys were the tools of the men behind the movement; and the men behind were priests and others who were feeding nothing but their own ambition.

No man knows even now how long the fire of rebellion had been burning underground before it showed through the surface; but it is quite obvious that, in spite of the heroism shown by British and loyal native alike when the crash did come, the rebels must have won—and have won easily by sheer weight of numbers—had they only used their amazing system solely for the broad, comprehensive purpose for which it was devised.

But the sense of power that its ramifications and extent gave birth to also whetted the desires of individuals. Each man of any influence at all began to scheme to use the system for the furtherance of his individual ambition. Instead of bending all their energy and craft to the one great object of hurling an unloved conqueror back whence he came, each reigning prince strove to scheme himself head and shoulders above the rest; and each man who wanted to be prince began to plot harder than ever to be one.

So in Howrah the Maharajah's brother, Jaimihr, with a large following and organization of his own, began to use the secret system of which he by right formed an integral part and to set wheels working within the wheels which in course of time should spew him up on the ledge which his brother now occupied. Long before the rebellion was ready he had all his preparations made and waited only for the general conflagration to strike for his own hand. And he was so certain of success that he dared make plans as well for Rosemary McClean's fate.

There is a blindness, too, quite unexplainable that comes over whole nations sometimes. It is almost like a plague in its mysterious arrival and departure. As before the French Revolution there were almost none of the ruling classes who could read the writing on the wall, so it was in India in the spring of '57. Men saw the signs and could not read their meaning. As in France, so in India, there were a few who understood, but they were scoffed at; the rest—the vast majority who held the reins of power—were blind.

Rosemary McClean discovered that her pony had gone lame, and was angry with the groom. The groom ran away, and she put that down to native senselessness. Duncan McClean sent one after another of the little native children to find him a man who would take a letter to Mount Abu. The children went and did not come back again, and he put that down to the devil, who would seem to have reclaimed them.

Both of them saw the watchers, posted at every vantage-point, insolently wakeful; both of them knew that Jaimihr had placed them there. But neither of them looked one inch deeper than the surface, nor supposed that their presence betokened anything but the prince's unreachable ambition. Neither of them thought for an instant that the day could possibly have come when Britain would be unable to protect a woman of its own race, or when a native—however powerful—would dare to do more than threaten.

Joanna disappeared, and that led to a chain of thought which was not creditable to any one concerned. They reasoned this way: Rosemary had seen Mahommed Gunga hold out a handful of gold coins for the old woman's eyes to glitter at, therefore it was fair to presume that he had promised her a reward for bringing word to the man whom, it was now known, he had left behind. She had brought word to him and had disappeared. What more obvious than to reason that the man had gladly paid her, and had just as gladly ridden off, rejoicing at the thought that he could escape doing service?

"So much," they argued, "for native constancy! So much for Mahommed Gunga's boast that he knew of men who could be trusted! And so much for Joanna's gratitude!"

The old woman had been saved by Rosemary McClean from the long-drawn-out hell that is the life portion of most Indian widows, even of low caste; she had had little to do, ever, beyond snooze in the shade and eat, and run sometimes behind the pony—a task which came as easily to her as did the other less active parts of her employment. Her desertion, particularly at a crisis, made Rosemary McClean cry, and set her father to quoting Shakespeare's "King Lear."

> "Blow, blow, thou winter wind!
> Thou art not so unkind
> As man's ingratitude!"

All Scotsmen seem to have a natural proclivity for quoting the appropriate dirge when sorrow shows itself. The Book of Lamentations—Shakespeare's sadder lines—roll off their tongues majestically and seem to give them consolation—as it were to lay a sound, unjoyous basis for the proper enjoyment of the songs of Robbie Burns.

The poor old king of the poet's imagining, declaiming up above the cliffs of Dover, could have put no more pathos into those immortal lines than did Duncan McClean as he paced up and down between the hot walls of the darkened room. The dry air parched his throat, and his ambition seemed to shrivel in him as he saw the brave little woman who was all he had sobbing with her head between her hands.

He turned to the Bible, but he could find no precedent in any of its pages for abandoning a quest like his in the teeth of disaster or adversity. He read it for hour after crackling hour, moistening his throat from time to time with warm, unappetizing water from the improvised jar filter; but when the oven blast that makes the Indian summer day a hell on earth had waned and died away, he had found nothing but admonishment to stand firm. There had been women, too, whose deeds were worthy of record in that book, and he found no argument for deserting his post on his daughter's account either. In the Bible account, as he read it, it had always been the devil who fled when things got too uncomfortable for him, and he was conscious of a tight-lipped, stern contempt for the devil.

He had about made up his mind what line to take with his daughter, when she ceased her sobbing and looked up through swollen eyes to relieve him of the necessity for talking her over to his point of view. What she said amazed him, but not because it came to him as a new idea. She said, in different words, exactly what was passing in his own mind, and it was as though her tears and his search of the Scriptures had brought them both to one clear-cut conclusion.

"Why are we here, father?" she asked him suddenly; and because she took him by surprise he did not answer her at once. "We are here to do good, aren't we?" That was no question; it was the beginning of a line of argument. Her father held his tongue, and laid his Bible down, and listened on. "How much good have we done yet?"

She paused, but the pause was rhetorical, and he knew it; he could see the light behind her eyes that was more than visionary; it was the light of practical Scots enthusiasm, unquenched and undiscouraged after a battle with fear itself. She began to be beautiful again as the spirit of unconquerable courage won its way.

"Have we won one convert? Is there one, of all those you have taught who is with us still?"

The answer was self-evident. There was none. But there was no sting for him in what she asked. Rather her words came as a relief, for he could feel the strength behind them. He still said nothing.

"Have we stopped one single suttee? Have we once, in any least degree, lessened the sufferings of one of those poor widows?"

"Not once," he answered her, without a trace of shame. He knew, and she knew, how hard the two of them had tried. There was nothing to apologize for.

"Have we undermined the power of the Hindoo priests? Have we removed one trace of superstition?"

"No," he said quietly.

"Have we given up the fight?"

He looked hard at her. Gray eyes under gray brows met gray eyes that shone from under dark, wet lashes, and deep spoke unto deep. Scotsman recognized Scotswoman, and the bond between them tightened.

"It seems to me"—there was a new thrill in her voice—"that here is our opportunity! *Either* Jaimihr wants to frighten us away *or* he is in earnest with his impudent attentions to me. In either case let us make no attempt to go away. Let us refuse to go away. Let us stay here at all costs. If he wishes us to go away, then he must have a reason and will show it, or else try to force us. If he is really trying to make love to me, then let him try; if he has pluck enough, let him seize me. In either case we shall force his hand. I am willing to be the bait. The moment that he harms either you or me, the government will *have* to interfere. If he kills us, so much the better, for that would mean swift vengeance and a British occupation. That would stop suttee for all time, and we would have given our lives for something worth while. As we are, we cannot communicate with our government, and Jaimihr thinks he has us in his grasp. Let him think it! Let him go ahead! Sooner or later the government *must* find out that we are missing. Then—!" Her eyes blazed at the thought of what would happen then.

Her father looked at her for about a minute, sadness and pride in her fighting in him for the mastery. Then he rose and crossed the little space between them.

"Lassie!" he said. "Lassie!"

She took his hand—the one little touch of human sentiment lacking to disturb his emotional balance. The Scots will talk readily enough of sorrow, but at showing it they are a grudging race of men. Unless a Scotsman thinks he can gain something for his cause by showing what emotion racks him, he will swallow down the choking flood of grief, and keep a straight face to the world and his own as well. Duncan McClean turned from her—drew his hand away—and walked to open the slit shutters. A moment later he came back, once more master of himself.

"As things are, dear," he said gently, "how would it be possible for us to get away?"

"'We canna gang awa'!'" she quoted, with a smile.

"No, lassie. We must stay here and be brave. This matter is not in our hands. We must wait, and watch, and see. If opportunity should come to us to make our escape, we will seize it. Should it not come—should Jaimihr, or some other of them, make occasion to molest us—it may be—it might be that—surely the day of martyrs is not past—it might be that—well, well, in either case we will eventually win. Should they kill us, the government must send here to avenge us; should we get away, surely our report will be listened to. A month or two—perhaps only a week or two—even a day or two, who knows?—and the last suttee will have been performed!"

He stood and stroked her head—then stooped and kissed it—an unusual betrayal of emotion from him.

"Ye're a brave lassie," he said, leaving the room hurriedly, to escape the shame of letting her see tears welling from his eyes—salt tears that scalded as they broke their hot-wind-wearied bounds.

Five minutes later she arose, dry-eyed, and went to stand in the doorway, where an eddy or two of lukewarm evening breeze might possibly be stirring. But a dirtily clad Hindoo, lounging on a raised, railless store veranda opposite, leered at her impudently, and she came inside again—to pass the evening and the sultry, black, breathless night out of sight, at least, of the brutes who shut her off from even exercise.

CHAPTER XIV

So, I am a dog? Hence I must come
    To do thy bidding faster?
Must tell thee— Nay, a dog stays dumb!
    A dog obeys one master!

NOT many yards from where the restless elephants
stood lined under big brick arches—in an age-old
courtyard, three sides of which were stone-carved
splendor and the fourth a typically Eastern mess of
stables, servants' quarters, litter, stink, and noisy
confusion—a stone door, slab-hewn, gave back the
aching glitter of the sun. Its only opening—a narrow slit quite near the top—was barred. A man—his
face close-pressed against them—peered through the
interwoven iron rods from within.

Jaimihr, in a rose-pink pugree still, but not at
all the swaggering cavalier who pranced, high-
booted, through the streets—a down-at-heel prince,
looking slovenly and heavy-eyed from too much
opium—sat in a long chair under the cloister which
faced the barred stone door. He swished with a
rhino riding-whip at the stone column beside him,
and the much-swathed individual of the plethoric
paunch who stood and spoke with him kept a very
leery eye on it; he seemed to expect the binding

swish of it across his own shins, and the thought seemed tantalizing.

"It is not to be done," said Jaimihr, speaking in a dialect peculiar to Howrah. "That—of all the idiotic notions I have listened to—is the least worth while! Thy brains are in thy belly and are lost amid the fat! If my brother Howrah only had such counsellors as thou—such monkey folk to make his plans for him—the jackals would have finished with him long ago."

"Sahib, did I not bring word, and overhear, and trap the man?"

"Truly! Overheard whisperings, and trapped me a hyena I must feed! Now thou sayest, 'Torture him!' He is a Rangar, and of good stock; therefore, no amount of torturing will make him speak. He is that pig Mahommed Gunga's man; therefore, there is nothing more sure than that Mahommed Gunga will be here, sooner or later, to look for him—Mahommed Gunga, with the half of a Hindoo name, the whole of a Moslem's fire, and the blind friendship of the British to rely on!"

"But if the man be dead when Mahommed Gunga comes?"

"He will be dead when Mahommed Gunga comes, if only what we await has first happened. But this rising that is planned hangs fire. Were I Maharajah I would like to see the Rangar who dare flout me or ask questions! I would like but to set eyes on that Rangar once! But I am not yet Maharajah; I am a prince—a younger brother—surrounded, counselled, impeded, hampered, rendered laughable by fat idiots!"

"My belly but shows your highness's generosity. At whose cost have I grown fat?"

"Ay, at whose cost? I should have kept thee slim, on prison diet, and saved myself a world of useless problems! Cease prattling! Get away from me! If I have to poison this Ali Partab, or wring his casteless neck, I will make thee do it, and give thee to Mahommed Gunga to wreak vengeance on. Leave me to think!"

The fat former occupant of the room above the arch of the caravansary waddled to the far end of the cloister, and sat down, cross-legged, to grumble to himself and scratch his paunch at intervals. His master, low-browed and irritable, continued to strike the stone column with his cane. He was in a horrid quandary.

Mahommed Gunga was one of many men he did not want, for the present, to offend seriously. Given a fair cause for quarrel, that irascible ex-Risaldar was capable of going to any lengths, and was known, moreover, to be trusted by the British. Nobody seemed to know whether or not Mahommed Gunga reciprocated the British regard, and nobody had cared to ask him except his own intimates; and they, like he, were men of close counsel.

The Prince had given no orders for the capture of Ali Partab; that had been carried out by his men in a fit of ill-advised officiousness. But the Prince had to solve the serious problem caused by the presence of Ali Partab within a stone-walled cell.

Should he let the fellow go, a report would be
certain to reach Mahommed Gunga by the speediest
route. Vengeance would be instantly decided on,
for a Rajput does not merely accept service; he
repays it, feudal-wise, and smites hip and thigh for
the honor of his men. The vengeance would be sure
to follow purely Eastern lines, and would be complicated; it would no doubt take the form of siding
in some way or other with his brother the Maharajah.
There would be instant, active doings, for that was
Mahommed Gunga's style! The fat would be in the
fire months, perhaps, before the proper time.

The prisoner's presence was maddening in a million ways. It had been the Prince's plan (for he
knew well enough that Mahommed Gunga had left
a man behind) to allow the escape to start; then
it would have been an easy matter to arrange an
ambush—to kill Ali Partab—and to pretend to ride
to the rescue. Once rescued, Miss McClean and
her father would be almost completely at his mercy,
for they would not be able to accuse him of anything but friendliness, and would be obliged to return to whatever haven of safety he cared to offer
them. Once in his palace of their own consent,
they would have had to stay there until the rising
of the whole of India put an end to any chance of
interference from the British Government.

But now there was no Ali Partab outside to try
to escort them to some place of safety; therefore,
there was little chance that the missionaries would
try to make a bolt. Instead of being in the position
of a cat that watches silently and springs when the

mouse breaks cover, he was in the unenviable condition now of being forced to make the first move.
Over and over again he cursed the men who had
made Ali Partab prisoner, and over and over again
he wondered how—by all the gods of all the multi-
tudinous Hindoo mythology—how, when, and by
what stroke of genius he could make use of the
stiff-chinned Rangar and convert him from being
a rankling thorn into a useful aid.

He dared not poison him—yet. For the same
reason he dared not put him to the torture, to discover, or try to discover, what Mahommed Gunga's
real leanings were in the matter of loyalty to the
Raj or otherwise. He dared not let the man go,
for forgiveness is not one of the virtues held in high
esteem by men of Ali Partab's race, and wrongful
arrest is considered ground enough for a feud to the
death. It seemed he did not dare do anything!

He racked his opium-dulled brain for a suspicion
of a plan that might help solve the difficulty, until
his eye—wandering around the courtyard—fell on
the black shape of a woman. She was old and bent,
and she was busied, with a handful of dry twigs,
pretending to sweep around the stables.

"Who is that mother of corruption?" demanded
Jaimihr; and a man came running to him.

"Who is that eyesore? I have never seen her,
have I?"

"Highness, she is a beggar woman. She sat by
the gate, and pretended to a power of telling for-
tunes—which it would seem she does possess in

some degree. It was thought better that she should
use her gift in here, for our advantage, than outside
to our disadvantage. So she was brought in and
set to sweeping."

"By the curse of the sin of the sack of Chitor, is
my palace, then, a midden for the crawling offal of
all the Howrah streets? First this Rangar—next a
sweeper hag—what follows? What bring you next?
Go, fetch the street dogs in!"

"Highness, she is useful and costs nothing but
the measure or two of meal she eats."

"A horse eats little more!" the angry Prince retorted, perfectly accustomed to being argued with
by his own servants. That is the time-honored
custom of the East; obedience is one thing—argument another—both in their way are good, and
both have their innings. "Bring her to me—nay!
—keep her at a decent distance—so!—am I dirt for
her broom?"

He sat and scowled at her, and the old woman
tried to hide more of her protruding bones under
the rag of clothing that she wore; she stood, wrig-
gling in evident embarrassment, well out in the sun.

"What wiltst thou steal of mine?" the Prince demanded suddenly.

"I am no thief." Bright, beady eyes gleamed
back at him, and gave the lie direct to her shrinking
attitude of fear. But he had taken too much opium
overnight, and was in no mood to notice little dis-
tinctions. He was satisfied that she should seem
properly afraid of him, and he scowled angrily when

one of his retainers—in slovenly undress—crossed the courtyard to him. The man's evident intention, made obvious by his manner and his leer at the old woman, was to say something against her; the Prince was in a mood to quarrel with any one, on any ground at all, who did not cower to him.

"Prince, she it is who ran ever with the white woman, as a dog runs in the dust."

"What does she here, then?"

"Ask her!" grinned the trooper. "Unless she comes to look for Ali Partab, I know not."

He made the last part of his remark in a hurried undertone, too low for the old woman to hear.

"Let her earn her meal around the stables," said the Prince. A sudden light dawned on him. Here was a means, at least, of trying to make use of Ali Partab. "Go—do thy sweeping!" he commanded, and the hag slunk off.

For ten minutes longer, Jaimihr sat still and flicked at the stone column with his whip; then he sent for his master of the horse, whose mistaken sense of loyalty had been the direct cause of Ali Partab's capture. He had acted instantly when the fat Hindoo brought him word, and he had expected to be praised for quick decision and rewarded; he was plainly in high dudgeon as he swaggered out of a dark door near the stables and advanced sulkily toward his master.

"Remove the prisoner from that cell, taking great care that the hag yonder sees what you do—yes, that hag—the new one; she is a spy. Bring the prisoner in to me, where I will talk with him; afterward place him in a different cell—put him where we kept the bear that died—there is a dark corner beside it, where a man might hide; hide a man there when it grows dark. And give the hag access. Say nothing to her; let her come and go as she will; watch, and listen."

Without another word, the Prince got up and shuffled in his decorated slippers to a door at one end of the cloister. Five minutes later Ali Partab —high-chinned, but looking miserable—was led between two men through the same door, while the old woman went on very ostentatiously with her sweeping about the yard. She even turned her back, to prove how little she was interested.

Ali Partab was hustled forward into a high-ceilinged room, whose light came filtered through a scrollwork mesh of chiselled stone where the wall and ceiling joined. There were no windows, but six doors opened from it, and every one of them was barred, as though they opened into treasure-vaults. The Prince sat restlessly in a high, carved wooden chair; there was no other furniture at all, and Ali Partab was left standing between his guards. The Prince drew a pistol from inside his clothing.

"Leave us alone!" he ordered; and the guards went out, closing the door behind them.

"I gave no orders for your capture," said Jaimihr, with a smile.

"Then, let me go," grinned Ali Partab.

"First, I must be informed on certain matters."

Ali Partab still grinned, but the muscles of his face changed their position slightly, and it took no expert in physiognomy to read that questions he would answer must be very tactfully asked.

"Ask on!"

"You are Mahommed Gunga's man?"

"Yes. It is an honorable service."

"Did he order you to stay here?"

"Here—in this palace? Allah forbid!"

"Did he order you to stay in Howrah?"

"He gave me certain orders. I obeyed them until your men invited swift death for themselves and you by interfering with me!"

"What were the orders?"

Ali Partab grinned again—this time insolently.

"To make sure that the Jaimihr-sahib did not make away with the treasure of his brother Howrah!" he answered.

"If you were released now what would you proceed to do?"

"To obey my orders."

Jaimihr changed his tactics and assumed the frequently successful legal line of pretending to know far more than he really did.

"I am told by one who overheard you speak that you were to take the missionary and his daughter to Alwa's place. How much is my brother Howrah paying for Mahommed Gunga's services in this matter? It is well known that he and Alwa between them could call out all the Rangars in the district for whichever side they chose. Since they are not

on my side, they must be for Howrah. How much¹
does he pay? I might offer more."

"I know not," said Ali Partab, perfectly ready to
admit anything that was not true.

"It is true, then, that Howrah has designs on the
missionary's daughter? Alwa is to keep her prisoner until the great blow is struck, and Howrah
dare take possession of her?"

"That is not my business," answered Ali Partab,
with the air of a man who knew all of the secret
details but would not admit it. Jaimihr began to
think that he had lit at random on the answer to
the riddle.

"Where is Mahommed Gunga?"

"I know not."

"At Alwa's place?"

"Am I God that I should know where any man
is whom I cannot see?"

"Oh! So he is at Alwa's, eh?" That overdose of
opium had rendered Jaimihr's brain very dull indeed; he considered himself clever, and overlooked
the fact that Ali Partab would be almost surely
lying to him. In India men never tell the truth to
chance-met strangers or to their enemies; the truth
is a valuable thing, to be shared cautiously among
friends.

"If Mahommed Gunga is at Alwa's," reasoned
Jaimihr, "then he is much too close at hand to
take any chances with. I must keep this man close
confined." He raised his voice in a high-pitched
command, and the guards opened the door in-

stantly; at a sign from the Prince they seized Ali Partab by the wrists.

"I will send a message to Mahommed Gunga for thee," said Jaimihr. "On his answer will depend your release or otherwise." He nodded. The guards took their prisoner out between them—led him past the wrinkled old woman in the courtyard—and halted him in a far corner, where an evil-smelling cage of a place stood open to receive him. A moment later, in order to make sure, the master of the horse sent for the old woman and made her sweep out the cell a little; then he drove her away with a fierce injunction not to let herself be caught anywhere near the cell again unless ordered. Following the line of eastern reasoning, had he not given that order he would not have known what her object could be should she make her way toward the cell; but now, if she risked his wrath by disobeying, he would know beyond the least shadow of a doubt that she had a message to deliver to the prisoner—the man who was hidden in the dark corner need entertain no hope of keeping the secret to himself for purposes of sale or blackmail!

They trust each other wonderfully—with an almost childlike confidence—in a household such as Jaimihr's!

CHAPTER XV

Ho! I am king! All lesser fry
Must cringe, and crawl, and cry to me,
And none have any rights but I,—
Except the right to lie to me.

JAIMIHR was not the only man who would have dearly liked to know of the whereabouts of Mahommed Gunga. It had been reported to Maharajah Howrah, by his spies, that the redoubtable ex-Risaldar of horse had visited his relatives in Howrah City, and, though he had not been able to ascertain a word of what had passed, he was none the less anxious.

He knew, of course—for every soul in Howrah knew—that Jaimihr was plotting for the throne. He knew, too, that the priests of Siva, who with himself were joint keepers of the wickedly won, tax-swollen treasure, had sounded Jaimihr; they had tentatively hinted that they might espouse his cause, provided that an equitable division of the treasure were arranged beforehand. The question uppermost in Maharajah Howrah's mind was whether the Rangars—the Moslem descendants of once Hindoo Rajputs, who formed such a small but valuable proportion of the local population—could or could not be induced to throw in their lot with him.

No man on the whole tax-ridden countryside believed or considered it as a distant possibility that the Rangars would strike for any hand except their own; they were known, on the other hand, to be more or less cohesive, and it was considered certain that, whichever way they swung, when the priest-pulled string let loose the flood of revolution, they would swing all together. The question, then, was how to win the favor of the Rangars. It was not at all an easy question, for the love lost between Hindoos and Mohammedans is less than that between dark-skinned men and white—a lot less.

Within two hours of its happening he had been told of the capture of Ali Partab; and he knew—for that was another thing his spies had told him—that Ali Partab was Mahommed Gunga's man. Apparently, then, Ali Partab—a prisoner in Jaimihr's palace-yard—was the only connecting link between him and the Rangars whom he wished to win over to his side. He was as anxious as any to help overwhelm the British, but he naturally wished to come out of the turmoil high and dry himself, and he was, therefore, ready to consider the protection of individual British subjects if that would please the men whom he wanted for his friends.

Mahommed Gunga was known to have carried letters for the missionaries. He was known to have engaged a new servant when he rode away from Howrah and to have left his trusted man behind.

Miss McClean was known to have conversed with the retainer, immediately after which the man had been seized and carried off by Jaimihr's men. Jaimihr was known to have placed watchers round the mission house and—once—to have killed a man in Miss McClean's defence. The deduction was not too far-fetched that the retainer had been left as a protection against Jaimihr, and consequently that the Rangars, at the behest of Mahommed Gunga, had decided on at least the white girl's safety.

Therefore, he argued, if he now proceeded to protect the McCleans, he would, at all events, not incur the Rangars' enmity.

It was a serious decision that he had to make, for, for one thing, he dared not yet make any move likely to incite his strongly supported brother to open rebellion; he dared not, therefore, interfere at present with the watchers near the mission house. To openly befriend the Christian priests would be to set the whole Hindoo population against himself, for it had been mainly against suttee and its kindred horrors that the missionaries had bent all their energy.

The great palace of Howrah was ahum. Elephants with painted tusks, and loaded to the groaning-point under howdahs decked with jewels and gold-leaf, came and went through the carved entrance-gates. Occasionally camels, loaded too until their legs all but buckled underneath them, strutted with their weird, mixed air of foolishness and dig-

nity, to be disburdened of great cases that eight men
could scarcely lift; on the outside the cases were
marked "Hardware," but a horde of armed and
waiting malcontents scattered about the countryside
could have given a more detailed and accurate
guess at what was in them.

Men came and went—men almost of all castes
and many nationalities. Priests—not all of them
fat, but every single one fat-smiling—sunned themselves, or waited in the shade until they could have
audience; no priest of any Hindoo temple had to
wait long to be admitted to that Rajah's presence,
and there was an everlasting chain of them, each with
his axe to grind, coming and going by day and night.

Color rioted in the blazing sun and deep, dark
shadows lurked in all the thousand places where the
sun could never penetrate. It was India in essence
—noise and blaze and flouted splendor, with a background and underground of mystery. Any but the
purblind British could have told at half a glance,
merely by the attitude of Howrah's armed sepoys,
that a concerted movement of some kind was afoot
—that there was a tight-held thread of plan running
through the whole confusion; but no man—not even
a native—could have guessed what secret plotting
might be going on within the acres of the straggling
palace.

From the courtyard there was no least hint obtainable even of the building's size; its shape could only
have been marked down from a bird's-eye view aloft.
Even the roof was so uneven, and so subdivided by

traced and deep-carved walls and ramparts, that a
sentry posted at one end could not have seen the
next man to him, perhaps some twenty feet away.
Building had been piled on building—other buildings had been added end to end and crisscrosswise
—and each extension had been walled in as new
centuries saw new additions, until the many acres
were a maze of bricks and stone and fountain-
decorated gardens that no lifelong palace denizen
could have learned to know in their entirety.

Within—one story up above the courtyard din—
in a spacious, richly decorated room that gave on to
a gorgeous roof-garden, the Maharajah sat and let
himself be fanned by women, who were purchasable
for perhaps a tenth of what any of the fans had cost.
Another woman, younger than the rest, played wild
minor music to him on an instrument not much
unlike a flute; they were melancholy notes—beautiful—but sad enough to sow pessimism's seed in
any one who listened.

His divan—carved, inlaid, and gilded—faced the
wide, awning-hung opening to the garden. Round
him on all three sides was a carved stone screen
through whose interstices came rustlings and whisperings that told of the hidden life which sees and
is not seen. The women with the fans and flute
were mere court accessories; the real nerves of Asia
—the veiled intriguers whom none may know but
whose secret power any man may feel—could be
heard like caged birds crowding on their perches.

Now and then glass bracelets tinkled from behind

the screen; ever and again the music stopped, until another girl appeared to play another melancholy air. But the even purring of the fans went on incessantly, and the poor, priest-ridden fool who owned it all scowled straight in front of him, his brows lined deep in thought.

It is a strange malady, that which seizes men whom fate has elevated to a throne. It acts as certain Indian drugs are known to do—deprives its victim of the power to act, but intensifies his ability to think, and theorize, and feel. Howrah, with untold treasure in his vaults, with an army of five thousand men, with the authority and backing that a hundred generations give, could long for more—could fear the loss of what he did have—but could not act.

The priests held him fear-bound. His brother held him hate-bound. His women—and not even he knew, probably, how many of them languished in the secret warren inside those palace walls—kept him restless in a net of this-and-that-way-tugged intrigue. Flattery—and that is by far the subtlest poison of the East—blinded him utterly to his own best course, and kept him blind. Luxury unmanned him; he who had once held the straightest spear in western India, and for the love of feeling red blood racing in his veins had ridden down panthers on the maidan, was flabby now; deep, dark rings underlined his eyes and the once steel-sinewed wrist trembled.

His brother Jaimihr in his place, unsapped yet by decadent delights, would have loosed his five thou-

sand on the countryside—butchered any who opposed him—pressed into service those who merely
lagged—and would have plunged India in a welter
of blood before the priests had time to mature
their plans and arrange to keep all the power and
plunder to themselves. But Jaimihr had to stalk
lesser game and content himself with pricking at
the ever-growing hate that gradually rendered the
Maharajah decisionless and sorry only for himself.

A first glimpse at Howrah, particularly in the
shaded room, showed a handsome man, black-
bearded, lean, and lithe; a second look, undazzled
by his jewelry or by the studied magnificence of each
apparently unstudied movement, betrayed a man
whose lightest word was law, but who feared to give
the word. Where muscles had been were unfilled
folds of skin that shook; where a firm if selfish
mouth had once smiled merrily beneath a pointed
black mustache, a mouth still smiled, but meanly;
the selfishness was there, but the firmness had faded.

His eyes, though, were his most marked feature.
They were hungry eyes, pathetic as a caged beast's
and as savage. No one could see them without pity-
ing him, and no man in his senses would have accepted their owner's word on any point at all. A
man looks as he did when the fire of a burning velt
has circled him and there is no way out. There was
fear behind them, and the look of restless search for
safety that is nowhere.

In one of the many-columned courtyards of the
palace was a chained, mad elephant whose duty

was to kneel on the Rajah's captive enemies. In another courtyard was a big, square tank with a weedy, slippery stone ramp at one end; in the tank were alligators; down the ramp other of the Rajah's enemies, tight-bound, would scream and struggle and slide from time to time. But they were only little enemies who died in that way; the greater ones, who had power or influence, lived on and plotted, because the owner of the execution beasts was afraid to put them to their use.

Below, in damp, unlit dungeons, there were silken cords suspended from stone ceilings; their ends were noosed, and the nooses hung ten feet above the floor; those told only, though, of the fate of women who had schemed unwisely—favorites of a week, perhaps, who had dared to sulk, listeners through screens who had forgotten to forget. No men died ever by the silken cord, and no tales ever reached the outside world of who did die down in the echoing brick cellars; there was a path that led underground to the alligator tank and a trap-door that opened just above the water edge. Night, and the fungus-fouled long jaws, and slimy, weed-filled water —the creak of rusty hinges—a splash—the bang of a falling trap—a swirl in the moonlit water, and ring after heavy, widening ring that lapped at last against the stone would write conclusion to a tragedy. There would be no record kept.

Howrah was childless. That, of all the hell-sent troubles that beset him, was the worst. That alone was worse than the hoarded treasure whose secret he and his brother and the priests of Siva shared. Only in India could it happen that a line of Rajahs, drag-net-armed—oblivious to the duties of a king, and greedy only of the royal right to tax—could pile up, century by century, a hoard of gold and jewels—to be looked at. The secret of that treasure made the throne worth plotting for—gave the priests, who shared the secret, more than nine-tenths of their power for blackmail, pressure, and intrigue—and grew, like a cancer, into each succeeding Rajah's mind until, from a man with a soul inside him, he became in turn a heartless, fear-ridden miser.

Any childless king is liable to feel the insolent expectancy betrayed by the heir apparent. But Jaimihr—who had no sons either—was an heir who understood all of the Indian arts whereby a man of brain may hasten the succession. Worry, artfully stirred up, is the greatest weapon of them all, and never a day passed but some cleverly concocted tale would reach the Rajah, calculated to set his guessing faculties at work.

Either of the brothers, when he happened to be thirsty, would call his least-trusted counsellor to drink first from the jewelled cup, and would watch the man afterward for at least ten minutes before daring to slake his thirst; but Jaimihr had the moral advantage of an aspirant; Howrah, on the defensive, wilted under the nibbling necessity for wakefulness, while Jaimihr grinned.

What were five thousand drilled, armed men to

a king who feared to use them? Of what use was a waiting countryside, armed if not drilled, if he was not sure that his brother had not won every man's allegiance? Being Hindoo, priest-reared, priest-fooled, and priest-flattered, he knew, or thought he knew, to an anna the value he might set on Hindoo loyalty or on the loyalty of any man who did not stand to gain in pocket by remaining true; and, as many another fear-sick tyrant has begun to do, he turned, in his mind at least, to men of another creed—which in India means of another race, practically—wondering whether he could not make use of them against his own.

Like every other Rajah of his line, he longed to have sole control of that wonderful treasure that had eaten out his very manhood. Miser though he was, he was prepared at least to bargain with outsiders with the promise of a portion of it, if that would give him possession of it all. He had learned from the priests who took such full advantage of him an absolute contempt for Mohammedans; and their teaching, as well as his own trend of character, made him quite indifferent to promises he might make, for the sake of diplomacy, to men of another creed. It began to be obvious to him that he would lose nothing by courting the favor of the Rangars, and of Alwa in particular, and that he might win security by coaxing them to take his part. Of one thing he was certain: the Rangars would do anything at all, if by doing it they could harm the Hindoo priests.

But, being of the East Eastern, and at that Hindoo,
he could not have brought himself to make overtures
direct and go straight to the real issue. He had
to feel his way gingerly. The thousand horses in
his stables, he reflected, would mount a thousand of
the Rangars and place at his disposal a regiment of
cavalry which would be difficult to beat; but a
thousand mounted Mohammedans might be a worse
thorn in his side than even his brother or the priests.
He decided to write to Alwa, but to open negotia-
tions with a very thin and delicately inserted wedge.

He could write. The priests had overlooked that
opportunity, and had taught him in his boyhood;
in that one thing he was their equal. But the
other things that they had taught him, too, offset his
penmanship. He was too proud to write—too lazy,
too enamoured of his dignity. He called a court
official, and the man sat very humbly at his feet—
listened meekly to the stern command to secrecy
—and took the letter from dictation.

Alwa was informed, quite briefly, that in view of
certain happenings in Howrah City His Highness the
Maharajah had considered it expedient to set a guard
over the Christian missionaries in the city, for their
safety. The accompanying horse was a gift to the
Alwa-sahib. The Alwa-sahib himself would be a
welcome guest whenever he might care to come.

The document was placed in a silver tube and
sealed. Within the space of half an hour a horseman
was kicking up the desert dust, riding as though he
carried news of life-and-death importance, and with

another man and a led horse galloping behind him.
Five minutes after the man had started, in a cell
below the temple of Siva, the court official who had
taken down the letter was repeating it word for word
to a congeries of priests. And one hour later still,
in a room up near the roof of Jaimihr's palace, one
of the priests—panting from having come so fast—
was asking the Rajah's brother what he thought
about it.

"Did he say nothing?" asked Jaimihr.

"Nothing, sahib."

The priest watched him eagerly; he would have
to bear back to the other priests an exact account
of the Prince's every word, and movement, and
expression.

"Then I, too, say nothing!" answered Jaimihr.

"But to the priests of Siva, who are waiting,
sahib?"

"Tell them I said nothing."

CHAPTER XVI

Eyes in the dark, awake and keen,
　See and may not themselves be seen;
But—and this is the tale I tell—
　What if the dark have eyes as well?

BESIDE the reeking bear's cage in which Ali Partab stood and swore was a dark, low corner space in which at one time and another sacks and useless impedimenta had been tossed, to become rat-eaten and decayed. In among all the rubbish, cross-legged like the idol of the underworld, a nearly naked Hindoo sat, prick-eared. He was quite invisible long before the sun went down, for that was the dingiest corner of the yard; when twilight came, he could not have been seen from a dozen feet away.

Joanna, sweeping, sweeping, sweeping, in the courtyard, with her back very nearly always turned toward the cage, appeared to take no notice of the falling darkness; unlike the other menials, who hurried to their rest and evening meal, she went on working, accomplishing very little but seeming to be very much in earnest about it all. Very, very gradually she drew nearer to the cage. When night fell, she was within ten feet of it. A few lamps were lit then, here and there over doorways, but nobody appeared to linger in the courtyard; no footfalls resounded; nothing but the neigh of stabled horses and the chatter around the big, flat supper pans broke on the evening quiet.

Joanna drew nearer. Ali Partab came forward to the cage bars, but said nothing; it was very dark inside the cage, and even the sharp-eyed old woman could not possibly have seen his gestures; when he stood, tight-pressed, against the bars she might have made out his dark shape dimly, but unless he chose to speak no signal could possibly have passed from him to her. He said nothing, though, and she—still sweeping, with her back toward him—passed by the cage, and stooped to scratch at some hard-caked dirt or other close to the rubbish hole where the Hindoo waited. Still scratching, still working with her twig broom, still with her back toward the rubbish hole, she approached until the darkest shadow swallowed her.

There were two in the dark then—she and the man who listened. He, motionless as stone, had watched her; peering outward at the lesser darkness, he lost sight of her for a second as she backed into the deepest shadow unexpectedly. Before he could become accustomed to the altered focus and the deeper black, her beady eyes picked out the whites of his. Before he could move she was on him—at his throat, tearing it with thin, steel fingers. Before he could utter a sound, or move, she had drawn a short knife from her clothing and had driven it to the hilt below his ear. He dropped without a gurgle, and without a sound she gathered up her broom again and swept her way back past the cage-bars, where Ali Partab waited.

"Was any there?" he whispered.

"There was one."

"And——?"

"He was."

"Good! Now will the reward be three mohurs instead of two!"

"Where are they?"

"These pigs have taken all the money from me. Now we must wait until Mahommed Gunga-sahib comes. His word is pledged."

"He said two mohurs."

"I—Ali Partab—pledge his word for three."

"And who art thou? The bear in the cage said: 'I will eat thee if I get outside!'"

"Mother of corruption! Listen! Alwa must know! Canst thou escape from here? Canst thou reach the Alwa-sahib?"

"If the price were four mohurs, there might be many things that I could do."

"The price is three! I have spoken!"

"'I would eat honey were I outside!' said the bear."

"Hag! The bear died in the cage, and they sold his pelt for how much? Alive, he had been worth three mohurs, but he died while they bargained for him!—Quick!"

"I am black, sahib, and the night is black. I am old, and none would believe me active. They watch the gates, but the bats fly in and out."

"Find out, then, what has happened to my horses, left at the caravansary; give that information to the Alwa-sahib. Tell the Miss-sahib at the mission where I am. Tell her whither I have sent thee. Tell the Alwa-sahib that a Rangar—by name Ali Partab—sworn follower of the prophet, and servant of the Risaldar Mahommed Gunga—is in need and asks his instant aid. Say also to the Alwa-sahib that it may be well to rescue the Miss-sahib first, before he looks for me, but of that matter I am no judge, being imprisoned and unable to ascertain the truth. Hast thou understood?"

"And all that for three mohurs?"

"Nay. The price is now two mohurs again. It will be one unless——"

"Three, sahib! It was three!"

"Then run! Hasten!"

The shadows swallowed her again. She crept where they were darkest—lay still once, breathless, while a man walked almost over her—reached the outer wall, and felt her way along it until she reached low eaves that reached down like a jagged saw from utter blackness. Less than a minute later she was crawling monkeywise along a roof; before another five had passed she had dropped on all fours in the dust of the outer road and was running like a black ghost—head down—an end of her loin-cloth between her teeth—one arm held tight to her side and the other crooked outward, swinging—striding, panting, boring through the blackness.

She wasted little time at the caravansary. The

gate was shut and a sleepy watchman cursed her for breaking into his revery.

"Horses? Belonging to a Rangar? Fool! Does not the Maharajah-sahib impound all horses left ownerless? Ask them back of him that took them! Go, night-owl! Go ask him!"

Almost as quickly as a native pony could have eaten up the distance, she dropped panting on the door-step of the little mission house. She was panting now from fright as well as sheer exhaustion. There were watchers—two sets of them. One man stood, with his back turned within ten paces of her, and another—less than two yards away from him— stood, turned half sideways, looking up the street and whistling to himself. There was not a corner or an angle of the little place that was not guarded.

She had tried the back door first, but that was locked, and she had rapped on it gently until she remembered that of evenings the missionary and his daughter occupied the front room always and that they would not have heard her had she hammered. She tapped now, very gently, with her fingers on the lower panel of the door, quaking and trembling in every limb, but taking care to make her little noise unevenly, in a way that would be certain to attract attention inside.

Tap-tap-tap. Pause. Tap-tap. Pause. Tap-tap-tap-tap-tap. Pause. Tap-tap.

The door opened suddenly. Both watchers turned and gazed straight into the lamplight that streamed out past the tall form of Duncan McClean.

He stared at them and they stared back again.
Joanna slunk into the deep shadow at one side of
the steps.

"Is it necessary for you to annoy me by rapping
on my door as well as by spying on me?" asked the
missionary in a tone of weary remonstrance.

The guards laughed and turned their backs with
added insolence. In that second Joanna shot like
a black spirit of the night straight past the missionary's legs and collapsed in a bundle on the floor behind him.

"Shut the door, sahib!" she hissed at him.
"Quick! Shut the door!"

He shut it and bolted it, half recognizing something in the voice or else guided by instinct.

"Joanna!" he exclaimed, holding up a lamp above
her. "You, Joanna!"

At the name, Rosemary McClean came running
out—looked for an instant—and then knelt by the
old woman.

"Father, bring some water, please, quickly!"

The missionary went in search of a water-jar, and
Rosemary McClean bent down above the ancient,
shrivelled, sorry-looking mummy of a woman—
drew the wrinkled head into her lap—stroked the
drawn face—and wept over her. The spent, age-
weakened, dried-out widow had fainted; there was
no wakened self-consciousness of black and white
to interfere. This was a friend—one lone friend of
her own sex amid all the waste of smouldering hate
—some one surely to be wept over and made much

of and caressed. The poor old hag recovered consciousness with her head pillowed on a European
lap, and Duncan McClean—no stickler for conven-
tion and no believer in a line too tightly drawn—
saw fit to remonstrate as he laid the jar of water
down beside them.

"Why," she answered, looking up at him, "father,
I'd have kissed a *dog* that got lost and came back
again like this!"

They picked her up between them, after they had
let her drink, and carried her between them to the
long, low sitting-room, where she told them—after
considerable make-believe of being more spent than
she really was—after about a tenth "sip" at the
brandy flask and when another had been laughingly
refused—all about Ali Partab and what his orders
to her were.

"I wonder what it all can mean?" McClean sat
back and tried to summarize his experiences of
months and fit them into what Joanna said.

"What does *that* mean?" asked his daughter,
leaning forward. She was staring at Joanna's forearm and from that to a dull-red patch on the woman's loin-cloth. Joanna answered nothing.

"Are you wounded, Joanna? Are you sure?
That's blood! Look here, father!"

He agreed that it was blood. It was dry and it
came off her forearm in little flakes when he rubbed
it. But not a word could they coax out of Joanna
to explain it, until Rosemary—drawing the old
woman to her—espied the handle of her knife pro-

jecting by an inch above the waist-fold of her cloth.
Too late Joanna tried to hide it. Rosemary held
her and drew it out. Beyond any shadow of a
doubt, there was blood on the blade still, and on
the wooden hilt, and caked in the clumsy joint between the hilt and blade.

"Joanna—have you killed any one?"

Joanna shook her head.

"Tell me the truth, Joanna. Whose blood is
that?"

"A dog's, Miss-sahib. A street dog attacked me
as I ran hither."

"I wish I could believe it!"

"I too!" said her father, and he took Joanna to
one side and cross-examined her. But he could get
no admission from her—nothing but the same statement, with added details each time he made her tell
it, that she had killed a dog.

They fed her, and she ate like a hyena. No
caste prejudices or forbidden foods troubled her;
she ate whatever came her way, Hindoo food, or
Mohammedan, or Christian, and reached for more
—and finished, as hyenas finish, by breaking bones
to get the marrow out. At midnight they left her,
curled dogwise on a mat in the hall, to sleep; and
at dawn, when they came to wake her, she was gone
again—gone utterly, without a trace or sign of explanation. The doors, both front and back, were
locked.

It was two days later when they found a hole
torn through the thatch, through which she had es-

caped; and though they searched the house from cellar up to roof, and turned all their small possessions over, they could not find (and they were utterly glad of it) that she had stolen anything.

"Thank God for that!" said the missionary.

"I've finished disbelieving in Joanna!" said his daughter with a grimace that went always with irrevocable decision.

"I've come to the conclusion," said McClean, "that there are more than just Joanna to be trusted. There is Ali Partab, and—who knows how many?"

CHAPTER XVII

Against all fear; against the weight of what,
For lack of worse name, men miscall the Law;
Against the Tyranny of Creed; against the hot,
Foul Greed of Priest, and Superstition's Maw;
Against all man-made Shackles, and a man-made Hell—
Alone—At last—Unaided—
                    I REBEL!

No single, individual circumstance, but a chain of
happenings in very quick succession, brought about
a climax, forcing the hand of Howrah and his brother
and for the moment drawing the McCleans, father
and daughter, into the toothed wheel of Indian action. As usual in India, the usual brought about
the unexpected, and the unexpected fitted strangely
into the complex, mysteriously worked-out whole.

Two days after Joanna left the mission house,
through a hole made in the thatch, the spirit of revolt took hold of Rosemary McClean again. The
stuffy, narrow quarters—the insolent, doubled, un-
explained, but very obvious, guard that lounged
outside—the sense of rank injustice and helplessness
—the weird feeling of impending horror added onto
stale-grown ghastliness—youth, chafing at the lack
of liberty—stirred her to action.

Without a word to her father, who was writing

reports that seemed endless at the little desk by the
shaded window, she left the house—drew with a
physical effort on all her reserve of strength and
health—faced the scorching afternoon wind, as
though it were a foe that could shrink away before
her courage, and walked, since she had no pony
now, in any direction in which chance or her momentary whim might care to lead her.

"I won't cry again—and I won't submit—and
I'll see what happens!" she told herself; and the
four who followed her at a none-too-respectful
distance—two of the Maharajah's men in uniform
and two shabby-looking ruffians of Jaimihr's—
grinned as they scented action. Like their masters
they bore no love for one another; they were there
now, in fact, as much to watch one another as the
missionaries; they detected the possibility of an
excuse to be at one another's throats, and gloated as
they saw two messengers, one of either side, run off
in a hurry to inform the rival camps.

It was neither plan nor conscious selection that
led Rosemary McClean toward the far end of the
maidan, where the sluggish, narrow, winding Howrah River sucked slimily beside the burning ghats.
When she realized where her footsteps were leading
her she would have turned in horror and retreated,
for even a legitimately roasting corpse that died
before the Hindoo priests had opportunity to introduce it to the flames is no sight for eyes that are
civilized.

But, when she turned her head, the sight of her

hurrying escort perspiring in her wake—(few natives like the heat and wind one whit better than their conquerors)—filled her with an unexpected, probably unjustifiable, determination not to let them see her flinch at any kind of horror. That was the spirit of sahibdom that is not always quite commendable; it is the spirit that takes Anglo-Saxon women to the seething, stenching plains and holds them there high-chinned to stiffen their men-folk by courageous example, but it leads, too, to things not quite so womanly and good.

"I'll show them!" muttered Rosemary McClean, wiping the blown dust from her eyes and facing the wind again that now began to carry with it the unspread taint—the awful, sickening, soul-revolting smell inseparable from Hindoo funeral rites. There were three pyres, low-smouldering, close by the river-bank, and men stirred with long poles among the ashes to make sure that the incineration started the evening before should be complete; there was one pyre that looked as though it had been lit long after dawn—another newly lit—and there were two pyres building.

It was those two new ones that held her attention, and finally decided her to hold her course. She wanted to make sure. The smell of burning—the unoutlined, only guessed-at ghastliness—would probably have killed her courage yet, before she came close enough to really see; but the suspicion of a greater horror drew her on, as snakes are said to draw birds on, by merely being snakes, and with red-rimmed eyes smarting from smoke as well as wind she pressed forward.

The ghats were deserted-looking, for the funeral rites of those who burned were practically over until the time should come to scatter ashes on the river-surface; only a few attendants hovered close to the fires to prod them and occasionally throw on extra logs. Only round the two new pyres not yet quite finished was anything approaching a crowd assembled, and there a priest was officiously directing the laying of the logs. It was the manner of their laying and the careful building of a scaffold on each side of either pyre that held Rosemary McClean's attention—called all the rebellious womanhood within her to interfere—and drew her nearer.

Soon the priest noticed her—a cotton-skirted wraith amid the smoke—and shouted to the guards behind; one of them answered, laughing coarsely, and Rosemary understood enough of the dialect he used to grit her teeth with shame and anger. The men left off building, and, directed by the priest, came toward her in a ragged line to cut her off from closer approach; she stood, then—examined the new pyres as carefully as she could—walked to another vantage-point and viewed them sideways—then turned her back.

"Oh, the brutes!" she ejaculated. There were tears in her voice, as well as helpless anger. "There is not one devil, there are a million, and they all live here!"

She looked back again once, trembling with an

overmastering hate, directed less at the priest who grinned back at her than at the loathsome rite he represented. In two actual words, she cursed him. It was the first time she had ever cursed anybody in her life, and the wickedness of doing it swept over her as a relief. She revelled in it. She was glad she had cursed him. Her little, light, graceful body that had been quivering grew calm again, and she turned to hurry home with an unexpected sense of having pulled some lever in the mechanism that would bring about results. She neither knew nor cared what results, nor how they were to happen; she felt that that curse of hers, her first, had landed on the mark!

But she had come further than she thought. Distance, hot wind, and emotion had exhausted her far more, too, than she had had time to realize. Before a mile of the homeward journey had been accomplished, she was forced against her stubborn Scots will to sit down on a big stone by the roadside and rest, while the four that followed came up close, grinning and passing remarks in anything but undertones. If the meaning of the words escaped her, their gestures left little to be misunderstood. A crowd of stragglers drew together near the four— laughed with them—took sides in the coarse-worded argument about Jaimihr's known ambition—and shamed her into pressing on homeward.

But she was forced to rest again, and then again. Physical sickness prevented her from obeying instinct, reason, will, that all three urged her on. No

false pride now told her to dare the insolence of the
guards; nothing appealed to her but the desire to
hurry, hurry, hurry, and do whatever should appear
to need doing when she reached the mission house.
She had no plan in her head. She only knew that
she had cursed a man, and that the curse was potent.
But her feet dragged, and her vitality died down. It
was sundown when she reached the mission house,
and she could hear the rising, falling, intermittent
din of drums before she saw her father in the doorway.

"Father!" She ran to him, and he caught her in
his arms to save her from falling headlong. "Father,
there is going to be a suttee to-night! Hear the
drums, father! Hear the drums! It'll be to-night!
That's to stop the screams from being heard! Listen to them, father—two suttees, side by side—I've
seen the pyres and the scaffolds—do they jump into
the flames, father, from the scaffolds?—tell me!
No—don't tell me—I won't listen! Take me away
from here—away—away—away—take me away,
d'you hear!"

He carried her inside, and laid her on the caned
couch in the living-room, looking like a great, big,
helpless, gray-haired baby, as any man is prone to
do when he has hysteria to deal with in a woman
whom he loves.

"I cursed a man, father! I cursed a man! I
did! I said 'Damn you!' I'm glad! Oh——"

"Don't, little girl—don't! Lassie mine, don't!
Never mind what you saw or what you said—be

calm now—there is something we must do; we must act; I have determined we must act. We must act to-night. But we can't do anything with you in this state."

Slowly, gradually he calmed her—or probably she grew calm, in spite of his attentions, for he was too upset himself to exercise much soothing sway over anybody else. At last, though, she fell into a fitful sleep, and he sat beside her, holding rigid the left hand that she clutched, letting it stiffen and grow cold and numb for fear of waking her.

Outside a full moon rose majestically, pure and silvery as peace herself, bathing the universe in blessings. And each month, when the full moon rose above the carved dome of Siva's temple, there was a ceremony gone through that commemorated cruelty, greed, poisoning, throat-slitting, hate, and all the hell-invented infamy that suckles always at the breast of stagnant treasure.

Since history has forgotten when, at each full moon, the priests of Siva had gone with circumstantial ceremony to view the hoarded wealth tied up by jealousy and guarded jealously in Howrah's palace. With them, as the custom that was stronger than a thousand laws dictated, went the Maharajah and his brother Jaimihr—joint owners with the priests.

There had not been one Maharajah, since the first of that long line, who would not have given the lives of ten thousand men for leave to broach that treasure; nor, since the first heir apparent shared the secret with the priests and the holder of the throne, had

there been one prince in line—son—brother—cousin
—who would not have drenched the throne with his
relation's blood with that same purpose.

Heir after heir could have agreed with Maharajah,
but the priests had stood between. That treasure
was their fulcrum; the legacy, dictated by a dead,
misguided hand, intended as a war reserve to stay
the throne of Howrah in its need, and trebly locked
to guard against profligacy, had placed the priests
of Siva in the position of dictators of Howrah's
destiny. A word from them, and a prince would
slay his father—only to discover that the promises
of Siva's priests were something less to build on than
the hope of loot. There would be another heir apparent to be let into the secret—another man to
scheme and hunger for the throne—another party
to the bloody three-angled intrigue which kept the
Siva-servers fat and the princes lean.

Past masters of the art by which superstitious
ignorance is swayed, the priests could swing the
allegiance of the mob whichever way they chose;
even the soldiers, loyal enough to their masters under
ordinary circumstances, would have rebelled at as
much as a hint from holy Siva. It was the priests
who made it possible for Jaimihr to dare take his part
in the ceremony; without them he would not have
entered his brother's palace-yard unless five thousand
men at least were there to guard his back; but, if
there was danger where the priests were, there was
safety too.

As the custom was, he rode to the temple of Siva

first with a ten-man guard; there, when the priests
had finished droning age-old anthems to the echoing
roof, when his brother, the Maharajah, also with a
ten-man guard, had joined him, and the two had
submitted to the sanctifying rites prescribed, eleven
priests would walk with them in solemn mummery
to the palace-entrance—censer-swinging, chanting,
blasphemously acting duty to their gods and state.

The moon—and that, too, was custom—rested
with her lower rim one full hand's breadth above the
temple dome as viewed from the palace-gate, when
a gong clanged resonantly, died to silence, music
of pipes and cymbals broke on the evening quiet,
and the strange procession started from the temple
door, the Maharajah leading.

Generally it passed uninterrupted over the inter-
vening street to the palace-entrance, between the
ranks of a salaaming, silent crowd, and disappeared
from view. This time, though, for the first time in
living memory, and possibly for the first time in all
history, the unforeseen, amazing happened. The procession stopped. Moon-bathed, between the carved
posts of the palace-gate, two people blocked the
way.

The music ceased. The sudden silence framed
itself against the distant thunder of a hundred
drums. The crowd—all heads bowed, as decreed—
drew in its breath and held it. A sea of pugrees
moved as brown eyes looked up surreptitiously—
stared—memorized—and then looked down again.
There was no precedent for this happening, and

even the Maharajah and the priests were at a
momentary loss—stood waiting, staring—and said
nothing.

"Maharajah-sahib!—I must interrupt your ceremony. I must have word with you at once!"

It was Duncan McClean, bareheaded, holding his
daughter's hand. They had no weapons; they
were messengers of peace, protesting, or so they
looked. No longer timid, but resigned to what
might happen—they held each other's hands, and
blocked the way of Siva's votaries—Siva's tools—
and Siva's ritual.

Jaimihr whispered to his brother—the first time
he had dared one word to him in person for years
—the high priest of the temple pressed forward
angrily, saying nothing, but trying to combine
rage and dignity with an attempt to turn the incident to priestly advantage. Surely this was a
crisis out of which the priests *must* come triumphant;
they held all the cards—knew how and when rebellion was timed, and could compare, as the prin-
cipals themselves could not do, Howrah's strength
with Jaimihr's. And the priests had the crowd to
back them—the ignorant, superstitious crowd that
can make or dethrone emperors.

But some strange freak of real dignity—curios-
ity perhaps, or possibly occasion-spurred desire to
act of his own initiative and keep the high priest in
his place—impelled the Maharajah in that minute.
Men said afterward that Jaimihr had whispered to
him advice which he knew was barbed because it

was his brother whispering, and that he promptly did the opposite; but, whatever the motive, he drew himself up in all his jewelled splendor and demanded: "What do you people wish?"

The McCleans were given no time to reply. The priests did not see fit to let the reins of this occasion slip; the word went out, panic-voiced, that sacrilege to Siva was afoot.

"Slay them! Slay them!" yelled the crowd. "They violate the sacred rites!"

There were no Mohammedans among that crowd to take delight in seeing Hindoo priests discomfited and Hindoo ritual disturbed. There came no counter-shout. The crowd did not, as so often happens, turn and rend itself; and yet, though a surge from behind pressed forward, the men in front pressed back.

"Slay them! Slay the sacrilegious foreigners!" The yell grew louder and more widely voiced, but no man in the front ranks moved.

The Maharajah looked from the company of guards that lined the palace-steps to the priests and his brother and the crowd—and then to the McCleans again.

He remembered Alwa and his Rangars, thought of the messenger whom he had sent, remembered that a regiment of lance-armed horsemen would be worth a risk or two to win over to his side, and made decision.

"You are in danger," he asserted, using a pronoun not intended to convey politeness, but—

Eastern of the East—counteracting that by courtesy of manner. "Do you ask my aid?"

"Yes, among other things," Duncan McClean answered him. "I wish also to speak about a Rangar, who I know is held prisoner in a cage in the Jaimihr-sahib's palace."

"Speak of that later," answered Howrah. "Guard!"

He made a sign. A spoken word might have told the priests too much, and have set them busy forestalling him. The guards rushed down the steps, seized both McCleans, and half-carried, half-hustled them up the palace-steps, through the great carved doors, and presently returned without them.

"They are my prisoners," said the Maharajah, turning to the high priest. "We will now proceed."

The crowd was satisfied, at least for the time being. Well versed in the kind of treatment meted out to prisoners, partly informed of what was preparing for the British all through India, the crowd never doubted for an instant but that grizzly vengeance awaited the Christians who had dared to remonstrate against time-honored custom. It looked for the moment as though the high priest's word had moved the Maharajah to order the arrest, and the high priest realized it. By skilful play and well-used dignity he might contrive to snatch all the credit yet. He ordered; the pipes and cymbals started up again at once; and, one by one—Maharajah, Jaimihr, high priest, then royal guard, Jaimihr's guard, priest again—the procession wound ahead, jewelled and egretted, sabred and spurred, priest-robed, representative of all the many cancers eating at the heart of India.

Chanting, clanging, wailing minor dirges to the night, it circled all the front projections of the palace, turned where a small door opened on a courtyard at one side, entered, and disappeared.

CHAPTER XVIII

Oh, is it good, my soldier prince, and is the wisdom clear,
To guard thy front a thousand strong, while ten may take thy
    rear?

Now, because it was impregnable to almost anything except a yet-to-be-invented air-ship, the Alwa-
sahib owned a fortress still, high-perched on a crag
that overlooked a glittering expanse of desert.
More precious than its bulk in diamonds, a spring
of clear, cold water from the rock-lined depths of
mother earth gushed out through a fissure near the
summit, and round that spring had been built, in
bygone centuries, a battlemented nest to breed and
turn out warriors. Alwa's grandfather had come
by it through complicated bargaining and dowry-
contracts, and Alwa now held it as the rallying-point
for the Rangars thereabout.

But its defensibility was practically all the crag
fort had to offer by way of attraction. Down at
its foot, where the stream of rushing water splashed
in a series of cascades to the thirsty, sandy earth,
there were an acre or two of cultivation—sufficient,
in time of peace, to support an attenuated garrison
and its horses. But for his revenues the Alwa-sahib
had to look many a long day's march afield.

Leagues of desert lay between him and the nearest farm he owned, and since—more in the East
than anywhere—a landlord's chief absorption is the
watching of his rents, it followed that he spent the
greater part of his existence in the saddle, riding
from one widely scattered tenant to another.

It was luck or fortuitous circumstance—Fate, he
would have called it, had he wasted time to give it
name—that brought him along a road where, many
miles from Howrah City, he caught sight of Joanna.
Needless to say, he took no slightest notice of her.

Dog-weary, parched, sore-footed, she was hurrying along the burning, sandy trail that led in the
direction of Alwa's fort. The trail was narrow,
and the horsemen whose mounts ambled tirelessly
behind Alwa's plain-bred Arab pressed on past him,
to curse the hag and bid her make horse-room for
her betters. She sunk on the sand and begged of
them. Laughingly, they asked her what a coin
would buy in all that arid waste.

"Have the jackals, then, turned tradesman?"
they jeered; but she only mumbled, and displayed
her swollen tongue, and held her hands in an attitude of pitiful supplication. Then Alwa cantered
up—rode past—heard one of his men jeering—drew
rein and wheeled.

"Give her water!" he commanded.

He sat and watched her while she knelt, face
upward, and a Rangar poured lukewarm water
from a bottle down her tortured throat. He held
it high and let the water splash, for fear his dignity

might suffer should he or the bottle touch her.
Strictly speaking, Rangars have no caste, but they
retain by instinct and tradition many of the Hindoo
prejudices. Alwa himself saw nothing to object to
in the man's precaution.

"Ask the old crows' meat whither she was running."

"She says she would find the Alwa-sahib."

"Tell her I am he."

Joanna fawned and laid her wrinkled forehead in
the dust.

"Get up!" he growled. "Thy service is dis-
honor and my ears are deaf to it! Now, speak!
Hast thou a message? Who is it sends a rat to
bring me news?"

"Ali Partab."

"Soho! And who is Ali Partab? He needs to
learn manners. He has come to a stern school for
them!"

"Sahib—great one—Prince of swordsmen!—Ali
Partab is Mahommed Gunga-sahib's man. He bid
me say that he is held a prisoner in a bear-cage in
Jaimihr's palace and needs aid."

Alwa's black beard dropped onto his chest as he
frowned in thought. He had nine men with him.
Jaimihr had by this time, perhaps, as many as nine
thousand, for no one knew but Jaimihr and the
priests how many in the district waited to espouse
his cause. The odds seemed about as stupendous as
any that a man of his word had ever been called
upon to take.

A moment more, and without consulting any one, he bade one of his men dismount.

"Put that hag on thy horse!" he commanded. "Mount thou behind another!"

The order was obeyed. Another Rangar took the led horse, and Joanna found herself, perched like a monkey on a horse that objected to the change of riders, between two troopers whose iron-thewed legs squeezed hers into the saddle.

"To Howrah City!" ordered Alwa, starting off at an easy, desert-eating amble; and without a word of comment, but with downward glances at their swords and a little back-stiffening which was all of excitement that they deigned to show, his men wheeled three and three behind him.

It was no affair of Alwa's that a full moon shone that night—none of his arranging that on that one night of the month Jaimihr and his most trusted body-guard should go with the priests and the Maharajah to inspect the treasure. Alwa was a soldier, born to take instant advantage of chance-sent opportunity; Jaimihr was a schemer, born to indecision and the cunning that seeks underhanded means but overlooks the obvious. Because the streets were full of men whose allegiance was doubtful yet, because he himself would be too occupied to sit like a spider in a web and watch the intentions of the crowd unfold, Jaimihr had turned out every retainer to his name, and had scattered them about the city, with orders, if they were needed, to rally on a certain point.

He did think that at any minute a disturbance

might break out which would lead to civil war, and he saw the necessity for watchfulness at every point; but he did not see the rather obvious necessity for leaving more than twenty men on guard inside his palace. Not even the thoughtfulness of Siva's priests could have anticipated that ten horsemen would be riding out of nowhere, with the spirit in them that ignores side issues and leads them only straight to their objective.

Alwa, as a soldier, knew exactly where fresh horses could be borrowed while his tired ones rested. A little way beyond the outskirts of the city lived a man who was neither Mohammedan nor Hindoo —a fearful man, who took no sides, but paid his taxes, carried on his business, and behaved—a Jew, who dealt in horses and in any other animal or thing that could be bought to show a profit.

Alwa had an utterly complete contempt for Jews, as was right and proper in a Rangar of the blood. He had not met many of them, and those he had had borne away the memory of most outrageous insult gratuitously offered and rubbed home. But this particular Jew was a money-lender on occasion, and his rates had proved as reasonable as his acceptance of Alwa's unwritten promise had been prompt. A man who holds his given word as sacred as did Alwa respects, in the teeth of custom or religion, the man who accepts that word; so, when the chance had offered, Alwa had done the Jew occasional favors and had won his gratitude. He now counted on the Jew for fresh horses.

To reach him, he had to wade the Howrah River,

less than a mile from where the burning ghats
glowed dull crimson against the sky; the crowd
around the ghats was the first intimation he received
that the streets might prove less densely thronged
than usual. It was the Jew, beard-scrabbling and
fidgeting among his horses, who reminded him that
when the full moon shone most of the populace,
and most of Jaimihr's and Howrah's guards, would
be occupied near Siva's temple and the palace.

He left his own horses, groomed again, and gor-
ging their fill of good, clean gram in the Jew's ram-
shackle stable place. Joanna he turned loose, to
sneak into any rat-hole that she chose. Then,
with their swords drawn—for if trouble came it
would be certain to come suddenly—he and his
nine made a wide-ringed circuit of the city, to a
point where the main street passing Jaimihr's palace
ended in a rune of wind-piled desert sand. From
the moment when they reached that point they did
not waste a second; action trod on the heel of
thought and thought flashed fast as summer lightning.

They lit through the deserted street, troubling
for speed, not silence; the few whom they passed
had no time to determine who they were, and no
one followed them. A few frightened night-wander-
ers ran at sight of them, hiding down side streets,
but when they brought up at last outside Jaimihr's
palace-gate they had so far escaped recognition.
And that meant that no one would carry word to
Jaimihr or his men.

It was death-dark outside the bronze-hinged double gate; only a dim lamp hung above from chains, to show how dark it was, and the moon —cut off by trees and houses on a bluff of rising ground—lent nothing to the gloom.

"Open! The Jaimihr-sahib comes!" shouted Alwa, and one of his horsemen legged up close beside the gate.

Some one moved inside, for his footsteps could be heard; whoever he was appeared to listen cautiously.

"Open for the Jaimihr-sahib!" repeated Alwa.

Evidently that was not the usual command, or otherwise the gates would have swung open on the instant. Instead, one gate moved inward by a fraction of a foot, and a pugreed head peered cautiously between the gap. That, though, was sufficient. With a laugh, the man up closest drove his sword-hilt straight between the Hindoo's eyes, driving his horse's shoulder up against the gate; three others spurred and shoved beside him. Not thirty seconds later Alwa and his nine were striking hoof sparks on the stone of Jaimihr's courtyard, and the gates—that could have easily withstood a hundred-man assault with battering-rams—had clanged behind them, bolted tight against their owner.

"Where is the bear cage?" demanded Alwa. "It is a bear I need, not blood!"

The dozen left inside to guard the palace had recovered quickly enough from their panic. They were lining up in the middle of the courtyard, ready to defend their honor, even if the palace should be lost. It was barely probable that Jaimihr's temper would permit them the privilege of dying quickly should he come and find his palace looted; a Rangar's sword seemed better, and they made ready to die hard.

"Where is Ali Partab?"

There was no answer. The little crowd drew in, and one by one took up the fighting attitude that each man liked the best.

"I say I did not come for blood! I came for Ali Partab! If I get him, unharmed, I ride away again; but otherwise——"

"What otherwise?" asked the captain of the guard.

"This palace burns!"

There was a momentary consultation—no argument, but a quickly reached agreement.

"He is here, unharmed," declared the captain gruffly.

"Bring him out!"

"What proof have we that he is all you came for?"

"My given word."

"But the Jaimihr-sahib——"

"You also have my given word that unless I get Ali Partab this palace burns, with all that there is in it!"

Distrustful still, the captain of the guard called out to a sweeper, skulking in the shadow by the stables, to go and loose Ali Partab.

"Send no sweepers to him!" ordered Alwa. "He has suffered indignity enough. Go thou!"

The captain of the guard obeyed. Two minutes later Ali Partab stood before Alwa and saluted.

"Sahib, my master's thanks!"

"They are accepted," answered Alwa, with almost regal dignity. "Bring a lamp!" he ordered.

One of the guard brought a hand-lantern, and by its light Alwa examined Ali Partab closely. He was filthy, and his clothing reeked of the disgusting confinement he had endured.

"Give this man clothing fit for a man of mine!" commanded Alwa.

"Sahib, there is none; perhaps the Jaimihr-sahib——"

"I have ordered!"

There was a movement among Alwa's men—a concerted, horse-length-forward movement, made terrifying by the darkness—each man knew well enough that the men they were bullying could fight; success, should they have to force it at the sword-point, would depend largely on which side took the other by surprise.

"It is done, sahib," said the leader of the guard, and one man hurried off to execute the order. Ten minutes later—they were ten impatient minutes, during which the horses sensed the fever of anxiety and could be hardly made to stand—Ali Partab stood arrayed in clean, new khaki that fitted him reasonably well.

"A sword, now!" demanded Alwa. "Thy sword! This man had a sword when he was taken! Give him thine, unless there is a better to be had."

There was nothing for it but obedience, for few things were more certain than that Alwa was not there to waste time asking for anything he would not fight for if refused. The guard held out his long sword, hilt first, and Ali Partab strapped it on.

"I had three horses when they took me," he asserted, "three good ones, sound and swift, belonging to my master."

"Then take three of Jaimihr's!"

It took ten minutes more for Ali Partab and two of Alwa's men to search the stables and bring out the three best chargers of the twenty and more reserved for Jaimihr's private use. They were wonders of horses, half-Arab and half-native-bred, clean-limbed and firm—worth more, each one of them, than all three of Mahommed Gunga's put together.

"Are they good enough?" demanded Alwa.

"My master will be satisfied," grinned Ali Partab.

"Open the gate, then!" Alwa was peering through the blackness for a sight of firearms, but could see none. He guessed—and he was right—that the guard had taken full advantage of their master's absence, and had been gambling in a corner while their rifles rested under cover somewhere else. For a second he hesitated, dallying with the notion of disarming the guard before he left, then decided that a fight was scarcely worth the risking now, and with ten good men behind him he wheeled and scooted through the wide-flung gates into outer gloom.

He galloped none too fast, for his party was barely out of range before a ragged volley ripped from the palace-wall; one of his men, hampered and delayed by a led horse that was trying to break away from him, was actually hit, and begged Alwa to ride back and burn the palace after all. He was grumbling still about the honor of a Rangar, when Alwa called a halt in the shelter of a deserted side street in order to question Ali Partab further.

Ali Partab protested that he did not know what to say or think about the missionaries. He explained his orders and vowed that his honor held him there in Howrah until Miss McClean should consent to come away. He did not mention the father; he was a mere side issue—it was Alwa who asked after him.

"A tick on the belly of an ox rides with the ox," said Ali Partab.

"Lead on, then, to the mission house," commanded Alwa, and the ten-man troop proceeded to obey. They had reached the main street again, and were wheeling into it, when Joanna sprang from gutter darkness and intercepted them. She was all but ridden down before Ali Partab recognized her.

"The mohurs, sahib!" she demanded. "Three golden mohurs!"

"Ay, three!" said Ali Partab, giving her a hand and yanking her off the ground. She sprang across his horse's rump behind him, and he seemed to have less compunction about personal defilement than the others had.

"Is she thy wife or thy mother-in-law?" laughed Alwa.

"Nay, sahib, but my creditor! The mother of confusion tells me that the Miss-sahib and her father are in Howrah's palace!"

They halted, all together in a cluster in the middle of the street—shut in by darkness—watched, for all they knew, by a hundred enemies.

"Of their own will or as prisoners?"

"As prisoners, sahib."

"Back to the side street! Quickly! Jaimihr's rat's nest is one affair," he muttered; "Howrah's beehive is another!"

CHAPTER XIX

Now, secrets and things of the Councils of Kings
Are deucid expensive to buy,
For it wouldn't look nice if a Councillor's price
Were anything other than high.
Be advised, though, and note that the price they will quote
Is less at each grade you go deeper,
And—(Up on its toes it's the Underworld knows!)—
The cheapest of all is the Sweeper.

JOANNA—when Alwa forgot about her and loosed
her to run just where she chose—had sneaked,
down alleys and over roof-tops, straight for the mission house. She found there nothing but a desultory guard and an impression, rather than the
traces, of an empty cage. About two minutes of
cautious questioning of neighbors satisfied her where
the missionaries were; nothing short of death
seemed able to deprive her of ability to flit like a
black bat through the shadows, and the distance to
Howrah's palace was accomplished, by her usual
bat's entry route, in less time than a pony would
have taken by the devious street. Before Alwa had
thundered on Jaimihr's gate Joanna had mingled
in the crowd outside the palace and was shrewdly
questioning again.

She arrived too late to see McClean and his

daughter seized; what she did hear was that they were prisoners, and that the Maharajah, Jaimihr, and the priests were all of them engaged in the secret ceremony whose beginning was a monthly spectacle but whose subsequent developments—supposed to be somewhere in the bowels of the earth—were known only to the men who held the key.

Like a rat running in the wainscot holes, she tried to follow the procession; like everybody else, she knew the way it took from the palace gate, and—as few others were—she was aware of a scaling-place on the outer wall where a huge baobab drooped century-scarred branches nearly to the ground on either side. The sacred monkeys used that route, and where they went Joanna could contrive to follow.

It was another member of the sweeper caste, lurking in the darkness of an inner courtyard, who pointed out the bronze-barred door to her through which the treasure guardians had chanted on their way; it was he, too, who told her that Rosemary McClean and her father had been rushed into the palace through the main entrance. Also, he informed her that there was no way—positively no way practicable even for a monkey or a bird—of following further. He was a sweeper—intimate acquaintance of creeper ladders, trap-doors, gutters, drains, and byways; she realized at once that there would be no wisdom in attempting to find within an hour what he had not discovered in a lifetime.

So Joanna, her beady eyes glittering between the

wrinkled folds of skin, slunk deeper in a shadow and began to think. She, the looker-on, had seen the whole play from its first beginning and could judge at least that part of it which had its bearing on her missionary masters. First, she knew what Jaimihr's ambition was—every man in Howrah knew how he planned to seize Miss McClean when the moment should be propitious—and her Eastern wisdom warned her that Jaimihr, foiled, would stop at nothing to contrive vengeance. If he could not seize Miss McClean, he would be likely to use every means within his power to bring about her death and prevent another from making off with his prize. Jaimihr, then, was the most pressing danger.

Second, as a Hindoo, she knew well how fiendishly the priests loathed the Christian missionaries; and it was common knowledge that the Maharajah was cross-hobbled by the priests. The Maharajah was a fearful man, and, unless the priests and Jaimihr threatened him with a show of combination, there was a slight chance that he might dread British vengeance too much to dare permit violence to the McCleans. Possibly he might hold out against the priests alone; but before an open alliance between Jaimihr and the priests he would surrender for his own throne's sake.

So far Joanna could reason readily enough, for there was a vast fund of wisdom stored beneath her wrinkled ugliness. But her Eastern limitation stopped her there. She could not hold loyalty to more than one cause, or to more than one offshoot of that cause, in the same shrewd head at once. She decided that at all costs Jaimihr must be got out of the way so that the Maharajah might be left to argue with the priests alone. For the moment no other thought occurred to her.

The means seemed ready to her hand. A peculiarity of the East, which is democratic in most ways under the veneer of swaggering autocracy, is that servants of the very lowest caste may speak, and argue on occasion, with men who would shudder at the prospect of defilement from their touch. There was nothing in the least outrageous in the proposition that the sweeper, waiting in a corner for the procession to emerge again so that he might curl on his mat and sleep undisturbed when it had gone, should dare to approach Jaimihr and address him. He would run no small risk of being beaten by the guards; but, on the other hand, should he catch Jaimihr's ear and interest him, he would be safe.

"Wouldst thou win Jaimihr's favor?" asked Joanna, creeping up beside him, and whispering with all the suggestiveness she could assume.

"Who would not? Who knows that within a week he will not be ruler?"

"True. I have a message for him. I must hurry back. Deliver it for me."

"What would be the nature of the message?"

"This. His prisoner is gone. A raid has taken place. In his absence, while his men patrolled the city, certain Rangars broke into his palace—looted

—and prepared to burn. Bid him hurry back with all the men he can collect."

"From whom is this message?"

"From the captain of the guard."

"And I am to deliver it? Thou dodderest! Mother of a murrain, have I not trouble sufficient for one man? Who bears bad news to a prince, or to any but his enemy? I—with these two eyes—I saw what happened to the men who bore bad news to Howrah once. I—with this broom of mine—I helped clean up the mess. Deliver thine own message!"

"Nay. Afterward I will say this—to the Jaimihr-sahib in person. There is one, I will tell him, a sweeper in the palace, who refused to bear tidings when the need was great."

"If his palace is burned and his wealth all ashes, who cares what Jaimihr hears?"

"There is no glow yet in the sky," said Joanna, looking up. "The palace is not yet in flames; they loot still."

"What if it be not true?"

"Will Jaimihr not be glad?"

"Glad to see me, the bearer of false news, impaled—or crushed beneath an elephant—ay—glad, indeed."

"The reward, were the Jaimihr-sahib warned in time, would be a great one."

"Then, why waitest thou not to have word with him. Art thou above rewards?"

"Have no fear! He will know in good time who it was brought *thee* the news."

They argued for ten minutes, Joanna threaten-
ing and coaxing and promising rewards, until at
last the man consented. It was the thought, thoroughly encouraged by Joanna, that the penalty for
not speaking would be greater than the beating he
might get for bearing evil news that at last convinced him; and it was not until she had won him
over and assured herself that he would not fail that
it dawned on Joanna just what an edged tool she
was playing with. While getting rid of Jaimihr, she
was endangering the liberty and life of Alwa—the
one man able to do anything for the McCleans!

That thought sent her scooting over housetops,
diving down dark alleyways, racing, dodging, hiding, dashing on again, and brought her in the nick
of time to a ditch, from whose shelter she sprang
and seized the hand of Ali Partab. That incident,
and her intimation that the missionaries were in
Howrah's palace, took Alwa back up the black, blind
side street; and before he emerged from it he saw
Jaimihr and his ten go thundering past, their eyes
on the sky-line for a hint of conflagration, and their
horses—belly-to-the-earth—racing as only fear, or
enthusiasm, or grim desperation in their riders' minds
can make them race.

A little later, in groups and scattered fours, and
one by one, his heavy-breathing troopers followed,
cursing the order that had sent them abroad without their horses, damning—as none but a dismounted cavalryman can damn—the earth's uneven-
ness, their swords, their luck, their priests, the

night, their boots, and Jaimihr. Forewarned, Alwa
held on down the pitch-dark side street, into whose
steep-sided chasm the moon's rays would not reach
for an hour or two to come, and once again he led
his party in a sweeping, wide-swung circle, loose-
reined and swifter than the silent night wind—this
time for Howrah's palace. There was his given
word, plighted to Mahommed Gunga, to redeem.

CHAPTER XX

Ha! my purse may be lean, but my 'scutcheon is clean,
And I'm backed by a dozen true men;
I've a sword to my name, and a wrist for the same;
Can a king *frown* fear into me, then?

It is the privilege of emperors, and kings and princes, that—however little real authority they have, or however much their power is undermined by men behind the throne—they must be accorded dignity. They must be, on the face of things, obeyed.

Inspection of the treasure finished and an hour-long mummery of rites performed, the thirty wound their way, chanting, in single file back again. The bronze-enforced door, that was only first of half a hundred barriers between approach and the semi-sacred hoard, at last clanged shut and was locked with three locks, each of whose individual keys was in the keeping of a separate member of the three— Maharajah, Prince, and priest. The same keys fitted every door of the maze-made passages, but no one door would open without all three.

Speaking like an omen from the deepest shadow, the sweeper called to Jaimihr.

"Sahib, thy palace burns! Sahib, thy prisoner runs! Haste, sahib! Call thy men and hasten

back! Thy palace is in flames—the Rangars come
to——"

As a raven, disturbed into night omen-croaking,
he sent forth his news from utter blackness into
nerve-strung tension. No one member of the thirty
but was on the alert for friction or sudden treachery;
they were all eyes for each other, and the croaking
fell on ears strained to the aching point. He had
time to repeat his warning before one of Jaimihr's
men stepped into the darkness where he hid and
dragged him out.

"Sahib, a woman came but now and brought the
news. It was from the captain of the guard. The
Rangars came to take their man away. They broke
in. They burn. They loot. They——"

But Jaimihr did not wait another instant to hear
the rest. To him this seemed like the scheming of his
brother. Now he imagined he could read between
the lines! That letter sent to Alwa had been mis-
reported to him, and had been really a call to come
and free the prisoner and wreak Rangar vengeance!
He understood! But first he must save his palace,
if it could be saved. The priests must have de-
ceived him, so he wasted no time in arguing with
them; he ran, with his guards behind him, to the
outer wall of Siva's temple where the horses waited,
each with a saice squatting at his head. The saices
were sent scattering among the crowd to give the
alarm and send the rest of his contingent hurrying
back; Jaimihr and his ten drove home their spurs,
and streaked, as the frightened jackals run when a

tiger interrupts them at their worry, hell-bent-for-
leather up the unlit street.

Then Maharajah Howrah's custom-accorded dignity stood him in good stead. It flashed across his
worried brain that space had been given him by
the gods in which to think. Jaimihr—one facet of
the problem and perhaps the sharpest—would have
his hands full for a while, and the priests—wish
how they would—would never dare omit the after-
ritual in Siva's temple. He—untrammelled for an
hour to come—might study out a course to take
and hold with those embarrassing prisoners of his.

He turned—updrawn in regal stateliness—and
intimated to the high priest that the ceremony
might proceed without him. When the priests de-
murred and murmured, he informed them that he
would be pleased to give them audience when the
ritual was over, and without deigning another argument he turned through a side door into the
palace.

Within ten minutes he was seated in his throne-
room. One minute later his prisoners stood in front
of him, still holding each other's hands, and the
guard withdrew. The great doors opening on the
marble outer hall clanged tight, and in this room
there were no carved screens through which a hidden,
rustling world might listen. There was gold-in-
crusted splendor—there were glittering, hanging
ornaments that far outdid the peacocks' feathers
of the canopy above the throne; but the walls were
solid, and the marble floor rang hard and true.

There was no nook or corner anywhere that could conceal a man.

For a minute, still bejewelled in his robes of state and glittering as the diamonds in his head-dress caught the light from half a dozen hanging lamps, the Maharajah sat and gazed at them, his chin resting on one hand and his silk-clad elbow laid on the carved gold arm of his throne.

"Why am I troubled?" he demanded suddenly.

"You know!" said the missionary. His daughter clutched his hand tightly, partly to reassure him, partly because she knew that a despot would be bearded now in his gold-bespattered den, and fear gripped her.

"Maharajah-sahib, when I came here with letters from the government of India and asked you for a mission house in which to live and work, I told you that I came as a friend—as a respectful sympathizer. I told you I would not incite rebellion against you, and that I would not interfere with native custom or your authority so long as acquiescence and obedience by me did not run counter to the overriding law of the British Government."

Howrah did not even move his head in token that he listened, but his tired eyes answered.

"To that extent I promised not to interfere with your religion."

Howrah nodded.

"Once—twice—in all nine times—I came and warned you that the practice of suttee was and is illegal. My knowledge of Sanskrit is only slight, but there are others of my race who have had opportunity to translate the Sanskrit Vedas, and I have in writing what they found in them. I warned you, when that information reached me, that your priests have been deliberately lying to you—that the Vedas say: 'Thrice-blessed is she who dies of a broken heart because her lord and master leaves her.' They say nothing, absolutely nothing, about suttee or its practice, which from the beginning has been a damnable invention of the priests. But the practice of suttee has continued. I have warned the government frequently, in writing, but for reasons which I do not profess to understand they have made no move as yet. For that reason, and for no other, I have tried to be a thorn in your side, and will continue to try to be until this suttee ceases!"

"Why," demanded Howrah, "since you are a foreigner with neither influence nor right, do you stay here and behold what you cannot change? Does a snake lie sleeping on an ant-hill? Does a woman watch the butchering of lambs? Yet, do ant-hills cease to be, and are lambs not butchered? Look the other way! Sleep softer in another place!"

"I am a prisoner. For months past my daughter and I have been prisoners to all intents and purposes, and you, Maharajah-sahib, have known it well. Now, the one man who was left to be our escort to another place is a prisoner, too. You know that, too. And you ask me why I stay! Suppose you answer?"

Rosemary squeezed his hand again, this time less to restrain him than herself. She was torn between an inclination to laugh at the daring or shiver at the indiscretion of taking to task a man whose one word could place them at the mercy of the priests of Siva, or the mob. But Duncan McClean, a little bowed about the shoulders, peered through his spectacles and waited—quite unawed by all the splendor—for the Maharajah's answer.

"Of what man do you speak?" asked Howrah, still undecided what to do with them, and anxious above all things to disguise his thoughts. "What man is a prisoner, and how do you know it?"

Before McClean had time to answer him, a spear haft rang on the great teak double door. There was a pause, and the clang repeated—another pause—a third reverberating, humming metal notice of an interruption, and the doors swung wide. A Hindoo, salaaming low so that the expression of his face could not be seen, called out down the long length of the hall.

"The Alwa-sahib waits, demanding audience!"

There was no change apparent on Howrah's face. His fingers tightened on the jewelled cimeter that protruded, silk-sashed, from his middle, but neither voice nor eyes nor lips betrayed the least emotion. It was the McCleans whose eyes blazed with a new-born hope, that was destined to be dashed a second later.

"Has he guards with him?"

"But ten, Maharajah-sahib."

"Then remove these people to the place where they were, and afterward admit him—without his guards!"

"I demand permission to speak with this Alwa-sahib!" said McClean.

"Remove them!"

Two spear-armed custodians of the door advanced. Resistance was obviously futile. Still holding his daughter's hand, the missionary let himself be led to the outer hall and down a corridor, where, presently, a six-inch door shut prisoners and guards even from sound of what transpired beyond.

Alwa, swaggering until his long spurs jingled like a bunch of keys each time his boot-heels struck the marble floor, strode straight as a soldier up to the raised throne dais—took no notice whatever of the sudden slamming of the door behind him—looked knife-keenly into Howrah's eyes—and saluted with a flourish.

"I come from bursting open Jaimihr's buzzard roost!" he intimated mildly. "He held a man of mine. I have the man."

Merely to speak first was insolence; but that breach of etiquette was nothing to his manner and his voice. It appeared that he was so utterly confident of his own prowess that he could afford to speak casually; he did not raise his voice or emphasize a word. He was a man of his word, relating facts, and every line of his steel-thewed anatomy showed it.

"I sent a letter to you, by horseman, with a present," said Howrah. "I await the answer."

Alwa's eyes changed, and his attention stiffened. Not having been at home, he knew nothing of the letter, but he did not choose to acknowledge the fact. The principle that one only shares the truth with friends is good, when taken by surprise.

"I preferred to have confirmation of the matter from the Maharajah's lips in person, so—since I had this other matter to attend to—I combined two visits in one trip."

He lied, as he walked and fought, like a soldier, and the weary man who watched him from the throne detected no false ring.

"I informed you that I had extended my protection to the two missionaries, man and daughter."

"You did. Also, you did well." He tossed that piece of comfort to the despot as a man might throw table scraps to a starveling dog! "I have come to take away the missionaries."

"With a guard of ten!"

It was the first admission of astonishment that either man had made.

"Are you not aware that Jaimihr, too, has eyes on the woman?"

"I am aware of it. I have shown Jaimihr how deep my fear of him lies! I know, too, how deep the love lies between thee and thy brother, king of Howrah! I am here to remind you that many more than ten men would race their horses to a standstill to answer my summons—brave men, Maharajah-

sahib—men whose blades are keen, and straightly
held, and true. They who would rally round me
against Jaimihr would——"

"Would fight for me?"

"I have not yet said so." There was a little,
barely accentuated emphasis on the one word "yet."
The Maharajah thought a minute before he answered.

"How many mounted troopers could you raise?"

"Who knows? A thousand—three thousand—
according to the soreness of the need."

"You have heard—I know that you have heard
—what, even at this minute, awaits the British? I
know, for I have taken care to know, that a cousin
of yours—Mahommed Gunga—is interested for the
British. So—so I am interested to have word with
you."

Alwa laughed ironically.

"And the tiger asked the wolf pack where good
hunting was!" he mocked. "I and my men strike
which way suits us when the hour comes."

"My palace has many chambers in it!" hinted
Howrah. "There have been men who wondered
what the light of day was like, having long ago forgotten!"

"Make me prisoner!" laughed Alwa. "Count
then the hours until three thousand blades join
Jaimihr and help him grease the dungeon hinges
with thy fat!"

"Having looted Jaimihr's palace, you speak
thus?"

"Having whipped a dog, I wait for the dog to lick my hand."

"What is your purpose with these missionaries?"

"To redeem my given word."

"And then?"

"I would be free to pledge it again."

"To me?"

"To whom I choose."

"I will give thee the missionaries, against thy word to fight on my side when the hour comes."

"Against whom?"

"The British."

"I have no quarrel with the British, yet."

"I will give thee the missionaries, against thy word to support me on this throne."

"Against whom?"

"Against all comers."

"If I refuse, what then?"

"Jaimihr—who by this time must surely be thy very warmest friend!—shall attack thee unmolested. Pledge thy word—take thy missionary people—and Jaimihr must oppose thee and me combined."

"Should Jaimihr ride after me, what then?"

"If he takes many with him, he must leave his camp unguarded, or only weakly guarded. Then I would act. If he goes with few, how can he take thy castle?"

"Then I have your protection against Jaimihr, and the missionaries, against my promise to support you on the throne?"

"My word on it."

"And mine."

Howrah rose, stepped forward to the dais edge, and held his hand out.

"Nay!" swore Alwa, recoiling. "My word is given. I take no Hindoo's hand!"

Howrah glared for a moment, but thought better of the hot retort that rose to his lips. Instead he struck a silver gong, and when the doors swung open ordered the prisoners to be produced.

"Escape through the palace-grounds," he advised Alwa. "A man of mine will show the way."

"Remember!" said Alwa across his shoulder with more than royal insolence, "I swore to help thee against Jaimihr and to support thee on thy throne —but in nothing did I swear to be thy tool—remember!"

CHAPTER XXI

Howrah City bows the knee
(More or less) to masters three,
   King, and Prince, and Siva.
Howrah City comes and goes—
Buys and sells—and never knows
Which is friend, and which are foes—
   King, or Prince, or Siva.

THAT that followed Alwa's breakaway was all but the tensest hour in Howrah City's history. The inevitable—the foiled rage of the priests and Jaimihr's impudent insistence that the missionaries should be handed over to him—the Maharajah's answer—all combined to set the murmurings afoot. Men said that the threatened rebellion against the rule of Britain had broken loose at last, and a dozen other quite as false and equally probable things.

Jaimihr, finding that his palace was intact, and that only the prisoner and three horses from his stable were missing, placed the whole guard under arrest—stormed futilely, while his hurrying swarm flocked to him through the dinning streets—and then, mad-angry and made reckless by his rage, rode with a hundred at his back to Howrah's palace, scattering the bee-swarm of inquisitive but so far peaceful citizens right and left.

With little ceremony, he sent in word to Howrah

that he wanted Alwa and the missionaries; he stated
that his private honor was at stake, and that he
would stop at nothing to wreak vengeance. He
wanted the man who had dared invade his palace
—the man whom he had released—and the two who
were the prime cause of the outrage. And with just
as little ceremony word came out that the Maharajah
would please himself as to what he did with prisoners.

That message was followed almost instantly by
the high priest of Siva in person, angry as a turkey-
gobbler and blasphemously vindictive. He it was
who told Jaimihr of the unexpected departure
through the palace-grounds.

"Ride, Jaimihr-sahib! Ride!" he advised him.
"How many have you? A hundred? Plenty!
Ride and cut him off! There is but one road to
Alwa's place; he must pass by the northern ford
through Howrah River. Ride and cut him off!"

So, loose-reined, foam-flecked, breathing vengeance, Jaimihr and his hundred thundered through
the dark, hot night, making a bee-line for the point
where Alwa's band must pass in order to take the
shortest route to safety.

It was his word to the Jew that saved Alwa's
neck. He and his men were riding borrowed horses,
and he had promised to return them and reclaim
his own. They had moved at a walk through winding, dark palace-alleys, led by a palace attendant,
and debouched through a narrow door that gave
barely horse-room into the road where Jaimihr had
once killed a Maharati trader who molested Rose-

mary McClean. The missionary and his daughter were mounted on the horses seized in Jaimihr's stable; Joanna, moaning about "three gold mohurs, sahib—three, where are they?" was up behind Ali Partab, tossed like a pea on a drum-skin by the lunging movements of the wonder of a horse.

Instead of heading straight for home, in which case—although he did not know it—he would have been surely overhauled and brought to bay, he led at a stiff hand gallop to the Jew's, changed horses, crossed the ford by the burning ghats, and swooped in a wide half-circle for the sandy trail that would take him homeward. He made the home road miles beyond the point where Jaimihr waited for him—drew rein into the long-striding amble that desert-taught horses love—and led on, laughing.

"Ho!" He laughed. "Ho-ho! Here, then, is the end of Mahommed Gunga's scheming! Now, when he comes with arguments to make me fight on the British side, what a tale I have for him! Ho! What a swearing there will be! I will give him his missionary people, and say, 'There, Mahommed Gunga, cousin mine, there is my word redeemed—there is thy man into the bargain—there are three horses for thee—and I—I am at Howrah's beck and call!' Allah! What a swearing there will be!"

There was swearing, viler and more blasphemous than any of which Mahommed Gunga might be capable, where Jaimihr waited in the dark. He waited until the yellow dawn broke up the first dim

streaks of violet before he realized that Alwa had
given him the slip; and he cursed even the high
priest of Siva when that worthy accosted him and
asked what tidings.

"Another trick!" swore Jaimihr. "So, thou and
thy temple rats saw fit to send me packing for the
night! What devils' tricks have been hatched out
in my absence?"

The high priest started to protest, but Jaimihr
silenced him with coarse-mouthed threats.

"I, too, can play double when occasion calls for
it!" he swore. And with that hint at coming
trouble he clattered on home to his palace.

To begin with, when he reached home, he had the
guard beaten all but unconscious for having dared
let raiders in during the night before; then he sent
them, waterless and thirsty, back to the dungeon.
He felt better then, and called for ink and paper.

For hours he thought and wrote alternately,
tearing up letter after letter. Then, at last, he
read over a composition that satisfied him and set
his seal at the foot. He placed the whole in a silver
tube, poured wax into the joint, and called for the
fat man who had been responsible for Ali Partab's
capture.

"Dog!" he snarled. "Interfering fool! All this
was thy doing! Didst thou see the guard beaten
awhile ago?"

"I did. It was a lordly beating. The men are
all but dead but will live for such another one."

"Wouldst thou be so beaten?"

"How can I prevent, if your highness wishes?"

"Take this. It is intended for Peshawur but may be given to any British officer above the rank of major. It calls for a receipt. Do not dare come back, or be caught in Howrah City, without a receipt for that tube and its contents intact!"

"If Alwa and Mahommed Gunga are in league with my brother," muttered Jaimihr to himself when the fat Hindoo had gone, "then the sooner the British quarrel with both of them the better. Howrah alone I can dispose of easily enough, and there is yet time before rebellion starts for the British to spike the guns of the other two. By the time that is done, I will be Maharajah!"

It was less than three days later when the word came mysteriously through the undiscoverable "underground" route of India for all men to be ready.

"By the next full moon," went the message, from the priests alone knew where, "all India will be waiting. When the full moon rises then the hour is come!"

"And when that full moon rises," thought Jaimihr to himself, "my brother's funeral rites will be past history!"

For the present, though, he made believe to regret his recent rage, and was courteous to priest and Maharajah alike—even sending to his brother to apologize.

CHAPTER XXII

They've called thee by an evil word,
They've named thee traitor, friend o' mine.
Thou askest faith? I send my sword.
There is no greater, friend o' mine.

RALPH CUNNINGHAM said good-by to Brigadier-
General Byng (Byng the Brigadier) with more feeling of regret and disappointment than he cared
to show. A born soldier, he did his hard-mouthed
utmost to refrain from whining; he even pretended
that a political appointment was a recognizable advance along the road to sure success—or, rather,
pretended that he thought it was; and the Brigadier,
who knew men, and particularly young men, detected instantly the telltale expression of the honest gray eyes—analyzed it—and, to Cunningham's
amazement, approved the unwilling make-believe.

"Now, buck up, Cunningham!" he said, slapping
him familiarly on the shoulder. "You're making a
good, game effort to hide chagrin, and you're a good,
game ass for your pains. There isn't one man in all
India who has half your luck at this minute, if you
only knew it; but go ahead and find out for yourself! Go to Abu and report, but waste no more
time there than you can help. Hurry on to Howrah, and, once you're there, if Mahommed Gunga

tells you what looks like a lie, trust him to the hilt!"

"Is he coming with me, then?" asked Cunningham in some amazement.

"Yes—unofficially. He has relations in that neighborhood and wants to visit them; he is going to take advantage of your pack-train and escort. You'll have a small escort as far as Abu; after that you'll be expected to look out for yourself. The escort is made up of details travelling down-country; they'll leave you at Abu Road."

So, still unbelieving—still wondering why the Brigadier should go to all that trouble to convince him that politics in a half-forgotten native state were fair meat for a soldier—Cunningham rode off at the head of a variously made-up travelling party, grudging every step of that wonderful mare Mahommed Gunga had given him, that bore him away from the breeze-swept north—away from the mist-draped hills he had already learned to love—ever down, down, down into the hell-baked plains.

Each rest-house where he spent a night was but another brooding-place of discontent and regret; each little petty detail connected with the command of the motley party (mainly time-expired men, homeward bound), was drudgery; each Hindoo pugree that he met was but a beastly contrast, or so it seemed to him, to the turbans of the troop that but a week ago had thundered at his back.

More than any other thing, Mahommed Gunga's cheerfulness amazed him. He resented it. He did not see why the man who had expressed such interest in the good fortune of his father's son should not be sympathetic now that his soldier career had been nipped so early in the bud. He began to lose faith in Mahommed Gunga's wisdom, and was glad when the ex-Risaldar chose to bring up the rear of the procession instead of riding by his side.

But behind, in Peshawur, there was one man at least who knew Mahommed Gunga and his worth, and who refused to let himself be blinded by any sort of circumstantial evidence. The evidence was black—in black on white—written by a black-hearted schemer, and delivered by a big, fat black man, who was utterly road-weary, to the commissioner in person.

The sepoy mutiny that had been planned so carefully had started to take charge too soon. News had arrived of native regiments whose officers had been obliged against their will to disarm and disband them, and the loyalty of other regiments was seriously called in question.

But the men whose blindness was responsible for the possibility of mutiny were only made blinder by the evidence of coming trouble. With a dozen courses open to them, any one of which might have saved the situation, they deliberately chose a thirteenth—two-forked toboggan-slide into destruction. To prove their misjudged confidence in the native army, they actually disbanded the irregulars led by Byng the Brigadier—removed the European soldiers wherever possible from ammunition-magazine guard-

duty, replacing them with native companies—and
reprimanded the men whose clear sight showed
them how events were shaping.

They reprimanded Byng, as though depriving him
of his command were not enough. When he protested, as he had a right to do, they showed him
Jaimihr's letter.

"Mahommed Gunga told you, did he? Look at
this!"

The letter, most concisely and pointedly written,
considering the indirect phraseology and caution of
the East, deliberately accused Mahommed Gunga
and a certain Alwa, together with all the Rangars of
a whole province, of scheming with Maharajah Howrah to overthrow the British rule. It recommended
the immediate arrest of Mahommed Gunga and stern
measures against the Rangars.

"What do you propose to do about it?" inquired
Byng.

"It's out of our province. A copy of this letter
has been sent to the proper quarter, and no doubt
the story will be investigated. There have been all
kinds of stories about suttee being practised in Howrah, and it very likely won't be difficult to find a
plausible excuse for deposing the Maharajah and putting Jaimihr in his place. In the meantime, if Mahommed Gunga shows himself in these parts he'll
be arrested."

Byng did then the sort of thing that was fortunately characteristic of the men who rose in the nick
of time to seize the reins. He hurried to his quarters,

packed in its case the sword of honor that had once been given him by his Queen, and despatched it without a written line of comment to Mahommed Gunga. The native who took it was ordered to ride like the devil, overtake Mahommed Gunga on the road to Abu, present the sword without explanation, and return.

Cunningham, in spite of himself, had travelled swiftly. The moon lacked two nights of being full, and two more days would have seen him climbing up the fourteen-mile rock road that leads up the purple flanks of Abu, when the ex-trooper of irregulars cantered from a dust cloud, caught up Mahommed Gunga, who was riding, as usual, in the rear, and handed him the sword. He held it out with both hands. Mahommed Gunga seized it by the middle, and neither said a word for the moment.

In silence Mahommed Gunga drew the blade— saw Byng's name engraved close to the hilt—recognized the sword, and knew the sender—thought— and mistook the meaning.

"Was there no word?"

"None."

"Then take this word back. 'I will return the sword, with honor added to it, when the peace of India is won.' Say that, and nothing else."

"I would rest my horse for a day or two," said the trooper.

"Neither thou nor yet thy horse will have much rest this side of Eblis!" said Mahommed Gunga. "Ride!"

The trooper wheeled and went with a grin and a salute which he repeated twice, leaning back from the saddle for a last look at the man of his own race whom Byng had chosen to exalt. He felt himself honored merely to have carried the sword. Mahommed Gunga removed his own great sabre and handed it to one of his own five whom he overtook; then he buckled on the sword of honor and spurred until he rode abreast of Cunningham, a hundred yards or more ahead of the procession.

"Sahib," he asked, "did Byng-bahadur say a word or two about listening to me?"

"He did. Why?"

"Because I will now say things!"

The fact that the Brigadier had sent no message other than the sword was probably the Rajput's chief reason for talking in riddles still to Cunningham. The silence went straight to his Oriental heart—so to speak, set the key for him to play to. But he knew, too, that Cunningham's youth would be a handicap should it come to argument; what he was looking for was not a counsellor or some one to make plans, for the plans had all been laid and cross-laid by the enemy, and Mahommed Gunga knew it. He needed a man of decision—to be flung blindfold into unexpected and unexpecting hell wrath, who would lead, take charge, decide on the instant, and lead the way out again, with men behind him who would recognize decision when they saw it. So he spoke darkly. He understood that the sword meant "Things have started," so with a soldier's courage he proceeded to head Cunningham toward the spot where hell was loose.

"Say ahead!" smiled Cunningham.

"Yonder, sahib, lies Abu. Yonder to the right lies thy road now, not forward."

"I have orders to report at Abu."

"And I, sahib, orders to advise!"

"Are you advising me to disobey orders?"

The Rajput hesitated. "Sahib, have I anything to gain," he asked, "by offering the wrong advice?"

"I can't imagine so."

"I advise, now, that we—thou and I, sahib, and my five turn off here—yonder, where the other trail runs—letting the party proceed to Abu without us."

"But why, Mahommed Gunga?"

"There is need of haste, sahib. At Abu there will be delay—much talk with Everton-sahib, and who knows?—perhaps cancellation of the plan to send thee on to Howrah."

"I'd be damned glad, Mahommed Gunga, not to have to go there!"

"Sahib, look! What is this I wear?"

"Which?"

"See here, sahib—this."

For the first time Cunningham noticed the fine European workmanship on the sword-hilt, and realized that the Rajput's usual plain, workmanlike weapon had been replaced.

"That is Byng-bahadur's sword of honor! It reached me a few minutes ago. The man who brought it is barely out of sight. It means, sahib, that the hour to act is come!"

"But——"

"Sahib—this sending thee to Howrah is my doing! Since the day when I first heard that the son of Pukka Cunnigan-bahadur was on his way I have schemed and planned and contrived to this end. It was at word from me that Byng-bahadur signed the transfer papers—otherwise he would have kept thee by him. There are owls—old women—men whom Allah has deprived of judgment—drunkards —fools—in charge at Peshawur and in other places; but there are certain men who know. Byng-bahadur knows. I know—and I will show the way! Let me lead, sahib, for a little while, and I will show thee what to lead!"

"But——"

"Does this sword, sahib, mean nothing? Did Byng-bahadur send it me for fun?"

"But what's the idea? I can't disobey orders, and ride off to—God knows where—without some excuse. You'll have to tell me why. What's the matter? What's happening?"

"Byng-bahadur sent not one word to me when he sent this sword. To thee he said: 'Listen to Mahommed Gunga, even when he seems to lie!' I know that, for he told me he had said it. To me he said: 'Take charge, Mahommed Gunga, when the hour comes, and rub his innocent young nose hard as you like into the middle of the mess!' Ay, sahib, so said he. It is now that I take charge."

"But——"

"'But,' said the nylghau, and the wolf-pack had him! 'But,' said the tiger, and the trap-door shut! 'But,' said the Hindoo, and a priest betrayed him! But—but—but—I never knew thy father make much use of that word!"

"Yes—but—I have my orders, Mahommed Gunga!"

"Sahib—this sword is a sword of honor—it stands for Byng-bahadur's honor. I have it in my keeping. Mine own honor is a matter somewhat dear to me, and I have kept it clean these many years. Now I ask to keep thine honor, too, awhile —making three men's honor. If I fail, then thou and I and Byng-bahadur all go down together in good company. If I fail not, then, sahib—Allah is contented when his honor stands!"

Cunningham drew rein and looked him in the eyes. Gray eyes met brown and neither flinched; each read what men of mettle only can read when they see it—the truth, the fearlessness, the thought they understand because it lives with them. Cunningham held out his hand.

Some thirty minutes later Cunningham, Mahommed Gunga, and the five, with a much-diminished mule-train bumping in their wake, were headed westward on a dry, hot trail, while the time-expired and convalescent escort plodded south. The escort carried word that Cunningham had heard of trouble to the west, and had turned off to investigate it.

CHAPTER XXIII

Quoth little red jackal, famishing, "Lo,
Yonder a priest and a soldier go;
You can see farthest, and you ought to know,—
Which shall I wander with, carrion crow?"
The crow cawed back at him, "Ignorant beast!
Soldiers get glory, but none of the feast;
Soldiers work hardest, and snaffle the least.
Take my advice on it—Follow the priest!"

It was two hours after sunrise on the second day that followed Cunningham's desertion of his party when he and Mahommed Gunga first caught sight of a blue, baked rock rising sheer out of a fringe of green on the dazzling horizon. It was a freak of nature—a point pushed through the level crust of bone-dry earth, and left to glitter there alone.

"That is my cousin Alwa's place!" exclaimed Mahommed Gunga, and he seemed to draw a world of consolation from the fact.

The sight loosed his tongue at last; he rode by Cunningham, and deigned an explanation now, at least, of what had led to what might happen. He wasted little breath on prophecy, but he was eloquent in building up a basis from which Cunningham might draw his own deductions. They had ridden through the cool of the night in easy stages, and should have camped at dawn; but Mahommed Gunga had in-

sisted that the tired animals could carry them for
three hours longer.

"A soldier's horse must rest at the other end,
sahib," he had laughed. "Who knows that they
have not sent from Abu to arrest both thee and me?"
And he had not vouchsafed another word until, over
the desert glare, his cousin's aerie had blazed out,
beating back the molten sun-rays.

"It looks hotter than the horns of hell!" said
Cunningham.

"The horns of hell, sahib, are what we leave behind us! They grow hot now! Thy countrymen—
the men who hated thee so easily—heated them and
sit now between them for their folly!"

"How d'you mean? 'Pon my soul and honor,
Risaldar, you talk more riddles in five minutes than
I ever heard before in all my life!"

"There be many riddles I have not told yet—
riddles of which I do not know the answer. Read
me this one. Why did the British Government annex the state of Oudh? All of the best native
soldiers came from Oudh, or nearly all. They were
loyal once; but can a man be fairly asked to side
against his own? If Oudh should rise in rebellion,
what would the soldiers do?"

"Dunno, I'm sure," said Cunningham.

"Read me this one, then. By pacifying both Mohammedan and Hindoo and by letting both keep
their religion; by sometimes playing one against the
other and by being just, the British Government has
become supreme from the Himalayas to the ocean.

Can you tell me why they now issue cartridges for
the new rifles that are soaked in the fat of cows and
pigs, thus insulting both Mohammedan and Hindoo?"

"I didn't know it was so."

"Sahib, it is! These damned new cartridges and
this new drill—sahib, I—I who am loyal to the marrow of my bones—would no more touch those cartridges—nor bite them, as the drill decrees—than I
would betray thee! Pig's fat! Ugh!"

He spat with Mohammedan eloquence and wiped
his lips on his tunic sleeve before resuming.

"Then, like a flint and steel, to light the train
that they have laid, they loose these missionaries,
in a swarm, from one end of India to the other.
Why? What say one and all? Mohammedan and
Hindoo both say it is a plot, first to make them lose
their own religion by defilement, then to make
Christians of them! Foolishness to talk thus?
Nay! It was foolishness to act thus!

"Sahib, peace follows in the wake of soldiers, as
we know. Time and time again the peace of India
has been ripped asunder at the whim of priests!
These padre people, preaching new damnation every-
where, are the flint and steel for the tinder of the
cartridge fat!"

"I never knew you to croak before, Mahommed
Gunga."

"Nor am I croaking. I am praising Allah, who
has sent thee now to the place whence the wind will
come to fan the hell flames that presently will burn.
The wind will blow hot or cold—for or against the

government—according as you and I and certain
others act when opportunity arrives! See yonder!"

They had been seen, evidently, for horsemen—
looking like black ants on the desert—seemed to have
crawled from the bowels of the living rock and were
galloping in their direction.

"Friends?" asked Cunningham.

"Friends, indeed! But they have yet to discover
whether we are friends. They set me thinking,
sahib. Alwa is well known on this countryside,
and none dare raid his place; few would waste time
trying. Therefore, it is all one to him who passes
along this road; and he takes no trouble, as a rule, to
send his men out in skirmishing order when a party
comes in view. Why, then, does he trouble now?"

"Couldn't say. I don't know Alwa."

"I am thinking, sahib, that the cloud has burst
at last! A blood-red cloud! Alwa is neither scare-
monger nor robber; when he sends out armed men
to inspect strangers on the sky-line, there is war!
Sahib, I grow young again! Had people listened
to me—had they called me anything but fool when
I warned them—thou and I would have been cooped
up now in Agra, or in Delhi, or Lucknow, or Peshawur! Now we are free of the plains of Rajputana
—within a ride of fifty of my blood-relations, and
they each within reach of others! Ho! I can hear
the thunder of a squadron at my back again! I am
young, sahib—young! My old joints loosen! Allah
send the cloud *has* burst at last—I bring to two
thousand Rangars a new Cunnigan-bahadur! Thy

father's son shall learn what Cunnigan-bahadur taught!"

He lapsed into silence, watching the advancing horsemen, who swooped down on them in an ever-closing fan formation. His tired horse sensed the thrill that tingled through its rider's veins, and pranced again, curving his neck and straining at the bit until Mahommed Gunga steadied him. The five behind—even the mule-drivers too—detected excitement in the air, and the little column closed in on its leaders. All eyes watched the neck-and-neck approach of Alwa's men, until Cunningham at last could see their turbans and make out that they were Rangars, not Hindoos. Then he and the Risaldar drew rein.

There were twenty who raced toward them, but no Alwa.

"It is as I thought!" declared Mahommed Gunga. "It is war, sahib! He has summoned men from his estates. As a rule, he can afford but ten men for that fort of his, and he would not send *all* his men to meet us; he has a garrison up yonder!"

Like blown dust-devils the twenty raced to them, and drew up thundering within a lance-length. A sword-armed Rangar with a little gold lace on his sleeve laughed loud as he saluted, greeting Mahommed Gunga first. The Risaldar accepted his salute with iron dignity.

"Forgive him, sahib!" he whispered to Cunningham. "The jungli knows no better! He will learn whom to salute first when Alwa has said his say!"

But Cunningham was in no mood just then to stand on military ceremony or right of precedence. He was too excited, too inquisitive, too occupied with the necessity for keeping calm in the face of what most surely looked like the beginning of big happenings. These horsemen of Alwa's rode, and looked, and laughed like soldiers, new-stripped of the hobble ropes of peace, and their very seat in the untanned saddles—tight down, loose-swaying from the hips, and free—was confirmation of Mahommed Gunga's words.

They wheeled in a cloud and led the way, opening a little in the centre to let the clouds of sand their horses kicked up blow to the right and left of Cunningham and his men. Not a word was spoken —not a question asked or a piece of news exchanged —until the whole party halted at the foot of Alwa's fortress home—a great iron gate in front of them and garden land on either side—watered by the splashing streamlet from the heights above.

"Men of the house of Kachwaha have owned and held this place, sahib, since Allah made it!" whispered Mahommed Gunga. "Men say that Alwa has no right to it; they lie! His father's father won the dower-right!"

He was interrupted by the rising of the iron gate. It seemed solid, without even an eyehole in it. It was wide enough to let four horses under side by side, and for all its weight it rose as suddenly and evenly as though a giant's hand had lifted it. Immediately behind it, like an actor waiting for the stage-

curtain to rise, Alwa bestrode his war-horse in the
middle of a roadway. He saluted with drawn sabre,
and this time Cunningham replied.

Almost instantly the man who had led the gallopers and had saluted Mahommed Gunga spurred
his horse up close to Cunningham and whispered:
"Pardon, sahib! I did not know! Am I forgiven?"

"Yes," said Cunningham, remembering then that
a Rajput, and a Rangar more particularly, thinks
about points of etiquette before considering what
to eat. Alwa growled out a welcome, rammed his
sabre home, and wheeled without another word,
showing the way at a walk—which was all a wild
goat could have accomplished—up a winding road,
hewn out of the solid mountain, that corkscrewed
round and round upon itself until it gave onto the
battlemented summit. There he dismounted, ordered his men to their quarters, and for the first
time took notice of his cousin.

"I have thy missionary and his daughter, three
horses for thee, and thy man," he smiled.

"Did Ali Partab bring them?"

"Nay. It was I brought Ali Partab and the rest!
My promise is redeemed!"

Mahommed Gunga thrust his sword-hilt out and
smiled back at him. "I present Raff-Cunnigan-
sahib—son of Pukka-Cunnigan-bahadur!" he announced.

Alwa drew himself up to his full height and eyed
young Cunningham as a buyer eyes a war-horse,
inch by inch. The youngster, who had long since

!earned to actually revel in the weird sensation of a
hundred pairs of eyes all fixed on him at once, felt
this one man's gaze go over him as though he were
being probed. He thanked his God he had no fat
to be detected, and that his legs were straight, and
that his tunic fitted him!

"Salaam, bahadur," said Alwa slowly. "I knew
thy father. So — thou — art — his — son. Welcome. There is room here always for a guest. I have
other guests with whom you might care to speak. I
will have a room made ready. Have I leave to ask
questions of my cousin here?"

Cunningham bowed in recognition of his courtesy,
and walked away to a point whence he could look
from the beetling parapet away and away across
the desert that shone hot and hazy-rimmed on every
side. If this were a man on whom he must depend
for following—if any of all the more than hints
dropped by the Risaldar were true—it seemed to
him that his reception was a little too chilly to be
hopeful.

After a minute or two he turned his eyes away
from the dazzling plain below and faced about to
inspect the paved courtyard. Round it, on three
sides of a parallelogram, there ran a beautifully
designed and wonderfully worked-out veranda-
fronted building, broken here and there by cobbled
passages that evidently led to other buildings on the
far edge of the rock. In the centre, covered by a
.roof like a temple-dome in miniature, was the ice-
cold spring, whose existence made the fort tenable.

Under the veranda, on a long, low lounge, was a sight that arrested his attention—held him spellbound—drew him, tingling in a way he could not have explained—drew him—drew him, slow-footed, awkward, red—across the courtyard.

He heard Mahommed Gunga swear aloud; he recognized the wording of the belly-growled Rangar oath; but it did not occur to him that what he saw —what was drawing him—could be connected with it. He looked straight ahead and walked ahead—reached the edge of the veranda—took his helmet off—and stood still, feeling like an idiot, with the sun full on his head.

"I'd advise you to step into the shade," said a voice that laughed more sweetly than the chuckling spring. "I don't know who you are, but I'm more glad to see you than I ever was in my life to see anybody. I can't get up, because I'm too stiff; the ride to here from Howrah City all but killed me, and I'm only here still because I couldn't ride another yard. My father will be out in a moment. He's half-dead too."

"My name is Cunningham."

"I'm Miss McClean. My father *was* a missionary in Howrah."

She nodded to a chair beside her, and Cunningham took it, feeling awkward, as men of his type usually do when they meet a woman in a strange place.

"How in the world did you get in?" she asked him. "It's two days now since the Alwa-sahib told us that the whole country is in rebellion. How is it that you managed to reach here? According to Alwa, no white man's life is safe in the open, and he only told me to-day that he wouldn't let me go away even if I were well enough to ride."

"First I've heard of rebellion!" said Cunningham, aghast at the notion of hearing news like that at second hand, and from a woman.

"Hasn't Alwa told you?"

"He hasn't had time to, yet."

"Then, you'd better ask him. If what he says is true—and I think he tells the truth—the natives mean to kill us all, or drive us out of India. Of course they can't do it, but they mean to try. He has been more than kind—more than hospitable— more than chivalrous. Just because he gave his word to another Rangar, he risked his life about a dozen times to get my father and me and Ali Partab out of Howrah. But, I don't think he quite liked doing it—and—this is in confidence—if I were asked —and speaking just from intuition—I should say he is in sympathy with the rebellion!"

"How long have you been here?" asked Cunningham.

"Several days—ten, I think. It seemed strange at first and rather awful to be lodged on a rock like this in a section of a Rangar's harem! Yes, there are several women here behind the scenes, but I only see the waiting-women. I've forgotten time; the news about rebellion seems too awful to leave room for any other thought."

"Who was the Rangar to whom Alwa gave his word? Not Mahommed Gunga, by any chance?"

"Yes, Mahommed Gunga."

"Well, I'm—!" Cunningham clipped off the participle just in time. "There *is* something, then, in the talk about rebellion! That man's been talking in riddles to me ever since I came to India, and it looks as though he knew long in advance."

He was about to cross-examine Miss McClean rigorously, even at the risk of seeming either rude or else frightened; but before his lips could frame another question he caught sight of Mahommed Gunga making signals to him. He affected to ignore the signals. He objected to being kept in the dark so utterly, and wished to find out a little for himself before listening to what the Rangars had to say. But Mahommed Gunga started over to him.

He could not hear the remark Mahommed Gunga made to Alwa over his shoulder as he came.

"Had I remembered there was a woman of his own race here, I would have plunged him straight into the fighting! Now there will be the devil first to pay!"

"He has decision in at least one thing!" grinned Alwa.

"Something that I think thou lackest, cousin!" came the hot retort.

Alwa turned his back with a shake of his head and a thin-lipped smile—then disappeared through a green door in the side of what seemed like solid rock. A moment later Mahommed Gunga stood near Cunningham, saluting.

"We ask the favor of a consultation, sahib."

Cunningham rose, a shade regretfully, and followed into the rock-walled cavern into which Alwa had preceded them. It was nearly square—a hollow bubble in the age-old lava—axe-trimmed many hundred years ago. What light there was came in through three long slits that gave an archer's view of the plain and of the zigzag roadway from the iron gate below. It was cool, for the rock roof was fifty or more feet thick, and the silence of it seemed like the nestling-place of peace.

They sat down on wooden benches round the walls, with their soldier legs stretched out in front of them. Alwa broke silence first, and it was of anything but peace he spoke.

"Now—now, let us see whose throats we are to slit!" he started cheerfully.

CHAPTER XXIV

Achilles had a tender spot
That even guarding gods forgot,
   When clothing him in armor;
And I have proved this charge o' mine
For fear, and sloth, and vice, and wine,
   But clear forgot the charmer!

THE Alwa-sahib knew more English than he was
willing to admit. In the first place, he had the
perfectly natural dislike of committing his thoughts
to any language other than his own when anything
serious was the subject of discussion; in the second
place, he had little of Mahommed Gunga's last-
ditch loyalty. Not that Alwa could be disloyal;
he had not got it in him; but as yet he had seen no
good reason for pledging himself and his to the
British cause.

So for more than ten minutes he chose to sit in
apparent dudgeon, his hands folded in front of him
on the hilt of his tremendous sabre, growling out a
monologue in his own language for Mahommed
Gunga's benefit. Then Mahommed Gunga silenced
him with an uplifted hand, and turned to translate
to Cunningham.

"It would seem, sahib, that even while we rode
to Abu the rebellion was already raging! It burst

suddenly. They have mutinied at Berhampur, and slain their officers. Likewise at Meerut, and at all the places in between. At Kohat, in this province, they have slain every white man, woman, and child, and also at Arjpur and Sohlat. The rebels are hurrying to Delhi, where they have proclaimed a new rule, under the descendants of the old-time kings. Word of all this came before dawn to-day, by a messenger from Maharajah Howrah to my cousin here. My cousin stands pledged to uphold Howrah on his throne; Howrah is against the British; Jaimihr, his brother, is in arms against Howrah."

"Why did the Alwa-sahib pledge himself to Howrah's cause?"

Mahommed Gunga—who knew quite well—saw fit to translate the question. With a little sign of irritation Alwa growled his answer.

"He says, sahib, that for the safety of two Christian missionaries, for whom he has no esteem at all, he was forced to swear allegiance to a Hindoo whom he esteems even less. He says that his word is given!"

"Does he mean that he would like me and the missionaries to leave his home at once—do we embarrass him?"

Again Mahommed Gunga—this time with a grin —saw fit to ask before he answered.

"He says, 'God forbid,' sahib; 'a guest is a guest!'"

Cunningham reflected for a moment, then leaned forward.

"Tell him this!" he said slowly. "I am glad to be his guest, but, if this story of rebellion is true——"

"It is true, sahib! More than true! There is much more to be told!"

"Then, I can only accept his hospitality as the representative of my government! I stay here officially, or not at all. It is for him to answer!"

"Now, Allah be praised!" swore Mahommed Gunga. "I knew we had a man! That is well said, sahib!"

"The son of Cunnigan-bahadur is welcome here on any terms at all!" growled Alwa, when Mahommed Gunga had translated. "All the rebels in all India, all trying at once, would fail to take this fort of mine, had I a larger garrison. But what Rangar on this countryside will risk his life and estates on behalf of a cause that is already lost? If they come to hold my fort for me, the rebels will burn their houses. The British Raj is doomed. We Rangars have to play for our own stake!"

Then Mahommed Gunga rose and paced the floor like a man in armor, tugging at his beard and kicking at his scabbard each time that he turned at either end.

"What Rangar in this province would have had one yard of land to his name but for this man's father?" he demanded. "In his day we fought, all of us, for what was right! We threw our weight behind him when he led, letting everything except obedience go where the devil wanted it! What came of that? Good titles, good report, good feeling, peace!"

"And then, the zemindary laws!" growled Alwa.
"Then the laws that took away from us full two-thirds of our revenue!"

"We had had no revenue, except for Cunnigan-bahadur!"

It dawned on Cunningham exactly why and how he came to be there! He understood now that Mahommed Gunga had told nothing less than truth when he declared it had been through his scheming, and no other man's, that he—Cunningham—whose sole thought was to be a soldier, had been relegated to oblivion and politics! He understood why Byng had signed the transfer, and he knew—knew—knew —deep down inside him that his chance had come!

"It seems that another Cunningham is to have the honor of preserving Rangars' titles for them," he smiled. "How many horsemen could the Alwa-sahib raise?"

"That would depend!" Alwa was in no mood to commit himself.

"At the most—at a pinch—in case of direst need, and for a cause that all agreed on?"

"Two thousand."

"Horsed and armed?"

"And ready!"

"And you, Alwa-sahib—are you pledged to fight against the British?"

"Not in so many words. I swore to uphold Howrah on his throne. He is against the British."

"You swore to help smash his brother, Jaimihr?"

"If I were needed."

"And Jaimihr too is against the British?"

"Jaimihr is for Jaimihr, and has a personal affair with me!"

"I must think," said Cunningham, getting up. "I can think better alone. D'you mind if I go outside for a while, and come back later to tell you what I think?"

Alwa arose and held the door open for him—stood and watched him cross the courtyard—then turned and laughed at Mahommed Gunga.

"Straight over to the woman!" he grinned. "This leader of thine seems in leading-strings himself already!"

Mahommed Gunga cursed, and cursed again as his own eyes confirmed what Alwa said.

"I tried him all the ways there are, except that one way!" he declared. "May Allah forgive my oversight! I should have got him well entangled with a woman before he reached Peshawur! He should have been heart-broken by this time—rightly, he should have been desperate with unrequited love! Byng-bahadur could have managed it! Byng-bahadur *would* have managed it, had I thought to advise him!"

He stood, looking over very gloomily at Cunningham, making a dozen wild plans for getting rid of Miss McClean—by no means forgetting poison—and the height of Alwa's aerie from the plain below! He would have been considerably calmer, could he have heard what Cunningham and Miss McClean were saying.

The missionary was with her now—ill and exhausted from the combined effects of excitement, horror, and the unaccustomed ride across the desert —most anxious for his daughter—worried, to the verge of desperation, by the ghastly news of the rebellion.

"Mr. Cunningham, I hope you are the forerunner of a British force?" he hazarded.

But Cunningham was too intent on cross-examination to waste time on giving any information.

"I want you to tell me, quite quietly and without hurry, all you can about Howrah," he said, sitting close to Miss McClean. "I want you to understand that I am the sole representative of my government in the whole district, and that whatever can be done depends very largely on what information I can get. I have been talking to the Alwasahib, but he seems too obsessed with his own predicament to be able to make things quite clear. Now, go ahead and tell me what you know about conditions in the city. Remember, you are under orders! Try and consider yourself a scout, reporting information to your officer. Tell me every single thing, however unimportant."

On the far side of the courtyard Alwa and Mahommed Gunga had gone to lean over the parapet and watch something that seemed to interest both of them intently. There were twenty or more men, lined round the ramparts on the lookout, and they all too seemed spellbound, but Cunningham was too engrossed in Miss McClean's story of the hap-

penings in Howrah City to take notice. Now and
then her father would help her out with an inter-
jected comment; occasionally Cunningham would
stop her with a question, or would ask her to repeat
some item; but, for more than an hour she spun a
clear-strung narrative that left very little to imagination and included practically all there was to know.

"Do you think," asked Cunningham, "that this
brute Jaimihr really wants to make you Maharanee?"

"I couldn't say," she shuddered. "You know,
there have been several instances of European women
having practically sold themselves to native princes;
there have been stories—I have heard them—of
English women marrying Rajahs, and regretting it.
There is no reason why he should not be in earnest,
and he certainly seemed to be."

"And this treasure? Of course, I have heard
tales about it, but I thought they were just tales."

"That treasure is really there, and its amount
must be fabulous. I have been told that there
are jewels there which would bring a Rajah's ransom,
and gold enough to offset the taxes of the whole of
India for a year or two. I've no doubt the stories
are exaggerated, but the treasure is real enough,
and big enough to make the throne worth fighting
for. Jaimihr counts on being able to break the
power of the priests and broach the treasure."

"And Jaimihr is—er—in love with you!"

"He tried very hard to prove it, in his own ob-
jectionable way!"

"And Jaimihr wants the throne—and Howrah
wants to send a force against the British, but dare
not move because of Jaimihr—I have Mahommed
Gunga and five or six men to depend on—the Rangars are sitting on the fence—and the government
has its hands full! The lookout's bright! I think
I see the way through!"

"You are forgetting me." The missionary spread
his broad stooped shoulders. "I am a missionary
first, but next to that I have my country's cause
more at heart than anything. I place myself under
your orders, Mr. Cunningham."

"I too," said Miss McClean. She was looking
at him keenly as he gazed away into nothing through
slightly narrowed eyes. Vaguely, his attitude reminded her of a picture she had once seen of the
Duke of Wellington; there was the same mastery,
the same far vision, the same poise of self-contained
power. His nose was not like the Iron Duke's, for
young Cunningham's had rather more tolerance in
its outline and less of Roman overbearing; but the
eyes, and the mouth, and the angle of the jaw were
so like Wellesley's as to force a smile. "A woman
isn't likely to be much use in a case like this—but,
one never knows. My country comes first."

"Thanks," he answered quietly. And as he
turned his head to flash one glance at each of them,
she recognized what Mahommed Gunga had gloated
over from the first—the grim decision, that will
sacrifice all—take full responsibility—and use all
means available for the one unflinching purpose of

the game in hand. She knew that minute, and her father knew, that if she could be used—in any way at all—he would make use of her.

"Go ahead!" she nodded. "I'll obey!"

"And I will not prevent!" said Duncan McClean, smiling and straightening his spectacles.

Cunningham left them and walked over to the parapet, where the whole garrison was bending excitedly now above the battlement. There were more than forty men, most of them clustered near Alwa and Mahommed Gunga. Mahommed Gunga was busy counting.

"Eight hundred!" he exclaimed, as Cunningham drew near.

"Eight hundred what, Mahommed Gunga?"

"Come and see, sahib."

Cunningham leaned over, and beheld a mounted column, trailing along the desert road in wonderfully good formation.

"Where are they from?" he asked.

"Jaimihr's men, from Howrah!"

"That means," growled Alwa, "that the Hindoo pig Jaimihr has more than half the city at his back. He has left behind ten men for every one he brings with him—sufficient to hold Howrah in check. Otherwise he would never have dared come here. He hopes to settle his little private quarrel with me first, before dealing with his brother! Who told him, I wonder, that I was pledged to Howrah?"

"He reckons he has caught thee napping in this fort of thine!" laughed Mahommed Gunga. "He means to bottle up the Rangars' leader, and so checkmate all of them!"

The eight hundred horsemen on the plain below rode carelessly through Alwa's gardens, leaving trampled confusion in their wake, and lined up—with Jaimihr at their head—immediately before the great iron gate. A moment later four men rode closer and hammered on it with their lance-ends.

"Go down and speak to them!" commanded Alwa, and a man dropped down the zigzag roadway like a goat, taking short cuts from level to level, until he stood on a pinnacle of rock that overhung the gate. Ten minutes later he returned, breathing hard with the effort of his climb.

"Jaimihr demands the missionaries—particularly the Miss-sahib—also quarters and food!" he reported.

"Quarters and food he shall have!" swore Alwa, looking down at the Prince who sat his charger in the centre of the roadway. "Did he deign a threat?"

"He said that in fifteen minutes he will burst the gate in, unless he is first admitted!"

Duncan McClean walked over, limping painfully, and peered over the precipice.

"Unfriendly?" he asked, and Mahommed Gunga heard him.

"Thy friend Jaimihr, sahib! His teeth are all but visible from here!"

"And——?"

"He demands admittance—also thee and thy daughter!"

"And——?"

"Sahib—art thou a priest?"

"I am."

"One, then, who prays?"

"Yes."

"For dead men, ever? For the dying?"

"Certainly."

"Aloud?"

"On occasion, yes."

"Then pray now! There will be many dead and dying on the plain below in less than fifteen minutes! Hindoos, for all I know, would benefit by prayer. They have too many gods, and their gods are too busy fighting for ascendancy to listen. Pray thou, a little!"

There came a long shout from the plain, and Alwa sent a man again to listen. He came back with a message that Jaimihr granted amnesty to all who would surrender, and that he would be pleased to accept Alwa's allegiance if offered to him.

"I will offer the braggart something in the way of board and lodging that will astonish him!" growled Alwa. "Eight men to horse! The first eight! That will do! Back to the battlement, the rest of you!"

They had raced for the right to loose themselves against eight hundred!

Oh, duck and run—the hornets come!
Oh, jungli! Clear the way!
The nest's ahum—the hornets come!
The sharp-stinged, harp-winged hornets come!
Nay, jungli! When the hornets come,
  It isn't well to stay!

ALWA ordered ten men down into the bowels of the rock itself, where great wheels with a chain attached to them were forced round to lift the gate. Next he stationed a signaller, with a cord in either hand, above the parapet, to notify the men below exactly when to set the simple machinery in motion. His eight clattered out from the stables on the far side of the rock, and his own charger was brought to him, saddled.

Then, in a second, it was evident why Rajputs do not rule in Rajputana.

"I ride too with my men!" declared Mahommed Gunga.

"Nay! This is my affair—my private quarrel with Jaimihr!"

Mahommed Gunga turned to Ali Partab, who had been a shadow to him ever since he came.

"Turn out my five, and bring my charger!" he commanded.

"No, I say!" Alwa had his hand already on his

253

sabre hilt. "There is room for eight and no more. Four following four abreast, and one ahead to lead them. I and my men know how to do this. I and my men have a personal dispute with Jaimihr. Stay thou here!"

Mahommed Gunga's five and Ali Partab came clattering out so fast as to lead to the suspicion that their horses had been already saddled. Mahommed Gunga mounted.

"Lead on, cousin!" he exclaimed. "I will follow thy lead, but I come!"

Then Alwa did what a native nearly always will do. He turned to a man not of his own race, whom he believed he could trust to be impartial.

"Sahib—have I no rights in my own house?"

"Certainly you have," said Cunningham, who was wondering more than anything what weird, wild trick these horsemen meant to play. No man in his senses would have dared to ride a horse at more than foot-pace down the path. Was there another path? he wondered. At least, if eight men were about to charge into eight hundred, it would be best to keep his good friend Mahommed Gunga out of it, he decided.

"Risaldar!" The veteran was always most amenable to reason when addressed by his military title. "Who of us two is senior—thou or I?"

"By Allah, not I, sahib! I am thy servant!"

"I accept your service, and I order you to stay with your men up here with me!"

Mahommed Gunga saluted and dismounted, and

his six followed suit, looking as disappointed as children just deprived of a vacation. Alwa wheeled his horse in front of Cunningham and saluted too.

"For that service, sahib, I am thy friend!" he muttered. "That was right and reasonable, and a judgment quickly given! Thy friend, bahadur!" He spoke low on purpose, but Mahommed Gunga heard him, caught Cunningham's eye, and grinned. He saw a way to save his face, at all events.

"That was a trick well turned, sahib!" he whispered, as Alwa moved away. "Alwa will listen in future when Cunnigan-bahadur speaks!"

"Go down and tell Jaimihr that I come in person!" ordered Alwa, and the man dropped down the cliff side for the third time; they could hear his voice, high-pitched, resounding off the rock, and they caught a faint murmur of the answer. Below, Jaimihr could be seen waiting patiently, checking his restive war-horse with a long-cheeked bit, and waiting, ready to ride under the gate the moment it was opened. Rosemary McClean came over; she and Cunningham and the missionary leaned together over the battlement and watched.

"We might do some execution with rifles from here," Cunningham suggested; "I believe I'll send for mine." But Mahommed Gunga overheard him.

"Nay, sahib! No shooting will be necessary. Watch!"

There was a clatter of hoofs, and they all looked up in time to see the tails of the last four chargers disappearing round the corner, downward. They had gone—full pelt—down a path that a man might hesitate to take! From where they stood, there was an archer's view of every inch of the only rock-hewn road that led from the gate to the summit of the cliff; an enemy who had burst the gate in would have had to climb in the teeth of a searching hail of missiles, with little chance of shooting back.

They could see the gate itself, and Jaimihr on the other side. And, swooping—shooting—sliding down the trail like a storm-loosed avalanche, they could see the nine go, led by Alwa. No living creature could have looked away!

Below, entirely unconscious of the coming shock, the mounted sepoys waited behind Jaimihr in four long, straight lines. Jaimihr himself, with a heavy-hilted cimeter held upward at the "carry," was about four charger lengths beyond the iron screen, ready to spur through. Close by him were a dozen, waiting to ram a big beam in and hold up the gate when it had opened. And, full-tilt down the gorge, flash-tipped like a thunderbolt, gray-turbaned, reckless, whirling death ripped down on them.

They caught sound of the hammering hoofs too late. Two gongs boomed in the rock. The windlass creaked. Five seconds too late Jaimihr gathered up his reins, spurred, wheeled, and shouted to the men behind him. The great gate rose, like the jaws of a hungry monster, and the nine—streaking too fast down far too steep a slide to stop themselves—burst straight out under it and struck, as a wind blast smites a poppy-field.

Jaimihr was borne backward—carried off his horse. Alwa and the first four rode him down, and crashed through the four-deep line beyond; the second four pounced on him, gathered him, and followed. Before the lines could form again the whole nine wheeled—as a wind-eddy spins on its own axis—and burst through back again, the horses racing neck and neck, and the sabres cutting down a swath to screech and swear and gurgle in among the trampled garden stuff.

They came back in a line, all eight abreast, with Alwa leading only by a length. At the opening, four horses—two on either side—slid, rump to the ground, until their noses touched the rock. Alwa and four dashed through and under; the rest recovered, spun on their haunches, and followed. The gongs boomed again down in the belly of the rock, and the gate clanged shut.

"That was good," said Mahommed Gunga quietly. "Now, watch again!"

Almost before the words had left his lips, a hail of lead barked out from twenty vantage-points, and the smoke showed where some forty men were squinting down steel barrels, shooting as rapidly and as rottenly as natives of India usually do. They did little execution; but before Alwa and his eight had climbed up the steep track to the summit, patting their horses' necks and reviling Jaimihr as they came, the cavalry below had scampered out of range, leaving their dead and wounded where they lay.

"How is that for a start, sahib?" demanded Ma-

hommed Gunga exultantly, as two men deposited
the dishevelled Jaimihr on his feet, and the Prince
glared around him like a man awaking from a dream.
"How is that for a beginning?"

"As bad as could be!" answered Cunningham.
"It was well executed—bold—clever—anything you
like, Mahommed Gunga, but—if I'd been asked—
I'd have sooner made the devil prisoner! Jaimihr
is no use at all to us in here. Outside, he'd be a
veritable godsend!"

CHAPTER XXVI

There is war to the North should I risk and ride forth,
And a fight to the South, too, I'm thinking;
There is war in the East, and one battle at least
In the West between eating and drinking.
I'm allowed to rejoice in an excellent choice
Of plans for a soldier of mettle,
For all of them mean bloody war and rapine.
So—on which should a gentleman settle?

WITH his muscles strained and twisted (for his Rangar capturers had dragged him none too gently) and with his jewelled pugree all awry, Jaimihr did not lack dignity. He held his chin high, although he gazed at the bubbling spring thirstily; and, thirsty though he must have been, he asked no favors.

One of Alwa's men brought him a brass dipper full of water, after washing it out first thoroughly and ostentatiously. But Jaimihr smiled. His caste forbade. He waved away the offering much as Cæsar may have waved aside a crown, with an air of condescending mightiness too proud to know contempt.

"Go, help thyself!" growled Alwa; and Jaimihr walked to the spring without haste, knelt down, and dipped up water with his hand.

"Now to a cell with him!" commanded Alwa,

before the Prince had time to slake a more than
ordinary thirst. Jaimihr stood upright as four men
closed in on him, and looked straight in the eyes
of every one in turn. Rosemary McClean stepped
back, to hide herself behind Cunningham's broad
shoulders, but Jaimihr saw her and his proud smile
broadened to a laugh of sheer amusement. He let
his captors wait for him while he stared straight at
her, sparing her no fragment of embarrassment.

"I slew a man once to save thee, sahiba!" he
mocked. "Why slink away? Have I ever been
thy enemy?"

Then he folded his arms and walked off between
his guards, without even an acknowledgment of
Alwa's or any other man's existence on the earth.

Alwa spat as he wiped blood from his long sabre.
He imagined he was doing the necessary dirty work
out of Miss McClean's sight; but, except hospital
nurses, there are few women who can see dry blood
removed from steel without a qualm; she had
looked at Alwa to escape Jaimihr's gaze; now she
looked at Jaimihr's back to avoid the sight of what
Alwa was seeing fit to do. And with all the woman
in her she pitied the prisoner, who had said no less
than truth when he claimed to have killed a man
for her.

She knew that he would have killed a thousand
men for her with equal generosity and equal disregard of what she thought was right, and she
did not doubt that he would think himself both
justified and worthy of renown for doing it. She

could have begged his release that minute, had she thought for an instant that Alwa would consent, and but for Cunningham. She had grown aware of Cunningham's gray eyes, staring straight at her —summing her up—reading her. And she became conscious of the fact that she had met a man whose leave she would like to ask before deciding to act.

The mental acknowledgment brought relief for a few seconds. She was tired. The woman in her went out to the man in Cunningham, and she welcomed a protector. Then the Scots blood raced to the assistance of the woman, and she bridled instantly. Who, then, was this chance-met jackanapes, that she should lean on him or look to him for guidance?

The rebellion that had made her disobey her father back in Howrah City—the spirit that had kept her in Howrah City and had given Jaimihr back cool stare for stare—rallied her to resist—to ridicule—to rival Cunningham's pretensions. He saw her flush beneath his gaze, and turned away to where Mahommed Gunga watched from the parapet.

The leaders of Jaimihr's cavalry were arguing. They could be seen gathered together out of rifle-shot but in full view of Alwa's rock, and from their gestures they seemed to be considering the feasibility of an attack.

But it needed no warrior—it needed less even than ordinary intelligence—to know that as few as forty men could hold that fastness against two thousand. Eight hundred would have no chance against it. Even two thousand would need engineers, and ordnance, as well as plans.

Presently half of the little army rode away, back toward Howrah City, and the other half proceeded to bivouac where they could watch the iron-shuttered entrance and cut off the little garrison from all communication or assistance.

"We might as well resume our conference," suggested Alwa, with the courtly air of a man just arisen from a chair. No one who had not seen him ride would have dreamed that he was fresh from snatching a prisoner at the bottom of a neck-breaking defile. Cunningham nodded acquiescence and followed him, turning to stare again at Miss McClean before he strode away with long, even strides that had a reassuring effect on any one who watched him. She bridled again, and blushed. But she experienced the weird sensation of being read right through before Mahommed Gunga contrived adroitly to step into the line of view and so let Cunningham's attention fix itself on something else. The Risaldar had made up his mind that love was inopportune just then; and he was a man who left no stone unturned—no point un-watched—when he had sensed a danger. This might be danger and it might not be; so he watched. Cunningham was conscious of the sudden interruption of a train of thought, but he was not conscious of deliberate interference.

"That very young man is an old man," said Duncan McClean, wiping his spectacles as he walked beside his daughter to the deep veranda where their chairs were side by side. "He is a grown man. He has come to man's estate. Look at the set of that pair of shoulders. Mark his strength!"

"I expect any one of those Rajputs is physically stronger," answered Rosemary, in no mood to praise any one.

"I was thinking of the strength of character he expresses rather than of his actual muscles," said McClean.

"Bismillah!" Alwa was swearing behind the thick teak door that closed behind him and Cunningham and Mahommed Gunga. "We have made a good beginning! With the wolf in a trap, what has the goat to dread? Howrah may chuckle himself to sleep! And I—I, too, by the beard of God's prophet!—I, too, may laugh, for, with Jaimihr under lock and key, what need is there to ride to the aid of a Hindoo Rajah? I am free again!"

"Alwa-sahib!"

Cunningham had fixed him with those calm gray eyes of his, and Mahommed Gunga sat down on the nearest bench contented. He could wait for what was coming now. He recognized the blossoming of the plant that he had nursed through its growth so long.

"I listen," answered Alwa.

"I represent the British Government. I am the only servant of the Company within reach. Do you realize that?"

"Yes, sahib."

"I have no orders which entitle me to deal with any crisis such as this. But, when my orders were given me, no such crisis was contemplated. Therefore, on behalf of the Company, I assume full authority until such time as some one senior to me turns up to relieve me. Is all that clear to you?"

"Yes, sahib."

Mahommed Gunga went through considerable pantomime of being angry with a fly. He found it necessary to conceal emotion in some way or other. Alwa sat motionless and stared straight back at Cunningham.

"I understand, sahib," he repeated.

"You are talking to me, then, on that understanding?"

"Most certainly, huzoor."

"You can raise two thousand men?"

"Perhaps."

"Say fifteen hundred?"

"Surely fifteen hundred. Not a sabre less."

"All horsed and armed?"

"Surely, bahadur. Of what use would be a rabble? I was speaking in terms of men able to fight, as one soldier to another."

"Will you raise those men?"

"Of a truth, I must, sahib!" Alwa laughed. "Jaimihr's thousands will be in no mind to lie leaderless and let Howrah ride rough-shod over them! They know his charity of old! They will be here to claim their Prince within a day or two,

and without my fifteen hundred how would I stand?
Surely, bahadur, I will raise my fifteen hundred."

"Very well. Now I will make you a proposal.
On behalf of the Company I offer you and your
men pay at the rate paid to all irregular cavalry on
a war basis. In return, I demand your allegiance."

"To whom, sahib? To you or to the Company?"

"To the Company, of course."

"Nay! Not I! For the son of Cunnigan-bahadur I would slit the throats of half Asia, and then
of nine-tenths of the other half! But by the breath
of God—by my spurs and this sabre here—I have
had enough of pledging! I swore allegiance to
Howrah. Being nearly free of that pledge by Allah's sending, shall I plunge into another, like a
frightened bird fluttering from snare to snare?
Nay, nay, bahadur! For thyself, for thy father's
sake, ask any favor. It is granted. But thy Company may stew in the grease of its own cartridges
for aught I care!"

Cunningham stood up and bowed very slightly—
very stiffly—very punctiliously. Mahommed Gunga
leaped to his feet, and came to attention with a
military clatter. Alwa stared, inclining his head a
trifle in recognition of the bow, but evidently taken
by surprise.

"Then, good-by, Alwa-sahib."

Cunningham stretched out a hand.

"I am much obliged to you for your hospitality,
and regret exceedingly that I cannot avail myself
of it further, either for myself or for Mahommed

Gunga or for Mr. and Miss McClean. As the Company's representative, they, of course, look to me for orders and protection, and I shall take them away at once. As things are, we can only be a source of embarrassment to you."

"But—sahib—huzoor—it is impossible. You have seen the cavalry below. How can you—how could you get away?"

"Unless I am your prisoner I shall certainly leave this place at once. The only other condition on which I will stay here is that you pledge your allegiance to the Company and take my orders."

"Sahib, this is—why—huzoor——"

Alwa looked over to Mahommed Gunga and raised his eyebrows eloquently.

"I obey him! I go with him!" growled Mahommed Gunga.

"Sahib, I would like time to think this over."

"How much time? I thought you quick-witted when you made Jaimihr prisoner. Has that small success undermined your power of decision? I know my mind. Mahommed Gunga knows his, Alwa-sahib."

"I ask an hour. There are many points I must consider. There is the prisoner for one thing."

"You can hand him over to the custody of the first British column we can get in touch with, Alwa-sahib. That will relieve you of further responsibility to Howrah and will insure a fair trial of any issue there may be between yourself and Jaimihr."

Alwa scowled. No Rajput likes the thought of

litigation where affairs of honor are concerned. He
fel: he would prefer to keep Jaimihr prisoner for
the present.

"Also, sahib"—fresh facets of the situation kept
appearing to him as he sparred for time—"with
Jaimihr in a cage I can drive a bargain with his
brother. While I keep him in the cage, Howrah
must respect my wishes for fear lest otherwise I
loose Jaimihr to be a thorn in his side anew. If I
hand him to the British, Howrah will know that
he is safe and altogether out of harm's way; then
he will recall what he may choose to consider insolence of mine; and then——"

"Oh, well—consider it!" said Cunningham, saluting him and making for the door, close followed
by Mahommed Gunga. The two went out and
left Alwa to stride up and down alone—to wrestle
between desire and circumspection—to weigh uncomfortable fact with fact—and to curse his wits
that could not settle on the wisest and most creditable course. They turned into another chamber
of the tunnelled rock, and there until long after
the hour of law allowed to Alwa they discussed the
situation too.

"The point was well taken, sahib," said Mahommed Gunga, "but he should have been handled
rather less abruptly."

"Eh?"

"Rather less abruptly, sahib."

"Oh! Well—if his mind isn't clear as to which
side he'll fight on, I don't want him, and that's all!"

said Cunningham. And Mahommed Gunga bitted his impatience fiercely, praying the one God he believed in to touch the right scale of the two. Later, Cunningham strode out to pace the court-yard in the dark, and the Rajput followed him.

CHAPTER XXVII

The trapped wolf bared his fangs and swore,
"But set me this time free,
And I will hunt thee never more!
By ear and eye and jungle law,
I'll starve—I'll faint—I'll die before
I bury tooth in thee!"

WHILE Alwa raged alone, and while Mahommed Gunga talked to Cunningham in a rock-room near at hand, Rosemary McClean saw fit to take a hand in history. It was not her temperament to sit quite idle while others shaped her destiny; nor was she given to mere brooding over wrongs. When a wrong was being done that she could alter or alleviate it was her way to tackle it at once without asking for permission or advice.

From where her chair was placed under the long veranda she could see the passage in the rock that led to Jaimihr's cell. She saw his captors take him up the passage; she heard the door clang shut on him, and she saw the men come back again. She heard them laugh, too, and she overheard a few words of a jest that seemed the reason for the laughter.

In Rajputana, as in other portions of the East, men laugh with meaning as a rule, and seldom from mere amusement. Included in the laugh there usually lies more than a hint of threat, or hate, or cruelty. And, in partial confirmation of the jest she unintentionally overheard, she saw no servant go to the chuckling spring to fill a water-jar. She recalled that Jaimihr only sipped as much as he could dip up in the hollow of his hand, and that physical exertion and suffering of the sort that he had undergone produces prodigious thirst in that hot, dry atmosphere.

She waited until dark for Cunningham, growing momentarily more restless. She recalled that she was a guest of Alwa's, and as such not free to interfere with his arrangements or to suggest insinuations anent his treatment of prisoners. She recalled the pride of all Rajputs, and its accompanying corollary of insolence when offended. There would come no good—she *knew*—from asking anybody whether Jaimihr was allowed to drink or not.

Cunningham, with that middle-aged air of authority laid over the fire and ability of youth, would be able, no doubt, to enforce his wishes in the matter after finding out the truth about it. But Cunningham did not come; and she remembered from a short experience of her own what thirst was.

The men-at-arms were all on the ramparts now, watching the leaderless cavalry on the plain. They had even left the cell door unguarded, for it was held shut by a heavy beam that could not be reached from the inside; and they were all too few, even all of them together, to hold that rock against eight hundred. It was characteristic, though, and Eastern of the East, that they should omit to padlock the big beam. It pivoted at its centre on a big bronze pin, and even a child could move it from the outside; it was only from the inside that it was uncontrollable. From inside one could have jerked at the door for a week and the big beam would have lain still and efficient in its niche in the rock wall; but a little pressure underneath one end would send it swinging in an arc until it hung bolt upright. Then the same child who had pushed it up could have swung the teak door wide.

Rosemary, growing momentarily thirstier herself as she thought of the probable torture of the prisoner, walked down to the spring and filled a dipper, as she had done half a dozen times a day since she first arrived. She had carried almost all her own and her father's water, for Joanna was generally sleeping somewhere out of view, and no other body-servant had been provided for her. There was a fairly big brass pitcher by the spring. She filled it. Nobody noticed her.

Then she recalled that nobody would notice her if she were to carry the brass pitcher in the direction of her room, for she had done that often. She picked it up, and she reached the end of the veranda with it without having called attention to herself. She set it down then to make quite sure that she was unobserved.

But some movement of the cavalry on the plain below was keeping the eyes of the garrison employed.

Although a solitary lantern shone full on her, she reached the passage leading to the prisoner's cell unseen; and she walked on down it, making no attempt to hide or hurry, remembering that she was acting out of mercy and had no need to be ashamed. If she were to be discovered, then she would be, and that was all about it, except that she would probably be able to appeal to Cunningham to save her from unpleasant consequences. In any case, she reasoned, she would have done good. She was quite ready to get herself and her own in trouble if by doing it she could insure that a prisoner had water.

But she was not seen. And no one saw her set the jar down by the door. No one except the prisoner inside heard her knock.

"Have you water, Jaimihr-sahib?" she inquired.

The East has a hundred florid epithets for one used in the West; and in a land where water is as scarce as gold and far more precious the mention of water to a thirsty man calls forth a flood of thought such as only music or perhaps religion can produce in luckier climes. Jaimihr waxed eloquent; more eloquent than even water might have made him had another—had even another woman—brought it. He recognized her voice, and said things to her that roused all the anger that she knew. She had not come to be made love to.

She thought, though, of his thirst. She remembered that within an hour or two he might be raving for another reason and with other words. The

big beam lifted on her hands with barely more
effort than was needed to lift up the water-jar;
the door opened a little way, and she tried, while
she passed the water in, to peer through the darkness at the prisoner. But there were no windows
to that cell, and such dim light as there was came
from behind her.

"They have bound me, sahiba, in this corner,"
groaned Jaimihr. "I cannot reach it. Take it
away again! The certainty that it is there and
out of reach is too great torture!"

So she slipped in through the door, leaving it
open a little way—both her hands busy with the
brass pitcher and both eyes straining their utmost
through the gloom—advancing step by step through
mouldy straw that might conceal a thousand horrors.

"You wonder, perhaps, why I do not escape!"
said a voice. And then she heard the cell door
close again gently.

Now she could see Jaimihr, for he stood with
his back against the door, and his head was between her and the little six-inch grating that was
all the ventilation or light a prisoner in that place
was allowed.

"So you lied to me, even when I brought you
water?" she answered. She was not afraid. She
had nerve enough left to pity him.

"Yes. But I see that you did not lie. I am
still thirsty, sahiba."

He held out both hands, and she could see them

dimly. There were no chains on them, and he was not bound in any way. She gave him the jar.

"Let me pass out again before you drink," she ordered. "It is not known that I am in here, and I would not have it known."

She could have bitten out her tongue with mortification a moment afterward for letting any such admission escape her. She heard him chuckle as he drank; he choked from chuckling, and set the jar down to cough. Then, when he had recovered breath again, he answered almost patronizingly.

"Which would be least pleased with you, sahiba? The Rangars, or thy father, or the other Englishman? But never mind, sahiba, we are friends. I have proved that we are friends. Never have I taken water from the hands of any man or any woman not of my own caste. I would have died sooner. It was only thou, sahiba, who could make me set aside my caste."

"Let me pass!"

She certainly was frightened now. It dawned on her, as it had at once on him, that at the least commotion on his part or on hers a dozen Rangars would be likely to come running. And just as he had done, she wondered what explanation she would give in that case, and who would be likely to believe it. To have been caught going to the cell would have been one thing; to be caught in it would be another. He divined her thoughts.

"Have no fear, sahiba. Thou and I are friends."

She did not answer, for words would not come.

Besides, she was beginning to realize that words would be of little help to her. A woman who will tell nothing but the truth under any circumstances and will surely keep her promises is at a disadvantage when conversing with a man who surely will not tell the truth if he can help it and who regards his given word with almost equal disrespect.

"I have no fear, sahiba. I am not afraid to open this door wide and make a bid for liberty. It would not be wise, that is all, and thou and I must deal in wisdom."

His words came through the dark very evenly—spaced evenly—as though he weighed each one of them before he voiced it. She gathered the impression that he was thinking for his very life. She felt unable to think for her own. She felt impelled to listen—incredulous, helpless, frightened, —not a little ashamed. She was thinking more of the awful things those Moslem gentlemen would say about her should they come and discover her in Jaimihr's cell.

"Listen, sahiba! From end to end of India thy people are either dead, or else face to face with death. There is no escape anywhere for any man or woman—no hope, no chance. The British doom is sealed. So is the doom of every man who dared to side with them."

She shuddered. But she had to listen.

"There will be an army here within a day or two. My men—and I number them by thousands —will come and rip these Rangars from their roost.

Those that are not crucified will be thrown down
from the summit, and there shall be a Hindoo shrine
where they have worshipped their false god. Then,
sahiba, if thou art here—perhaps—there might—
yet—be a way—perhaps, yes?—a way, still, to escape me?"

She was trembling. She could not help beginning to believe him. Whatever might be true of
what he said was certainly not comforting.

"But, while my army comes in search of me,
my brother Howrah will be making merry with
my palace and belongings. There will be devastation and other things in my army's rear for which
there is no need and for which I have no stomach.
I detest the thought of them, sahiba. Therefore,
sahiba, I would drive a bargain. Notice, sahiba,
I say not one word of love, though love such as
mine is has seldom been offered to a woman. I
say no word of love—as yet. I say, help me to
escape by night, when I may make my way unseen back to my men: enable me to reach Howrah before my dear brother is aware of my trouble
and before his men can start plundering, and name
your own terms, sahiba!"

Name her own terms—name her own terms—
name her own terms! The words dinned through
her head and she could grasp no other thought.
She was alone in a cell with Jaimihr, and she could
get out of it if she would name her terms! She
must name them—she must hurry—what were
they? What were her terms? She could not think.

"Understand, sahiba. Certain things are sure. It is sure my men will come. It is sure that every Rangar on this rock will meet a very far from pleasant death——"

He grinned, and though she could not see him grin, she knew that he was doing it. She knew that he was even then imagining a hundred horrors that the Rangars would endure before they died. She might name her terms. She could save them.

"No!" she hissed hoarsely. "No! They are my terms! I name them! You must spare them—spare the Rangars—spare every man on this hill, and theirs, and all they have!"

"Truly are those thy terms, sahiba?"

"Truly! What others can I ask?"

"They are granted, sahiba!"

"Oh, thank God!"

She knew that he was speaking at least half the truth. She knew his power. She knew enough of Howrah City's politics to be convinced that he would not be left at the mercy of a little band of Rangars. She knew that there were not enough Rangars on the whole countryside to oppose the army that would surely come to his rescue. And whether he were dead or living, she knew well enough that the vengeance would be wreaked on every living body on the hill. Alwa might feel confident, not she. She trembled now with joy at the thought that she—she the most helpless and useless of all of them—might save the lives of all.

But then another phase of the problem daunted

her. She might help Jaimihr go. He might escape unobserved with her aid. But then? What then? What would the Rangars do to her? Had she sufficient courage to face that? It was not fear now that swept over her so much as wonder at herself. Jaimihr detected something different in her mental attitude, and, since almost any change means weakness to the Oriental mind, he was quick to try to take advantage of it. He guessed right at the first attempt.

"And what wilt thou do here, sahiba? When I am gone, and there is none here to love thee——"

"Peace!" she commanded. "Peace! I have suffered enough——"

"Thou wilt suffer more, should the Rangars learn——"

"That is my business! Let me pass! I have bargained, and I will try to fulfil my part!"

She stepped toward the door, but he held out both his arms and she saw them. She had no intention of being embraced by him, whatever their conspiracy.

"Stand back!" she ordered.

"Nay, nay, sahiba! Listen! Escape with me! These Rangars will not believe without proof that thou hast saved their lives by bargaining. They will show thee short shrift indeed when my loss is discovered. Come now and I will make thee Maharanee in a week!"

"I would be as safe with one as with the other!" she laughed, something of calm reflection returning to her. "And what proof have I in any case that you will keep your word, Jaimihr-sahib. I will keep mine—but who will keep yours, that has been so often broken?"

"Sahiba——"

"Show me a proof!"

"Here—now—in this place?"

"Convince me, if you can! I will give myself willingly if I can save my father by it and these Rangars and Mr. Cunningham; but your bare word, Jaimihr-sahib, is worth that!"

She snapped her fingers, and he swore beneath his breath. Then he remembered his ambition and his present need, and words raced to his aid—words, plans, oaths, treachery, and all the hundred and one tricks that he was used to. He found himself consciously selecting from a dozen different plans for tricking her.

"Sahiba"—he spoke slowly and convincingly. In the gloom she could see his brown eyes levelled straight at hers, and she saw they did not flinch— "there is none who knows better than thou knowest how my brother and I stand to each other." She shuddered at the reiterated second person singular, but he either did not notice it or else affected not to. "Thou knowest that there is no love between him and me, and that I would have his throne. The British could set me on that throne unless they were first overwhelmed. Wert thou my legal wife, and were I to aid the British in this minute of their need, they would not be overwhelmed, and afterward they would surely set me on the throne. Therefore I pledge my word to lead my men to the Company's aid, provided that these Rangars ride to *my* aid. My brother plans to overcome me first, and then take arms against the British. If the Rangars come to help me I will ride with them to the Company's aid afterward. That is my given word!"

"Then the throne of Howrah is your price, Jaimihr-sahib?"

"Thou art the price and the prize, sahiba! For thee I would win the throne!"

She actually laughed, and he winced palpably. There was no doubt that he loved her after a manner of his own, and her contempt hurt him.

"I have said all I can say," he told her. "I have promised all I can promise. What more is there to say or offer? If I stay here, I swear on the honor of a Rajput and a prince of royal blood, that every living man and woman on this rock, excepting thee only, shall be dead within a week. But if I escape by thy aid, and if, at thy instance, these Rangars and their friends ride to my help against my brother, then I will throw all my weight—men and influence—in the scale on the British side."

"And——?"

"And thou shalt be Maharanee!"

"Never!"

"But in case that the British should be beaten before we reach them, then, sahiba! Then in case of thy need!"

"Jaimihr-sahib, I will help you to escape to-night on the terms that you have named—that you spare these Rangars and every living body on this hill. Then I will do my utmost to persuade the Rangars to ride to your assistance on your condition, that you lead your men to help the British afterward. And if my action in helping you escape should make the Rangars turn against me and my immediate friends, I shall claim your protection. Is that agreed?"

"Sahiba—absolutely!"

"Then let me pass!"

Reluctantly he stood aside. She slipped out and let the bar down unobserved. But she had not recovered all her self-possession when she reached the courtyard.

"'Evening, Miss McClean," said Cunningham; and she all but fainted, she was strained to such a pitch of nervousness.

"Where have you come from, Miss McClean?" asked Cunningham. And she told him. She was not quite so stiff-chinned as she had been.

"What were you doing there?"

She told him that, too.

"Where is your father?"

"In his chair on the veranda, Mr. Cunningham. There, in that deep shadow."

"Come to him, please. I want your explanation in his presence."

She followed as obediently as a child. The sense of guilt—of fright—of impending judgment left her

as she walked with him, and gave place to a glow
of comfort that here should be a man on whom to
lean. She did not fight the new sensation, for she
was growing strangely weary of the other one. By
the time that they had reached her father, and he
was standing before Cunningham wiping his spectacles in his nervous way, she had completely recovered her self-possession, although it is likely she
would not have given any reason for it to herself.

Cunningham held a lantern up, so that he could
study both their faces. His own face muscles were
set rigidly, and he questioned them as he might
have cross-examined a spy caught in the act. His
voice was uncompromising, and his manner stern.

"Do you both understand how serious this situation is?" he asked.

"We naturally do," said Duncan McClean. The
Scotsman was beginning to betray an inclination to
bridle under the youngster's attitude, and to show an
equally pronounced desire not to appear to. "More
so, probably, than anybody else!"

"Are you positive—both of you—you too, Mr.
McClean—that all that talk about treasure in Howrah City is not mere imagination and legend?"

"Absolutely positive!" They both answered him
at once, both looking in his eyes across the unsteady
rays of the flickering, smoky lamp. "The amount
has been, of course, much exaggerated," said Mc-
Clean, "but I have no doubt there is enough there
to pay the taxes of all India for a year or two."

"Then I have another question to ask. Do you

both—or do you not—place yourselves at the service of the Company? It is likely to be dangerous —a desperate service. But the Company needs all that it can muster."

"Of course we do!" Again both answered in one breath.

"Do you understand that that involves taking my orders?"

This time Duncan McClean did the answering, and now it was he who seized the lamp. He held it high, and scanned Cunningham's face as though he were reading a finely drawn map.

"We are prepared—I speak for my daughter as well as for myself—to obey any orders that you have a right to give, young man."

"You misunderstand me," answered Cunningham. "I am offering you the opportunity to serve the Company. As the Company's senior officer in this neighborhood, I am responsible to the Company for such orders as I see fit to give. I could not have my orders questioned. I don't mind telling you that I'm asking you, as British subjects, no more than I intend to ask Alwa and his Rangars. You can do as much as they are going to be asked to do. You can't do more. But you can do less if you like. You are being given the opportunity now to offer your services unconditionally—that is to say in the only manner in which I will accept them. Otherwise you will remain non-combatants, and I shall take such measures for your safety as I see fit. Time presses. Your answer, please!"

"I will obey your legal orders," said McClean, still making full use of the lantern.

"I refuse to admit the qualification," answered Cunningham promptly. "Either you will obey, or you will not. You are asked to say which, that is all."

"I will obey," said Rosemary McClean quietly. She said it through straight lips and in a level voice that carried more assurance than a string of loud-voiced oaths.

"And you, sir?"

"Since my daughter sees fit to—ah—capitulate, I have no option."

"Be good enough to be explicit."

"I agree to obey your orders."

"Thank you." He seemed to have finished with McClean. He turned away from him and faced Rosemary, not troubling to examine her face closely as he had done her father's, but seeming none the less to give her full attention. "I understood you to say that you promised to help Prince Jaimihr to escape from his cell to-night?"

"WHAT?"

Duncan McClean could not have acted such amazement. Cunningham desired no further evidence that he had not been accessory to his daughter's visit to the prisoner. He silenced him with a gesture. And now his eyes seemed for the time being to have finished with both of them; in spite of the darkness they both knew that he had resumed the far-away look that seemed able to see things finished.

"Yes," said Rosemary. "I promised. I had to."

Her father gasped. But Cunningham appeared to follow an unbroken chain of thought, and she listened.

"Well. You will both realize readily that we, as British subjects, are ranged all together on one side, opposed to treachery, as represented by the large majority of the natives. That means that our first consideration must be to keep our given word. What we say—what we promise—what we boast—must tally with what we undertake, and at the least try, to do. You must keep your word to Jaimihr, Miss McClean!"

She stared back at Cunningham through wide, unfrightened eyes. Whatever this man said to her, she seemed unable to feel fear while she had his attention. Her father seemed utterly bewildered, and she held his hand to reassure him.

"On the other hand, we cannot be guilty of a breach of faith to our friend Alwa here. I must have a little talk with him before I issue any orders. Please wait here and—ah—do nothing while I talk to Alwa. Did you—ah—did you agree to marry Jaimihr, should he make you Maharanee?"

"No! I told him I would rather die!"

"Thank you. That makes matters easier. Now tell me over again from the beginning what you know about the political situation in Howrah. Quickly, please. Consider yourself a scout reporting to his officer."

Ten minutes later Cunningham heard a commotion by the parapet, and stalked off to find Alwa, close followed by Mahommed Gunga. The grim old Rajput was grinning in his beard as he recognized the set of what might have been Cunningham the elder's shoulders.

CHAPTER XXVIII

Ye may go and lay your praise
At a shrine of other days
By the tomb of him who gat, and her who bore me;
My plan is good—my way—
The sons of kings obey—
But, I'm reaping where another sowed before me.

JAIDEV SINGH was a five-K man, with the hair,
breeches, bangle, comb, and dagger that betoken
him who has sworn the vow of Khanda ka Pahul.
Every item of the Sikh ritual was devised with no
other motive than to preserve the fighting character of the organization. The very name Singh
means lion. The Sikh's long hair with the iron
ring hidden underneath is meant as a protection
against sword-cuts. And because their faith is
rather spiritual than fanatical—based rather on the
cause of things than on material effect—men of
that creed take first rank among fighting men.

Jaidev Singh arrived soon after the moon had
risen. The notice of his coming was the steady
drumming footfall of his horse, that slowed occasionally, and responded to the spur again immediately.

Close to the big iron gate below Alwa's eyrie there
were some of Jaimihr's cavalry nosing about among

the trampled gardens for the dead and wounded they had left there earlier in the afternoon. They ceased searching, and formed up to intercept whoever it might be who rode in such a hurry. Above them, on the overhanging ramparts, there was quick discussion, and one man left his post hurriedly.

"A horseman from the West!" he announced, breaking in on Alwa's privacy without ceremony.

"One?"

"One only."

"For us or them?"

"I know not, sahib."

Alwa—glad enough of the relief from puzzling his brain—ran to the rampart and looked long at the moving dot that was coming noisily toward his fastness but that gave no sign of its identity or purpose.

"Whoever he is can see them," he vowed. "The moon shines full on them. Either he is a man of theirs or else a madman!"

He watched for five more minutes without speaking. Cunningham and Mahommed Gunga, coming out at last in search of him, saw the strained figures of the garrison peering downward through the yellow moon rays, and took stand on either side of him to gaze, too, in spellbound silence.

"If he is their man," said Alwa presently, "he will turn now. He will change direction and ride for the main body of them yonder. He can see them now easily. Yes. See. He is their man!"

On a horse that staggered gamely—silhouetted

and beginning to show detail in the yellow light—
a man whose nationality or caste could not be recognized rode straight for the bivouacking cavalry,
and a swarm of them rode out at a walk to meet
him.

The tension on the ramparts was relaxed then.
As a friend in direst need the man would have been
welcome. As one of the enemy, with a message
for them, however urgent, he was no more than an
incident.

"By Allah!" roared Alwa suddenly. "That is
no man of theirs! Quick! To the wheels! Man
the wheels! Eight men to horse!"

He took the cord himself, to send the necessary
signal down into the belly of the rock. From his
stables, where men and horses seemed to stand
ready day and night, ten troopers cantered out,
scattering the sparks, the whites of their horses'
eyes and their drawn blades gleaming; without
another order they dipped down the breakneck
gorge, to wait below. The oncoming rider had
wheeled again; he had caught the cavalry, that
rode to meet him, unawares. They were not yet
certain whether he was friend or foe, and they were
milling in a bunch, shouting orders to one another.
He, spurring like a maniac, was heading straight
for the searching party, who had formed to cut
him off. He seemed to have thrown his heart over
Alwa's iron gate and to be thundering on hell's
own horse in quest of it again.

Alwa's eight slipped down the defile as quickly

as phantoms would have dared in that tricky moonlight. One of them shouted from below. Alwa
jerked the cord, and the great gate yawned, well-
oiled and silent. The oncomer raced straight for
the middle of the intercepting line of horsemen;
they—knowing him by this time for no friend—
started to meet him; and Alwa's eight, unannounced
and unexpected, whirled into them from the rear.

In a second there was shouting, blind confusion
—eddying and trying to reform. The lone galloper pulled clear, and Alwa's men drove his oppo-
nents, crupper over headstall, into a body of the
main contingent who had raced up in pursuit. They
rammed the charge home, and reeled through both
detachments—then wheeled at the spur and cut
their way back again, catching up their man at
the moment that his horse dropped dead beneath
him. They seized him beneath the arms and bore
him through as the great gate dropped and cut his
horse in halves. Then one man took the galloper up
behind his saddle, and bore him up the hill unques-
tioned until he could dismount in front of Alwa.

"Who art thou?" demanded the owner of the
rock, recognizing a warrior by his trade-marks, but
in no way moderating the natural gruffness of his
voice. Alwa considered that his inviolable hospitality should be too well known and understood to
call for any explanation or expression; he would
have considered it an insult to the Sikh's intelligence to have mouthed a welcome; he let it go
for granted.

"Jaidev Singh—galloper to Byng-bahadur. I
bring a letter for the Risaldar Mahommed Gunga,
or for Cunnigan-sahib, whichever I can find first."

"They are both here."

"Then my letter is for both of them."

Cunningham and Mahommed Gunga each took
one step forward, and the Sikh gave Cunningham a
tiny, folded piece of paper, stuck together along
one edge with native gum. He tore it open, read
it in the light of a trooper's lantern, and then read
it again aloud to Mahommed Gunga, pitching his
voice high enough for Alwa to listen if he chose.

"What are you two men doing?" ran the note.
"The very worst has happened. We all need men
immediately, and I particularly need them. One
hundred troopers now would be better than a thousand men a month from now. Hurry, and send
word by bearer.   S. F. BYNG."

"How soon can you start back?" asked Cunningham.

"The minute I am provided with a horse, sahib."

Cunningham turned to Alwa.

"Will you be kind enough to feed him, Alwa-
sahib?"

Alwa resented the imputation against his hospitality instantly.

"Nay, I was waiting for his money in advance!"
he laughed. "Food waits, thou. Thou art a Sikh
—thou eatest meat—meat, then, is ready."

The Sikh, or at least the true Sikh, is not hampered by a list of caste restrictions. All of his precepts, taken singly or collectively, bid him be nothing but a man, and no law forbids him accept the hospitality of soldiers of another creed. So Jaidev Singh walked off to feed on curried beef that would have made a Hindoo know himself for damned. Cunningham then turned on Alwa.

"Now is the time, Alwa-sahib," he said in a level voice. "My party can start off with this man and our answer, if your answer is no. If your answer is yes, then the Sikh can bear that answer for us."

"You would none of you ride half a mile alive!" laughed Alwa.

"I none the less require an answer, Alwa-sahib."

Alwa stared hard at him. That was the kind of talk that went straight to his soldier heart. He loved a man who held to his point in the teeth of odds. The odds, it seemed to him, were awfully against Cunningham.

"So was thy father," he said slowly. "My cousin *said* thou wast thy father's son!"

"I require an answer by the time that the Sikh has finished eating," said Cunningham. "Otherwise, Alwa-sahib, I shall regret the necessity of foregoing further hospitality at your hands."

"Bismillah! Am I servant here or master?" wondered Alwa, loud enough for all his men to hear. Then he thought better of his dignity. "Sahib," he insisted, "I will not talk here before my men. We will have another conference."

"I concede you ten minutes," said Cunningham, preparing to follow him, and followed in turn by Mahommed Gunga.

"Now," swore the Risaldar into his beard, "we shall see the reaching of decisions! Now, by the curse of the sack of Chitor we shall know who is on whose side, or I am no Rangar, nor the son of one!"

"I have a suggestion to make, sahib," smiled Alwa, closing the door of the rock-hewn chamber on the three of them.

"Hear mine first!" said Cunningham, with a hint of iron in his voice.

"Ay! Hear his first! Hear Chota-Cunnigan-ba-hadur!" echoed Mahommed Gunga. "Let us hear a plan worth hearing!" And Alwa looked into a pair of steady eyes that seemed to see through him—past him—to the finished work beyond.

"Speak, sahib."

"You are pledged to uphold Howrah on his throne?"

"Ha, sahib."

"Then, I guarantee you shall! You shall not go to the Company's aid until you have satisfactory guarantees that your homes and friends will not be assailed behind your backs."

"Guarantees to whose satisfaction, sahib?"

"Yours!"

"But with whom am I dealing?" Alwa seemed actually staggered. "Who makes these promises? The Company?"

"I give you my solemn word of honor on it!"

"It is at least a man who speaks!" swore Alwa.

"It is the son of Cunnigan-bahadur!" growled Mahommed Gunga, standing chin erect. He seemed in no doubt now of the outcome. He was merely waiting for it with soldierly and ill-concealed impatience.

"But, sahib——"

"Alwa-sahib, we have no time for argument. It is yes or no. I must send an answer back by that Sikh. He must—he shall take my answer! Either you are loyal to our cause or you are not. Are you?"

"By the breath of God, sahib, I am thinking you leave me little choice!"

"I still await an answer. I am calling on you for as many men as you can raise, and I have made you specific promises. Choose, Alwa-sahib. Yes or no?"

"The answer is yes—but——"

"Then I understand that you undertake to obey my orders without question until such time as a senior to me can be found to take over the command."

"That is contingent on the agreement," hesitated Alwa.

"I would like your word of honor, Alwa-sahib."

"I pledge that not lightly, sahib."

"For that very good reason I am asking for it. I shall know how far to trust when I have your word of honor!"

"I knew thy father! Thou art his son! I trusted him for good reason and with good result. I will trust thee also. My word is given, on thy conditions, sahib. First, the guarantees before we ride to the British aid!"

"And you obey my orders?"

"Yes. My word is given, sahib. The oath of a Rajput, of a Rangar, of a soldier, of a zemindar of the House of Kachwaha; the oath of a man to a man, sahib; the promise of thy father's friend to thy father's son! Bahadur"—he drew himself to his full height, and clicked his spurs together—"I am thy servant!"

Cunningham saluted. All three men looked in each other's eyes and a bond was sealed between them that nothing less than death could sever.

"Thank you," said Cunningham quite quietly. "And now, Alwa-sahib"— (he could strike while the iron glowed, could this son of Cunnigan!)— "for the plan. There is little time. Jaimihr must escape to-night!"

"Sahib, did I understand aright?"

Alwa's jaw had actually dropped. He looked as though he had been struck. Mahommed Gunga slammed his sabre ferule on the stone floor. He, too, was hard put to it to believe his ears.

"Jaimihr is the key to the position. He is nothing but a nuisance where he is. Outside he can be made to help us."

"Am I dreaming, or art thou, sahib?" Alwa stood with fists clinched on his hips and his legs apart—incredulous. "Jaimihr to go free? Why that Hindoo pig is the source of all the trouble in the district!"

"We are neither of us dreaming, Alwa-sahib. Jaimihr is the dreamer. Let him dream in Howrah City for a day or two, while we get ready. Let him lead his men away and leave the road clear for us to pass in and out."

"But——"

"Oh, I know. He is your prisoner, and your honor is involved, and all that kind of thing. I'm offering you, to set off against that, a much greater honor than you ever experienced in your whole life yet, and I've put my order in the shape of a request for the sake of courtesy. I ask you again to let me arrange for Jaimihr to escape."

"I was mad. But it seems that I have passed my word!" swore Alwa.

"I give you your word back again, then."

"Bismillah! I refuse it!"

"Then I do with Jaimihr as I like?"

"I gave my word, sahib."

"Thanks. You'll be glad before we've finished. Now I've left the raising of as many men as can be raised to you, Alwa-sahib. You will remember that you gave your promise on that count, too."

"I will keep that promise, too, sahib."

"Good. You shall have a road clear by to-night."

He stepped back a pace, awaited their salute with the calm, assured authority of a general of division, returned it, and left the two Rajputs looking in each other's eyes.

"What is this, cousin, that thou hast brought me to?" demanded Alwa.

Mahommed Gunga laughed and shook his sabre, letting it rattle in its scabbard.

"This? This is the edge of the war that I promised thee a year ago! This is the service of which I spoke! This is the beginning of the blood-spilling! I have brought thee the leader of whom we spoke in Howrah City. Dost remember, cousin? I recall thy words!"

"Ay, I recall them. I said then that I would follow a second Cunnigan, could such be found."

"And this is he!" vowed Mahommed Gunga. "Ho! But we Rangars have a leader! A man of men!"

"But this plan of his? This loosing of the trapped wolf—what of that?"

"I neither know nor care, as yet! I trust him! I am his man, as I was his father's! I have seen him; I have heard him; I have felt his pulse in the welter of the wrath of God. I know him. Whatever plans he makes, whatever way he leads, those are my plans, my road! I serve the son of Cunnigan!"

CHAPTER XXIX

Did he swear with his leg in a spring-steel trap
And a tongue dry-cracked from thirst?
Or down on his knees at his lady's lap
With the lady's lips to his own, mayhap,
And his head and his heart aburst?
Nay! I have listened to vows enough
And never the oath could bind
Save that, that a free man chose to take
For his own good reputation's sake!
They're qualified—they're tricks—they break—
They're words, the other kind!

MAHOMMED GUNGA had long ago determined to "go it blind" on Cunningham. He had known him longest and had the greatest right. Rosemary McClean, who knew him almost least of all, so far as length of time was concerned, was ready now to trust him as far as the Risaldar dared go; her limit was as long and as devil-daring as Mahommed Gunga's. Whatever Scots reserve and caution may have acted as a brake on Duncan McClean's enthusiasm were offset by the fact that his word was given; so far as he was concerned, he was now as much and as obedient a servant of the Company as either of the others. Nor was his attitude astonishing.

Alwa's was the point of view that was amazing,

unexpected, brilliant, soldierly, unselfish—all the things, in fact, that no one had the least right to expect it to turn out to be. Two or three thousand men looked to him as their hereditary chieftain who alone could help them hold their chins high amid an overwhelming Hindoo population; his position was delicate, and he might have been excused for much hesitation, and even for a point-blank refusal to do what he might have preferred personally. He and his stood to lose all that they owned—their honor—and the honor of their wives and families, should they fight on the wrong side. Even as a soldier who had passed his word, he might have been excused for a lot of wordy questioning of orders, for he had enough at stake to make anybody cautious.

Yet, having said his say and sworn a dozen God-invoking Rangar oaths before he pledged his word, and then having pledged it, he threw Rajput tradition and the odds against him into one bottomless discard and proceeded to show Cunningham exactly what his fealty meant.

"By the boots and beard of Allah's Prophet!" he swore, growing freer-tongued now that his liberty of action had been limited. "Here we stand and talk like two old hags, Mahommed Gunga! My word is given. Let us find out now what this fledgling general of thine would have us do. If he is to release my prisoner, at least I would like to get amusement out of it!"

So he and Mahommed Gunga swaggered across

the courtyard to where Cunningham had joined the McCleans again.

"We come with aid and not objections, sahib," he assured him. "If we listen, it may save explanations afterward."

So at a sign from Cunningham they enlarged the circle, and the East and West—bearded and clean-shaven, priest and soldiers, Christian and Mohammedan—stood in a ring, while almost the youngest of them—by far the youngest man of them—laid down the law for all. His eyes were all for Rose-mary McClean, but his gestures included all of them, and they all answered him with nods or grunts as each saw fit.

"Send for the Sikh!" commanded Cunningham.

Five minutes later, with a lump of native bread still in his fist, Jaidev Singh walked up and saluted.

"Where is Byng-bahadur now?" asked Cunningham.

"At Deeseera, sahib—not shut in altogether, but hard pressed. There came cholera, and Byng-bahadur camped outside the town. He has been striking, sahib, striking hard with all too few to help him. His irregulars, sahib, were disbanded at some one's orders just before this outbreak, but some of them came back at word from him. And there were some of us Sikhs who knew him, and who would rather serve him and die than fight against him and live. He has now two British regiments with him, sadly thinned—some of my people, some Goor-khas, some men from the North—not very many

more than two thousand men all told, having lost
heavily in action and by disease. But word is going
round from mouth to mouth that many sahibs have
been superseded, and that only real sahibs such as
Byng-bahadur have commands in this hour. Byng-
bahadur is a man of men. We who are with him
begin to have courage in our bones again. Is the
answer ready? Yet a little while? It is well, sahib,
I will rest. Salaam!"

"You see," said Cunningham, "the situation's
desperate. We've got to act. Alwa here stands
pledged to protect Howrah, and you have promised
to aid Jaimihr. Somebody's word has got to break,
and you may take it from me that it will be the
word of the weakest man! I think that that man
is Jaimihr, but I can't be sure in advance, and we've
got to accept his promise to begin with. Go to
him, Miss McClean, and make a very careful bargain with him along the line I mapped out for you.
Alwa-sahib, I want witnesses, or rather overhearers.
I want you and Mahommed Gunga to place yourselves near Jaimihr's cell so that you can hear what he
says. There won't be any doubt then about who has
broken promises. Are you ready, Miss McClean?"

She was trembling, but from excitement and not
fear. Both Rajputs saluted her as she started back
for the cell, and whatever their Mohammedan ideas
on women may have been, they chose to honor this
one, who was so evidently one of them in the hour
of danger. Duncan McClean seemed to be praying softly, for his lips moved.

When the cell-door creaked open, Alwa and Mahommed Gunga were crouched one on either side, listening with the ears of soldiers that do not let many sounds or words escape them.

"Jaimihr-sahib!" she whispered. "Jaimihr-sahib!"

"Ha! Sahiba!" Then he called her by half a dozen names that made the listening Rangars grin into their beards.

"Jaimihr-sahib"—she raised her voice a little now—"if I help you to escape, will you promise me my safety under all conditions?"

"Surely, sahiba!"

"Do you swear to protect every living person on this hill, including the Alwa-sahib and Cunningham-sahib?"

"Surely, sahiba."

"You swear it?"

"I swear it on my honor. There is no more sacred oath."

"Then, listen. I can help you to escape now. I have a rope that is long enough to lower you over the parapet. I am prepared to risk the consequences, but I want to bargain with you for aid for my countrymen."

Jaimihr did not answer.

"The Alwa-sahib and his Rangars stand pledged to help your brother!"

"I guessed at least that much," laughed Jaimihr.

"They would not help you against him under any circumstances. But they want to ride to the Com-

pany's aid, and they might be prepared to protect
you against him. They might guarantee the safety
of your palace and your men's homes. They might
exact a guarantee from Howrah."

Jaimihr laughed aloud, careless of the risk of being
overheard, and Rosemary knew that Cunningham's
little plan was useless even before it had been quite
expounded. She felt herself trembling for the consequences.

"Sahiba, there is only one condition that would
make me ride to the British aid with all my men."

"Name it!"

"Thou art it!"

"I don't understand you, Jaimihr-sahib," she
whispered, understanding all too well.

"Follow me. Come to me in Howrah. Then,
whatever these fool Rangars choose to do, I swear
by Siva and the Rites of Siva that I will hurry to
the Company's aid!"

Rosemary McClean shuddered, and he knew it.
But that fact rather added to his pleasure. The
wolf prefers a cowering, frightened prey even though
he dare fight on occasion. She was thinking against
time. Through that one small, overburdened head,
besides a splitting headache, there was flashing the
ghastly thought of what was happening to her
countrymen and women—of what would happen unless she hurried to do something for their aid. All
the burden of all warring India seemed to be resting on her shoulders, in a stifling cell; and Jaimihr
seemed to be the only help in sight.

"How many men could you summon to the Company's aid?" she asked him.

He laughed. "Ten thousand!" he boasted.

"Armed and drilled men—soldiers fit to fight?"

"Surely."

"I think that is a lie, Jaimihr-sahib. There is not time enough to waste on lies. Tell me the exact truth, please."

He contrived to save his face, or, rather, he contrived to make himself believe he did.

"I would need some to guard my rear," he answered. "I could lead five thousand to the British aid."

"Is that the truth?"

"On my honor, sahiba."

"And you wish to marry me?"

"Sahiba—I—I have no other wish!"

"I agree to marry you provided you will lead five thousand men to the Company's aid, but not until you have done so."

"You will come to Howrah?"

She could feel his excitement. The cell walls seemed to throb.

"Yes; but I shall come accompanied by my father, and Mr. Cunningham, and all the Rangars he can raise. And I shall hold you to your bargain. You must help the Company first. FIRST—d'you understand?"

"I understand."

It was Jaimihr's turn now to lay the law down. She had let him see her eagerness to gain his aid for the Company, and he saw the weakness of her case in an instant. He knew very well, too, that no woman of her breed would have thought of consenting to marry him unless her hand was forced. He decided immediately to force it further.

"I understand, sahiba. I, too, will hold thee to thy promise! Thou wilt come with an escort, as befits a prince's wife! But how should I know that the Rangars would prove friends of mine? How should I know that it is not all a trap?"

"You will have my promise to depend on."

"Truly! And there will be how many hundred men to override the promise of one woman? Nay! My word is good; my promise holds; but on my own conditions! Help me to escape. Then follow me to Howrah City. Come in advance of thy Rangar escort. By that I will know that the Rangars and this Cunningham are my friends—otherwise they would not let thee come. The Rangars are to exact guarantees from my brother? How should I know that they do not come to help my brother crush me out of existence? With thee in my camp as hostage I would risk agreement with them, but not otherwise. Escape with me now, or follow. But bring no Rangars, sahiba! Come alone!"

"I will not. I would not dare trust you."

Jaimihr laughed. "I have been reckoning, sahiba, how many hours will pass before my army comes to rip this nest of Alwa's from its roots, and defile the whole of it! If I am to spare the people on this rock, then I must hurry! Should my men come here to carry me away, they will be less merciful than I! Choose, sahiba! Let me go, and I will spare these Rangars until such time as they earn punishment anew. Or let me go, and follow me. Then I will fight with the Rangars and for the Company, with thee as the price of my alliance. Or leave me in this cell until my men come to rescue me. The last would be the simplest way! Or it would be enough to help me escape and wait until I have done my share at conquering the British. Then I could come and claim thee! Choose, sahiba; there are many ways, though they all end in one goal."

"If I am the price of your allegiance," said Rosemary, "then I will pay the price. Five thousand men for the British cause are dearer to me than my own happiness. I promise, Jaimihr-sahib, that I will come to you in Howrah. I shall come accompanied by one servant, named Joanna, and—I think —by my father; and the Rangars and Mr. Cunningham shall be at least a day's ride behind me. I give my word on that. But—I can promise you, on Mr. Cunningham's behalf, and on the Alwasahib's, and Mahommed Gunga's, that should you have made any attempt against my liberty—should you have offered me any insult or indignity—before they come—should you have tried to anticipate the terms of your agreement—then—then—there would be an end of bargaining and promises, Jaimihr-sahib, and your life would be surely forfeit! Do you understand?"

"Surely, sahiba!"

"Do you agree?"

"I already have agreed. They are my terms. I named them!"

"I would like to hear you promise, on your honor."

"I swear by all my gods and by my honor. I swear by my love, that is dearer to me than a throne, and by the name and the honor of a Rajput!"

"Be ready, then. I am going now to hide the rope in the shadow of the wall. It will take perhaps fifteen minutes. Be ready."

He made a quick movement to embrace her, but she slipped out and escaped him; and he thought better of his sudden plan to follow her, remembering that her word was likely to be good, whatever his might be. He elected to wait inside until she returned for him. He little knew that he missed the downward swing of Alwa's sabre, that was waiting, poised and balanced for him, in the darkness by the door.

"Bismillah! I would have had a right to kill him had he followed her and broken faith so early in the business!" Alwa swore, excusing his impatience to Mahommed Gunga. "Have no fear, sahib!" he counselled Cunningham a moment later, laying a heavy hand on the boy's arm. "Let her keep her promises. That Hindoo pig will not keep his! We will be after her, and surely—surely we will find good cause for some throat-slitting as well as the cancelling of marriage promises!"

"Do you understand, Alwa-sahib, that—if Jaimihr keeps his promise to her, she must keep hers to him? Do you realize that?"

"Allah! Listen to him! Yes, sahib. Truly, bahadur, I appreciate! I also know that I have given certain promises which I, too, must fulfil! She is not the only bargainer! I am worrying more about those guarantees that Howrah was to give —I am anxious to see how, with fifteen hundred, we are to get the better of a Rajah and his brother and their total of ten thousand! I want to see those promises performed! Ay! The Miss-sahib has done well. She has done her share. Let her continue. And do thou thy share, bahadur! I am at thy back with my men, but give us action!"

Cunningham held up a lantern, and looked straight at Duncan McClean. The missionary had held his daughter's hand while she recounted what had happened in the cell. Whatever he may have thought, he had uttered no word of remonstrance.

"Of course, we go to Howrah ahead of you," he answered to Cunningham's unspoken question.

Cunningham held out his right hand, and the missionary shook it.

"Hold the lamp, please," said Cunningham, and Mahommed Gunga seized it. Then Cunningham took paper and a pencil and read aloud the answer that he wrote to Byng-bahadur. He wrote it in Greek characters, for fear lest it might fall into the enemy's hands and be too well understood.

"I can be with you in one week, sir, and perhaps sooner. Unless we are all killed in the meantime we should number more than fifteen hundred when

we come. Expect either all or none of us. The
situation here is critical, but our course seems clear,
and we ought to pull through. Mahommed Gunga
sends salaams. Your obedient servant,

"RALPH CUNNINGHAM."

"Would God I could see the clear course!" laughed
Alwa.

"Call the Sikh, please."

The Sikh came running, and Cunningham gave
him the folded note.

"Have you a horse for him, Alwa-sahib?"

"That has been attended to, sahib," the Sikh
answered. "The Alwa-sahib has given me a wonder
of a horse."

"Very well, then, Jaidev Singh. Watch your
chance. Go to the parapet, and when you see by
their lanterns that the cavalry below have ridden
off, then race for all you're worth with that news
for Byng-bahadur!"

"Salaam, sahib!" said the Sikh.

"Salaam, Jaidev Singh. And now hide, everybody! Don't let Jaimihr get the impression that
we're playing with him."

A little later Miss McClean led Jaimihr through
a passage in the rock, off which axe-hewn cells led
on either side, to the far side of the summit, where
the parapet was higher but the wall was very much
less sheer. The Prince's arms were still too sore
from the wrenching he received when they took
him prisoner for him to dare trust himself hand

over hand on a rope; she had to make the rope fast
beneath his armpits, and then lower him slowly,
taking two turns with the rope round the waist of
a brass cannon. The Prince fended himself off the
ragged wall with hands and feet, and called up
instructions to her as loudly as he dared.

It was a tremendous drop. For the last fifty or
more feet the wall rose straight, overhung by a
ridge that rasped the rope. And the rope proved
fifteen feet or more too short. Rosemary paid out
as much of it as she dared, and then made the end
fast round the cannon, leaning over to see whether
Jaimihr would have sense enough or skill enough to
cut himself free and fall. But he hung where he
was and spun, and it was five minutes before Rosemary remembered that his weapons had all been
taken from him! It was scarcely likely that he
could bite the thick rope through with his teeth!

She stood then for two or three more minutes
wondering what to do, for she had no knife of her
own, and she had made the rope fast—woman-wise
—with a true landlubber's knot that tightened from
the strain until her struggling fingers could not make
the least impression on it. But Alwa walked up
openly—drew his heavy sabre—and saved the situation for her.

"That may help to jog his recollection of the bargain!" he laughed, severing the rope with a swinging cut and peering over to see, if he could, how
Jaimihr landed. By a miracle the Prince landed on
his feet. He sat down for a moment to recover

from the shock, and then walked off awkwardly to where his cavalry were sleeping by their horses.

He had some trouble in persuading the outposts who he really was, and there was an argument that could be quite distinctly heard from the summit of the rock and made Alwa roar with laughter before, finally, the whole contingent formed and wheeled and moved away, ambling toward Howrah City at a pace that betokened no unwillingness.

Five minutes later the Sikh's horse thundered out across the plain from under Alwa's iron gate; and the news, such as it was, was on its way to Byng-bahadur.

"A clear road at the price of a horse-hide rope!" laughed Alwa. "Now for some real man's work!"

Rosemary stole off to argue with her father and her conscience, but Alwa went to his troopers' quarters and told off ten good men for the task of manning the fortress in his absence. They were ten unwilling men; it needed all his gruff authority, and now and then a threat, to make them stay behind.

"I must leave ten men behind," he insisted. "It takes four men, even at a pinch, to lift the gate. And who shall guard my women? Nay, I should leave twenty, and I must leave ten. Therefore I leave the ten best men I have, and they who stay behind may know by that that I consider them the best!"

The remainder of his troopers he sent out one by one in different directions, with orders to rally every

Rangar they could find, and at a certain point he named. Then he and Mahommed Gunga said good-by to Cunningham and took a trail that led in the direction where most of the doubtfuls lived —the men who might need personal convincing—rousing—awakening from lethargy.

"You think I ought to stay behind?" asked Cunningham, who had already made his mind up but chose to consult Alwa.

"Surely, sahib. If for no other reason, then to make sure that that priest of thine and his daughter make tracks for Howrah City! While he is here he is a priest, and we Rangars have our own ideas on what they are good for! When he is there he will be a man manœuvring to save his own life and his daughter's reputation! See that he starts, sahib!"

He rode off then. But before Mahommed Gunga saw fit to follow him he legged his charger close to Cunningham for a final word or two.

"Have no fear now, bahadur—no anxiety! Three days hence there will be a finer regiment to lead than ever thundered in thy father's wake—a regiment of men, sahib, for a man to lead and love!—a regiment that will trust thee, sahib! See thou to the guarantees! Rung Ho, bahadur!"

"Rung Ho! See you again, Mahommed Gunga!"

CHAPTER XXX

Sabres and spurs and jingling bits—
  (Ho! But the food to feed them!)
Sinews and eyes and ears and wits—
  (Hey! But the troopers need them!)
Sahib, mount! Thy chargers fling
Foam to the night—thy trumpets sing—
Thy lance-butts on the stirrups ring—
  Mount, sahib! Blood them! Lead them!

IT was arranged that the McCleans, with old
Joanna, should start at dawn for Howrah City, and
they were, both of them, too overcome with mingled
dread and excitement to even try to sleep. Joanna,
very much as usual, snoozed comfortably, curled
in a blanket in a corner.

They would run about a hundred different risks,
not least of which was the chance of falling in with
a party of Howrah's men. In fact, if they should
encounter anybody before bringing up at Jaimihr's
palace it was likely that the whole plan would fizzle
into nothing.

Cunningham, after fossicking for a long time in
Alwa's armory—that contained, besides weapons of
the date, a motley assortment of the tools of war
that would have done great credit to a museum of
antiquities—produced two pistols. He handed one

to the missionary and one to Miss McClean, advising her to hide hers underneath her clothing. "You know what they're for?" he asked. "No. You'd gain nothing by putting up a fight. They're loaded. All you've got to do is jerk the hammer back and pull the trigger, and the best way not to miss is to hold the muzzle underneath your chin— this way—keeping the butt well out from you. You make sure when you do that. The only satisfaction you'll have, if it comes to suicide as a last resource, will be that you've tried to do your duty and the knowledge that you'll be avenged. I promise that. But I don't think you'll have any need to do it—if I did think it I'd have thought twice before sending you."

"How does such a very young man as you come to have all this responsibility?" asked Rosemary, taking the pistol without a shudder. She laughed then as she noticed Cunningham's discomfort and recognized the decency that hates to talk about itself.

"I suppose I know my own mind," he answered. "These other awfully decent fellows don't, that's all—if you except Mahommed Gunga. That chap's a wonder. 'Pon my soul, it seems he knew this was coming and picked me from the start to take charge over here. Seems, owing to my dad's reputation, these Rangars think me a sort of reincarnation of efficiency. I've got to try and live up to it, you know—same old game of reaping what you didn't sow and hoping it'll all be over before you wake up! Won't you try and get some sleep before morning?

No? Come and sit over by the parapet with me,
then."

He carried chairs for both of them to a point
whence he could sit and watch the track that led
to Howrah and so help out the very meagre garrison. There, until the waning moon dipped down
below the sky-line, they talked together—first about
the task ahead of each of them; then about the
sudden ghastliness of the rebellion, whose extent
not one of them could really grasp as yet; last,
and much longest, as familiarity gradually grew
between them, of youthful reminiscences and home
—of Eton and the Isle of Skye.

In the darkness and the comparative coolness that
came between the setting of the moon and dawn
Rosemary fell asleep, her head pillowed in her
father's lap. For a while, then, seeing her only
dimly through the night, but conscious, as he could
not help being, of her youth and charm and of the
act of self-sacrifice that she had undertaken without
remonstrance, he felt ashamed. He began to wonder whether there might not have been some other
way—whether he had any right, even for his country's sake, to send a girl on such a mission. Mis-
giving began to sap his optimism, and there was no
Mahommed Gunga now to stir the soldier in him and
encourage iron-willed pursuance of the game. He
began to doubt; and doubt bred silence.

He was wakened from a revery by Duncan
McClean, who raised his daughter tenderly and got
up on his feet.

"The dawn will be here soon, Mr. Cunningham. We had better get ready. Well—in case we never meet again—I'm glad I met you."

"Better start before the sun gets up," he answered, gripping the missionary's hand. He was a soldier again. He had had the answer to his thoughts! If the man who was to sacrifice his daughter—or risk her sacrifice—was pleased to have met him, there was not much sense in harboring self-criticism! He shook it off, and squared his shoulders, beginning again to think of all that lay ahead.

"Trust to the old woman to guide you and show you a place to rest at, if you must rest. You ought to reach Howrah at dusk to-morrow, for you'll find it quite impossible to travel fast—you're both of you too stiff, for one thing. Lie up somewhere—Joanna will know of a place—until the old woman has taken in a message to Jaimihr, and wait until he sends you some men to escort you through the outskirts of the city. I've got disguises ready for you—a pugree for you, Mr. McClean, and a purdah for your daughter—you'll travel as a Hindoo merchant and his wife. If you get stopped, say very little, but show this——"

He produced the letter written once by Maharajah Howrah to the Alwa-sahib and sent by galloper with the present of a horse. It was signed, and at the bottom of it was the huge red royal seal. "Now go and put the disguise on, while I see to the horses; I'm going to pick out quiet ones, if

possible, though I warn you they're rare in these
parts."

Some twenty minutes later he led their horses
for them gingerly down the slippery rock gorge, and
waited at the bottom while six men wound the gate
up slowly. Rosemary McClean was quite unrec-
ognizable, draped from head to foot in a travelling
veil that might have been Mohammedan or Hindoo,
and gave no outward sign as to her caste, or rank.
McClean, in the full attire of a fairly prosperous
Hindoo, but with no other mark about him to betoken that he might be worth robbing, rode in front
of her, high-perched on a native saddle. In front,
on a desert pony, rode Joanna, garbed as a man.

"She *ought* to be travelling in a carriage of some
kind," admitted Cunningham, "but we haven't got
a single wheeled thing here. If any one asks perti-
nent questions on the road, you'd better say that
she had an ekka, but that some Rangars took it from
you. D'you think you know the language well
enough to pass muster?"

"It's a little late to ask me that!" laughed Mc-
Clean. "Yes—I'm positive I do. Good-by."

They shook hands again and the three rode off,
cantering presently, to make the most of the coolness before the sun got up. Cunningham climbed
slowly up the hill and then watched them from
the parapet—wondering, wondering again whether
he was justified. As he put it to himself, it was
"the hell of a position for a man to find himself in!"
He caught himself wondering whether his thoughts

would have been the same, and whether his conscience would have racked him quite as much, had
Rosemary McClean been older, and less lovely, and
a little more sour-tongued.

He had to laugh presently at the absurdity of
that notion, for Jaimihr would never have bargained
for possession of a sour-faced, elderly woman. He
came to the conclusion that the only thing he could
do was to congratulate the Raj because, at the
right minute, the right good-looking woman had
been on the spot! But he did not like the circumstances any better; and before two hours had passed
the loneliness began to eat into his soul.

Like any other man whose race and breed and
training make him self-dependent, he could be alone
for weeks on end and scarcely be aware that he had
nobody to talk to. But his training had never yet
included sending women off on dangerous missions
any more than it had taught him to resist woman's
attraction—the charm of a woman's voice, the lure
of a woman's eyes. He did not know what was the
matter with him, but supposed that his liver must
be out of order or else that the sun had touched
him.

Taking a chance on the liver diagnosis, he had
out the attenuated garrison, and drilled it, both
mounted and dismounted, first on the hilltop—
where they made the walls re-echo to the clang of
grounded butts—and then on the plain below, with
the gate wide open in their rear and one man watching from the height above. When he had tired

them thoroughly, and himself as well, he set two
men on the lookout and retired to sleep; nor did
the droning and the wailing music of some women
in the harem trouble him.

They called him regularly when the guard was
changed, but he slept the greater part of that day
and stood watch all night. The next day, and the
third day, he drilled the garrison again, growing
horribly impatient and hourly more worried as to
what Byng-bahadur might be doing, and thinking of
him.

It was evening of the fourth day when a Rangar
woke him, squeezing at his foot and standing silent
by the cot.

"Huzoor—Mahommed Gunga comes!"

"Thank God!"

He ran to the parapet and watched in the fading
light a little dust cloud that followed no visible
track but headed straight toward them over the
desert.

"How d'you know that's Mahommed Gunga?"
he demanded.

"Who else, huzoor? Who else would ride from
that direction all alone and straight for this nest of
wasps? Who else but Alwa or Mahommed Gunga?
Alwa said he would not come, but would wait
yonder."

"It might be one of Alwa's men."

"We have many good men, sahib—and many
good horses—but no man or horse who could come
at that pace after traversing those leagues of desert!

That is Mahommed Gunga, unless a new fire-eater has been found. And what new man would know the way?"

Soon—staccato, like a drum-beat in the silence —came the welcome, thrilling cadence of the horse's hoofs—the steady thunder of a horse hard-ridden but not foundered. The sun went down and blackness supervened, but the sound increased, as one lone rider raced with the evening wind, head on.

It seemed like an hour before the lookout challenged from the crag that overhung the gate—before the would-be English words rang out; and all Asia and its jackals seemed to wait in silence for the answer.

"Howt-uh! Hukkums—thar!"

"Ma—hommed—Gunga—hai!"

"Hurrah!"

The cheer broke bonds from the depth of Cunningham's being, and Mahommed Gunga heard it on the plain below. There was a rush to man the wheels and sweat the gate up, and Cunningham started to run down the zigzag pathway. He thought better of it, though, and waited where the path gave out onto the courtyard, giving the signal with the cords for the gate to lower away again.

"Evening, Mahommed Gunga!" he said, almost casually, as the weary charger's nose appeared above the rise.

"Salaam, bahadur!"

He dismounted and saluted and then leaned against his horse.

"I wonder, sahib, whether the horse or I be weariest! Of your favor, water, sahib!"

Cunningham brought him water in a dipper, and the Rajput washed his horse's mouth out, then held out the dipper again to Cunningham for a fresh charge for himself.

"I would not ask the service, sahib, but for the moment my head reels. I must rest before I ride again."

"Is all well, Mahommed Gunga?"

"Ay, sahib! More than well!"

"The men are ready?"

"Horsed, armed, and waiting, they keep coming —there were many when I left—there will be three squadrons worthy of the name by the time we get there! Is all well at your end, sahib?"

"Yes, all's well."

"Did the padre people go to Howrah?"

"They started and they have not returned."

"Then, Allah be praised! Inshallah, I will grip that spectacled old woman of a priest by the hand before I die. He has a spark of manhood in him! Send me this good horse to the stables, sahib; I am overweary. Have him watered when the heat has left him, and then fed. Let them blanket him lightly. And, sahib, have his legs rubbed—that horse ever loved to have his legs rubbed. Allah! I must sleep four hours before I ride! And the Miss-sahib—went she bravely?"

"Went as a woman of her race ought to go, Mahommed Gunga."

"Ha! She met a man first of her own race, and
he made her go! Would she have gone if a coward
asked her, think you? Sahib—women are good—
at the other end of things! We will ride and fetch
her. Ha! I saw! My eyes are old, but they bear
witness yet!—Now, food, sahib—for the love of
Allah, food, before my belt-plate and my backbone
touch!"

"I wonder what the damned old infidel is dreaming of!" swore Cunningham, as Mahommed Gunga
staggered to the chamber in the rock where a serv-
ing-man was already heaping victuals for him.

"Have me called in four hours, sahib! In four
hours I will be a man again!"

CHAPTER XXXI

The freed wolf limped home to his lair,
And lay to lick his sore.
With wrinkled lip and fangs agnash—
With back-laid ear and eyes aflash—
"Twas something rather more than rash
To turn me loose!" he swore.

Now Jaimihr fondly thought he held a few cards
up his sleeve when he made his bargain with Rosemary McClean and let himself be lowered from the
Alwa-sahib's rock. He knew, better probably than
any one except his brother and the priests, how desperate the British situation had become throughout all India at an instant's notice, and he made
his terms accordingly.

He did not believe, in the first place, that there
would be any British left to succor by the time
matters had been settled sufficiently in Howrah to
enable him to dare leave the city at his rear. Afterward, should it seem wise, he would have no objection in the world to riding to the aid of a Company
that no longer existed.

In the second place, he entertained no least compunction about breaking his word completely in
every particular. He knew that the members of
the little band on Alwa's rock would keep their

individual and collective word, and therefore that
Rosemary McClean would come to him. He suspected, though, that there would prove to be a rider
of some sort to her agreement as regarded marrying him, for he had young Cunningham in mind;
and he knew enough of Englishmen from hearsay
and deduction to guess that Cunningham would
interject any obstacle his ingenuity could devise.

Natives of India do not like Englishmen to marry
their women. How much less, then, would a stiff-
necked member of a race of conquerors care to stand
by while a woman of his own race became the wife
of a native prince? He did not trust Cunningham,
and he recalled that he had had no promise from
that gentleman.

Therefore, he proposed to forestall Cunningham
if possible, and, if that were inconvenient or rash,
he meant to take other means of making Rosemary
McClean his, beyond dispute, in any case.

Next to Rosemary McClean he coveted most the
throne of Howrah. With regard to that he was
shrewd enough not to conceal from himself for a
second the necessity for scotching the priests of Siva
before he dare broach the Howrah treasure, and so
make the throne worth his royal while. Nor did he
omit from his calculations the public clamor that
would probably be raised should he deal too roughly
with the priests. And he intended to deal roughly
with them.

So the proposed allegiance of the Rangars suited
him in more ways than one. His army and his

brother's were so evenly matched in numbers and
equipment that he had been able to leave Howrah
without fear for the safety of his palace while his
back was turned. The eight hundred whom he had
led on the unlucky forray to Alwa's were scarcely
missed, and, even had the Maharajah known that
he was absent with them, there were still too many
men behind for him to dare to start reprisals. The
Maharajah was too complete a coward to do anything much until he was forced into it.

The Rangars, he resolved, must be made to take
the blame for the broaching of the treasure. He
proposed to go about the broaching even before hos-
tilities between himself and his brother had com-
menced, and he expected to be able to trick the
Rangars into seeming to be looting. To appear to
defend the treasure would probably not be difficult;
and it would be even less difficult to blame the
Rangars afterward for the death of any priest who
might succumb during the ensuing struggle. He
counted on the populace, more than on his own
organized forces, to make the Rangars powerless
when the time should come for them to try to take
the upper hand. The mob would suffer in the process, but its fanaticism—its religious prejudice and
numbers—would surely win the day.

As for Rosemary McClean, the more he considered her the more his brown eyes glowed. He had
promised to make her Maharanee. But he knew
too thoroughly what that would mean not to entertain more than a passing doubt as to the wisdom

of the course. He was as ready to break his word
on that point as on any other.

A woman of his own race, however wooed and
won, would have been content to accept the usual
status of whisperer from behind the close-meshed
screens. Not so an Englishwoman, with no friends
to keep her company and with nothing in the world
to do but think. She, he realized, would expect to
make something definite of her position, and that
would suit neither his creed (which was altogether
superficial), nor custom (which was iron-bound and
to be feared), nor prejudice (which was prodigious),
nor yet convenience (which counted most).

He came to the conclusion that the fate in store
for her was not such as she would have selected
had she had her choice. Nor were his conclusions
in regard to her such as would commend him in the
eyes of honest men.

But, after all, the throne was the fulcrum of his
plotting; and the lever had to be the treasure, if
his plans were to succeed beyond upsetting. He
changed his plans a dozen times over before he
arrived at last at the audacious decision he was
seeking.

Like many another Hindoo in that hour of England's need, he did not lose sight altogether of the
distant if actual possibility that the Company's servants might—by dint of luck and grit, and what the
insurance papers term the Act of God—pull through
the crisis. Therefore, he decided that under no
circumstances should Rosemary McClean be treated

cavalierly until the Rangars were out of the way and he could pose as her protector if need be.

He would be able to prove that Rosemary and her father had come to him of their own free will. He would say that they had asked him for protection from the Rangars. He had evidence that his brother Howrah had been in communication with the Rangars. So, should the Company survive and retain power enough to force an answer to unpleasant questions, he thought it would not be difficult to prove that he had been the Company's friend all along.

Under all the circumstances he considered it best to be false to everybody and strike for no hand but his own, and with that reconsidered end in view he decided on a master-stroke. He sent word to his brother, the Maharajah, saying that the Rangars had accepted service with the Company and purposed a raid on Howrah; therefore, he proposed that they unite against the common enemy and set a trap for the Rangars.

Howrah sent back to ask what proof he had of the Rangars' taking service with the British. Jaimihr answered that Cunningham and Mahommed Gunga were both on Alwa's crag. He also swore that as Alwa's prisoner he had been able to overhear the Rangars' plans.

The Maharajah was bewildered, as Jaimihr had expected that he would be. And with just as Eastern, just as muddle-headed, just as dishonest reasoning, he made up his mind to play a double game with everybody, too. He agreed to join Jaimihr in opposition to the Rangars. He agreed to send all his forces to meet Jaimihr's and together kill every Rangar who should show himself inside the city. And he privately made plans to arrive on the scene too late, and smash Jaimihr's army after it had been reduced in size and efficiency by its battle with Alwa's men.

Jaimihr, unknowingly, fitted his plan into his brother's by determining to get on the scene early enough to have first crack at the treasure. He meant to get away with that, leave his brother to deal with Alwa's men, circle round, and then attack his brother from the rear.

Finally, he made up his mind once and for all that Rosemary McClean must remain inviolate until he was quite certain that the English had been driven out of India. He expected that good news within a week.

He was delighted when Joanna, dressed as a man, turned up at his palace-gates and cajoled her way in past the guards. To be asked for an escort to bring the McCleans into Howrah fitted in with his rôle of protector as a key might fit a lock. Now they could never pretend—nobody could ever pretend—that he had seized them. He sent a carriage out for them, and when they arrived placed a whole wing of his palace at their disposal, treating them like royalty. He made no attempt to molest or interfere with either of them, except that he prevented them from going in and out; and he told off plenty of witnesses who would be able to swear subsequently that they had seen how well his guests were treated. He was taking no unnecessary chances at that stage of the game he played.

There were others, though, who plotted besides Jaimihr. There were, for instance, Siva's priests. It is not to be forgotten that in that part of India the priests had been foremost in fomenting the rebellion. They urged Howrah constantly to take the field against the British, and it was only the sure knowledge of his brother's intention to strike for the throne that prevented the Maharajah from doing what the priests urged.

He knew that Alwa and the Rangars would not help him unless Jaimihr first attacked him, for Alwa would be sure to stand on the strict letter of his oath. And he was afraid of the Rangars. He feared that they might protect him and depose him afterward. He reasoned that that, too, might be construed into a strict interpretation of the terms of Alwa's promise!

He consented to collect his army. He kept it under arms. He even paid it something on account of arrears of wages and served out rations. But, to the disgust of the priests who asked nothing better than dissenion between the brothers, he jumped at the idea of uniting with Jaimihr to defeat Alwa's men. He knew—just as the priests feared—that once he could trick and defeat Jaimihr he could treat the troublesome priests as cavalierly as he chose.

So the priests made a third knot in the tangle, and tried desperately at the last moment to recreate dissension between the rival royal camps.

"Jaimihr is getting ready to attack you!" they assured Howrah. "Attack him first!"

"I will wait until he does attack," the Maharajah answered. "For the moment we are friends and have a cause in common."

"Howrah's men will desert to you the moment you make a move to win the throne," they assured Jaimihr.

"Wait!" answered Jaimihr. "Wait but a day or two. I will move fast as I see fit when I am ready. For the present my cause and my brother's cause are one."

Spies brought in news to Maharajah, Prince, and priest of the hurried raising of a Rangar army. The Maharajah and the Prince laughed up their sleeves and the priests swore horribly; the interjection of another element—another creed—into the complication did not suit the priestly "book." They were the only men who were really worried about Alwa.

And another spy—Joanna—disappeared. No longer garbed as a man, she had hung about the palace, and—known to nearly all the sweepers—she had overheard things. Garbed as a man again, she suddenly evaporated in thin air, and Rosemary McClean was left without a servant or any means of communication with the outside world.

CHAPTER XXXII

The ringed wolf glared the circle round
Through baleful, blue-lit eye,
Not unforgetful of his debt.
"Now, heed ye how ye draw the net."
Quoth he: "I'll do some damage yet
Or ere my turn to die!"

THE mare that had been a present from Mahommed Gunga was brought out and saddled, together with a fresh horse for the Risaldar. The veteran had needed no summoning, for with a soldier's instinct he had wakened at the moment his self-allotted four hours had expired. He mounted a little stiffly, and tried his horse's paces up and down the courtyard once or twice before nodding to Cunningham.

"All ready, sahib."

"Ready, Mahommed Gunga."

But there was one other matter, after all, that needed attention first.

"That horse of mine that brought me hither"—the Risaldar picked out the man who waited with the gong cord in his hand—"is left in thy particular charge. Dost thou hear me? I will tell the Alwa-sahib what I now tell thee—that horse will be required of thee fit, good-tempered, light-mouthed,

331

not spur-marked, and thoroughly well groomed.
There will be a reward in the one case, but in the
other—I would not stand in thy shoes! It is a
trust!"

"Come along, Risaldar!" called Cunningham.
"We're wasting an awful lot of time!"

"Nay, sahib, but a good horse is like a woman,
to be loved and treated faithfully! Neither horse
nor woman should be sacrificed for less than duty!
Lead on, bahadur—I will join thee at the gate."

He had several directions to give for the horse's
better care, and Cunningham was forced to wait
at least five minutes for him at the foot of the steep
descent. Then for another minute the two sat their
horses side by side, while the great gate rose slowly,
grudgingly, cranked upward by four men.

"If we two ever ride under here again, bahadur,
we shall ride with honor thick on us," remarked
Mahommed Gunga. "God knows what thy plan
may be; but I know that from now on there will
be no peace for either of us until we have helped rip
it with our blades from the very belly of rebellion.
Ride!"

The gate clanged down behind them as—un-
touched by heel or spur—the two spring-limbed
chargers raced for their bits across the sand. They
went like shadows, casting other shadows—moon-
made—wind-driven—knee-to-knee.

"Now, sahib!"

The Risaldar broke silence after fifteen minutes.
Neither he nor Cunningham were of the type that

chatters when the time has come to loosen sabres
and sit tight.

"In the matter of what lies ahead—as I said,
neither I nor any man knows what this plan of
thine may be, but I and the others have accepted
thy bare word. These men who await thee—and
they are many, and all soldiers, good, seasoned
horsemen—have been told that the son of Cunnigan will lead them. Alwa has given his word, and
I mine, that in the matter of a leader there is nothing left to be desired. And my five men have told
them of certain happenings that they have seen.
Therefore, thou art awaited with no little keenness.
They will be all eyes and ears. It might be well,
then, to set the pace a little slower, for a man looks
better on a fresh horse than on a weary one!"

"I'm thinking, Mahommcd Gunga, of the two
McCleans and of General Byng, who is expecting
us. There is little time to lose."

"I, too, consider them, sahib. It is we Rangars
who must do the sabre work. ALL, sahib—ALL—
depends now on the impression created on the men
awaiting thee! Rein in a little. Thy father's name,
thine own, and mine and Alwa's weigh for much
on thy side; but have a sound horse between thy
legs and a trumpet in thy throat when we get there!
I have seen more than one officer have to fight
up-hill for the hearts of his troopers because his
tired horse stumbled or looked shabby on the first
parade. Draw rein a little, sahib."

So Cunningham, still saying nothing, drew back

into an easy canter. He was conscious of something, not at all like a trumpet, in his throat that was nearly choking him. He did not care to let Mahommed Gunga know that what was being mistaken for masterly silence was really emotion! He did not speak because he did not trust his voice.

"There are three squadrons, sahib—each of about five hundred men. Alwa has the right wing, I the left. Take thou the centre and command the whole. The horses are as good as any in this part of India, for each man has brought his best to do thee honor. Each man carries four days' rations in his saddle-bag and two days' rations for his horse. More horse feed is collecting, and they are bringing wagons, to follow when we give the word. But we thought there would be little sense in ordering wagons to follow us to Howrah City, knowing that thy plan would surely entail action. If we are to ride to the aid of Byng-bahadur it seemed better to pick up the wagons on the journey back again. That is all, sahib. There will be no time, of course, to waste on talk or drill. Take charge the moment that we get there— issue thy orders—and trust to the men understanding each command. Lead off without delay."

"All right," said Cunningham—two English words that went much further to allay the Risaldar's anxiety than any amount of rhetoric would have done. "But—d'you mean to tell me that the men don't understand words of command?"

"All of them do, sahib; but to many of them the English words are new. They all understand forma-

tions, and those who know the English words are
teaching the others while they wait for us. There
is not one man among them but has couched a lance
or swung a sabre in some force or other?"

"Good. Have they all got lances?"

"All the front-rank men are armed with lance
and sabre—the rear ranks have sabres only."

"Good."

After two hours of steady cantering the going
changed and became a quick succession of ever-
deepening gorges cleft in sandstone. Far away in
the distance to the left there rose a glow that showed
where Howrah City kept uneasy vigil, doubtless
with watch-fires at every street corner. It looked
almost as though the distant city were in flames.

Ahead of them lay the gloom of hell mouth and
the silence of the space beyond the stars.

It was with that strange, unclassified, unnamed
sixth sense that soldiers, savages, and certain hunt-
ers have that Cunningham became aware of life
ahead of him—massed, strong-breathing, ready-wait-
ing life, spring-bent in the quivering blackness.
A little farther, and he caught the ring of a curb-
chain. Then a horse whinnied and a hoarse voice
swore low at a restive charger. His own mare
neighed, throwing her head high, and some one
challenged through the dead-black night.

"How-ut! Hukkums—thar!"

A horseman appeared suddenly from nowhere,
and examined them at close quarters instead of
waiting for their answer. He peered curiously at

Cunningham—glanced at Mahommed Gunga—then
wheeled, spinning his horse as the dust eddies twist
in the sudden hot-wind gusts.

"Sahib-bahadur hai!" he shouted, racing back.

The night was instantly alive with jingling movement, as line after line of quite invisible light-horse-
men—self-disciplined and eager to obey—took up
their dressing. The overhanging cliff of sandstone
hid the moon, but here and there there was a gleam
of eyeballs in the dark—now man's, now horse's—
and a sheen that was the hint of steel held vertical.
No human being could have guessed the length of
the gorge nor the number of the men who waited
in it, for the restless chargers stamped in inch-deep
sand that deadened sound without seeming to lessen
its quantity.

"Salaam, bahadur!"

It was Alwa, saluting with drawn sabre, reining
back a pedigreed mare to get all the spectacular
emotion out of the encounter that he could.

"Here are fifteen hundred eight and fifty, sahib—
all Rangars—true believers—all true men—all pledged
to see thee unsinged through the flames of hell! Do
them the honor of a quick inspection, sahib!"

"Certainly!" smiled Cunningham.

"I have told them, sahib, that their homes, their
women, their possessions, and their honor are all
guaranteed them. Also pay. They make no other
terms."

"I guarantee them all of that," said Cunningham,
loud enough for at least the nearest ranks to hear.

"On thine own honor, sahib?"

"On my word of honor!"

"The promise is enough! Will you inspect them, sahib?"

"I'll take their salute first," said Cunningham.

"Pardon, bahadur!"

Alwa filled his lungs and faced the unseen lines.

"Rangars!" he roared. "Your leader! To Chota-Cunnigan-bahadur—son of Pukka-Cunnigan whom we all knew—general—salute—present—sabres!"

There was sudden movement—the ring of whipped-out metal—a bird's wing-beat—as fifteen hundred hilts rose all together to as many lips—and a sharp intake of breath all down the line.

It wasn't bad. Not bad at all, thought Cunningham. It was not done as regulars would have worked it. There was the little matter of the lances, that he could make out dimly here and there, and he could detect even in that gloom that half of the men had been caught wondering how to salute with lance and sabre both. But that was not their fault; the effort—the respect behind the effort—the desire to act altogether—were all there and striving. He drew his own mare back a little, and returned their salute with full military dignity.

"Reeeeeee—turn—sabres!" ordered Alwa, and that movement was accomplished better.

He rode once, slowly, down the long front rank, letting each man look him over—then back again along the rear rank, risking a kick or two, for there was little room between them and the cliff. He was not choking now. The soldier instinct, that is born in a man like statesmanship or poetry, but that never can be taught, had full command over all his other senses, and when he spurred out to the front again his voice rang loud and clear, like a trumpet through the night.

With fifty ground scouts scattered out ahead of them, they drummed out of the gorge and thundered by squadrons on the plain beyond—straight, as the jackal runs, for Howrah City. Alwa, leaving his own squadron, to canter at Cunningham's side, gave him all the new intelligence that mattered.

"Last evening I sent word on ahead to them of our coming, sahib! I sent one messenger to the Maharajah and one to Jaimihr, warning each that we ride to keep our plighted word. At the worst, we shall find both parties ready for us! We shall know before we reach the city who is our friend! News reached me, too, sahib, that the Maharajah and his brother have united against us—that Howrah will eat his promises and play me false. God send he does! I would like to have my hands in that Hindoo's treasure-chests! We none of us know yet, bahadur, what is this plan of thine——"

"You've been guessing awfully close to it, I think," laughed Cunningham.

"Aha! The treasure-chests, then! But—is there —have you information, sahib? Who knows, then —who has told where they are? Neither I nor my men know!"

"Send for Mahommed Gunga."

Mahommed Gunga left his squadron, too, to canter beside Alwa.

"I am all ears, sahib!" he asserted, reining his horse until his stride was equal to the others.

"The key to the situation is that treasure," asserted Cunningham. "Howrah wants it. Jaimihr wants it. The priests want it. I know that much, for certain, from the McCleans. All right. We're a new factor in the problem, and they all mistrust us nearly as much, if not more, than they mistrust one another. Good. They'll be all of them watching that treasure. It'll be near where they are, and I'm going to snaffle it or break my neck—and all your necks—in the deuced desperate attempt. Is that clear? Where the carcass is, there wheel the kites and there the jackals fight, as your proverb says. The easiest part will be finding the treasure. Then——"

They legged in closer to him, hanging on his words and too busy listening to speak.

"If Howrah thinks we're after the treasure and decides to fight without previous argument, that absolves you from your promise, doesn't it, Alwa-sahib?"

"Surely, sahib, provided our intention is not to evade the promise."

"Our intention is to prevent Howrah and his brother from fighting, to insure peace and protection on this whole countryside, and, if possible, to ride away with Jaimihr's army to the Company's aid."

"Good, sahib."

It seemed to occur to none of the three that fifteen hundred mounted men were somewhat few with which to accomplish such a marvel.

"If they are fighting already, we must interfere."

"We are ready, bahadur. Fighting is our trade!"

"But, before all things, we must keep our eyes well skinned for a hint of treachery on Jaimihr's part. I would rather quarrel with that gentleman than be his friend, but he happens to hold our promise. We've got to keep our promise, provided he keeps his. I think our first objective is the treasure."

"That, sahib, is an acrobat of a plan," said Alwa; "much jumping from one proposition to another!"

"It is no plan at all," said Cunningham. "It is a mere rehearsal of the circumstances. A plan is something quickly seized at the right second and then acted on—like your capture of Jaimihr. Wait awhile, Alwa-sahib!"

"Ay, wait awhile!" growled Mahommed Gunga. "Did I bring thee a leader to ask plans of thee, or a man of men for thee to follow? Which?"

"All the same," said Alwa, "I would rather halt and make a good plan. It would be wiser. I do not understand this one."

"I follow Cunnigan-bahadur!" said Mahommed Gunga; and he spurred off to his squadron. Alwa could see nothing better than to follow suit, for Cunningham closed his lips tight in a manner unmistakable. And whatever Alwa's misgivings might

have been, he had the sense and the soldierly determination not to hint at them to his men.

As dawn rose pale-yellow in the eastern sky they
thundered into view of Howrah City and drew
rein to breathe their horses. The sun was high before they had trotted near enough to make out details. But, long before details could be seen, it was
evident that an army was formed up to meet them
on the tree-lined maidan that lay between them and
the two-mile-long palace-wall. Beyond all doubt it
was Jaimihr's army, for his elephants were not so
gaudily harnessed as Howrah's, and his men were
not so brilliantly dressed.

As they dipped into the last depression between
them and the wall and halted for a minute's consultation, a khaki-clad, shrivelled figure of a man
leaped up from behind a sand-ridge, and raced toward
Cunningham, shouting to him in a dialect he had
no knowledge of and gesticulating wildly. A trooper
spurred down on him, brought him up all standing
with an intercepted lance, examined him through
puckered eyes, and then, roaring with laughter,
picked him up and carried him to Cunningham.

"A woman, sahib! By the beard of Abraham, a
woman!"

"Joanna!"

"Ha, sahib! Ha, sahib!——"

She babbled to him, word overtaking word and
choking all together in a dust-dry throat. Cunningham gave her water and then set her on the
ground.

"Translate, somebody!" he ordered. "I can't understand a word she says."

Babbled and hurried and a little vague it might be, but Joanna had the news of the minute pat.

"Jaimihr is looting the treasure now, sahib. He has tricked his brother. They were to join, and both fight against you, but Jaimihr tried to get the treasure out before either you or his brother came. He is trying now, sahib!"

"Miss McClean! Ask her where Miss McClean is! Ask for Miss Maklin, sahib!"

"Jaimihr has told her that thou and Alwa and Mahommed Gunga are all dead, and the British overwhelmed throughout all India! He has her with him in a carriage, under guard, for all his men are with him and he could spare no great guard for his palace. See! Look, sahib! Jaimihr's palace is in flames!"

Alwa all but fell from his charger, laughing volcanically. The Rajput, who never can agree, can always see the humor in other Rajputs' disagreement.

"Ho, but they are playing a great game with each other!" he shouted. But Cunningham decided he had wasted time enough. He shouted his orders, and in less than thirty seconds his three squadrons were thundering in the direction of Jaimihr's army and the palace-wall. They drew rein again within a quarter of a mile of it, to discover with amazed military eyes that Jaimihr had no artillery.

It was then, at the moment when they halted,

that Jaimihr reached a quick decision and the wrong one. He knew by now that his brother had won the first trick in the game of treachery, for he could see the smoke and flames of his burning palace from where he sat his horse. He decided at once that Alwa and his Rangars must have taken sides with the Maharajah, for how, otherwise, he reasoned, could the Maharajah dare let the Rangars approach unwatched and unmolested. It was evident to him that the Rangars were acting as part of a concerted movement.

He made up his mind to attack and beat off the new arrivals without further ceremony. He outnumbered them by four or five to one, and was on his own ground. Whatever their intentions, at least he would be able to pretend afterward that he had acted in defence of the sacred treasure; and then, with the treasure in his possession, he would soon be able to recompense himself for a mere burned and looted palace!

So he opened fire without notice, argument, or parley, and an ill-aimed volley shrieked over the heads of Cunningham's three squadrons.

Cunningham, unruffled and undecided still, made out through puckered eyes the six-horse carriage in which Miss McClean evidently was; it was drawn up close beside the wall, and two regiments were between it and his squadron. He was recalling the terms of the agreement made with Jaimihr; he remembered it included the sparing of all of Alwa's men, and not the firing on them.

A thousand of Jaimihr's cavalry swooped from the shelter of the infantry, opened out a very little, and, mistaking Cunningham's delay for fear, bore down with a cheer and something very like determination.

They were met some ten yards their side of the half-way mark by Cunningham's three squadrons, loosed and led by Cunningham himself. Outridden, outfought, outgeneralled, they were smashed through, ridden down, and whirled back reeling in confusion. About a hundred of them reached the shelter of the infantry in a formed-up body; many of the rest charged through it in a mob and threw it into confusion.

Too late Jaimihr decided on more reasonable tactics. Too late he gave orders to his infantry that no such confused body could obey. Before he could ride to rally them, the Rangars were in them, at them, through them, over them. The whole was disintegrating in retreat, endeavoring to rally and reform in different places, each subdivision shouting orders to its nearest neighbor and losing heart as its appeals for help were disregarded.

Back came Cunningham's close-formed squadrons, straight through the writhing mass again; and now the whole of Jaimihr's army took to its heels, just as part of the five-feet-thick stone palace-wall succumbed to the attacks of crowbars and crashed down in the roadway, disclosing a dark vault on the other side.

Jaimihr made a rush for the six-horse carriage,

and tried vainly to get it started. Cunningham
shouted to him to surrender, but he took no notice
of the challenge; he escaped being made prisoner
by the narrowest of margins, as the postilion next
him was cut down. The other postilions were unhorsed, and six Rangars changed mounts and seized
the reins. The Prince ran one man through the
middle, and then spurred off to try and overtake
his routed army, some of which showed a disposition to form up again.

"Sit quiet!" called Cunningham through the lat-
ticed carriage window. "You're safe!"

The heavy, swaying carriage rumbled round, and
the horses plunged in answer to the Rangars' heels.
A moment later it was moving at a gallop; two
minutes later it was backed against the wall, and
Rosemary McClean stepped out behind three pro-
tecting squadrons that had not suffered perceptibly
from what they would have scorned to call a battle.

"Now all together!" shouted Cunningham, whose
theories on the value of seconds when tackling re-
forming infantry were worthy of the Duke of Wellington, or any other officer who knew his business;
and again he led his men at a breakneck charge.
This time Jaimihr's disheartened little army did not
wait for him, but broke into wild confusion and
scattered right and left, leaving their elephants to
be captured. There were only a few men killed.
The lance-tipped, roaring whirlwind loosed itself for
the most part against nothing, and reformed unin-
jured to trot back again. Cunningham told off two

troops to pursue fugitives and keep their eyes open
for the Prince before he rode back to examine the
breach in the wall that Jaimihr had been to so much
trouble about making.

He had halted to peer through the break in the
age-old masonry when Mahommed Gunga spurred
up close to him, touched his arm, and pointed.

"Look, sahib! Look!"

Jaimihr—and no one but a wizard could have
told how he had managed to get to where he was
unobserved—was riding as a man rides at a tent-
peg, crouching low, full-pelt for Rosemary McClean!

Cunningham's spurs went home before the word
was out of Mahommed Gunga's mouth, and Mahommed Gunga raced behind him; but Jaimihr had
the start of them. Duncan McClean, looking ill
and weak and helpless, crowded his daughter to
the wall, standing between her and the Prince; but
Jaimihr aimed a swinging sabre at him, and the
missionary fell. His daughter stooped to bend over
him, and Jaimihr seized her below the arms. A
second later he had hoisted her to his saddle-bow
and was spurring hell-bent-for-leather for the open
country.

Two things prevented him from making his escape. Five of Alwa's men, returning from pursuing
fugitives, cut off his flight in one direction, and the
extra weight on his horse prevented him from getting clear by means of speed alone—as he might
have done otherwise, for Cunningham's mare was
growing tired.

Jaimihr rode for two minutes with the frenzy of a savage before he saw the futility of it. It was Cunningham's mare, gaining on him stride over stride, that warned him he would be cut down like a dog from behind unless he surrendered or let go his prize.

So he laughed and threw the girl to the ground. For a moment more he spurted, spurring like a fiend, then wheeled and charged at Cunningham. He guessed that but for Cunningham that number of Rangars would never have agreed on a given plan. He knew that it was he, and not Cunningham or Alwa or Rosemary McClean, who had broken faith. He had broken it in thought, and word, and action. And he had lost his prospect of a throne. So he came on like a man who has nothing to gain by considering his safety. He came like a real man at last. And Cunningham, on a tired mare, met him point to point.

They fought over a quarter of a mile of ground, for Jaimihr proved to be as useful with his weapon as Mahommed Gunga's teaching had made Cunningham. There was plenty of time for the reformed squadrons to see what was happening— plenty of time for Alwa, who considered that he had an account of his own to settle with the Prince, to leave his squadron and come thundering up to help. Mahommed Gunga dodged and reined and spurred, watching his opportunity on one side and Alwa on the other. It would have suited neither of them to have their leader killed at that stage of the game, but the fighting was too quick for either man to interfere.

Jaimihr charged Cunningham for the dozenth time and missed, charged past, to wheel and charge again, then closed with the most vindictive rush of all. Again Cunningham met him point to point. The two blades locked, and bent like springs as they wrenched at them. Cunningham's blade snapped. He snatched at his mare and spun her before Jaimihr could recover, then rammed both spurs in and bore down on the Prince with half a sabre. He had him on the near side at a disadvantage. Jaimihr spurred and tried to manœuvre for position, and the half sabre went home just below his ribs. He dropped bleeding in the dust at the second that Alwa and Mahommed Gunga each saw an opportunity and rushed in, to rein back face to face, grinning in each other's faces, their horses' breasts pressed tight against the charger that Jaimihr rode. The horse screamed as the shock crushed the wind out of him.

"You robbed me of my man, sahib, by about a sabre's breadth!" laughed Alwa.

"And you left your squadron leaderless without my permission!" answered Cunningham. "You, too, Mahommed Gunga!"

"But, sahib——"

"Do you prefer to argue or obey?"

Mahommed Gunga flushed and rode back. Alwa grinned and started after him. Cunningham, without another glance at the dead Prince, rode up to

Rosemary McClean, who was picking herself up and looking bewildered; she had watched the duel in speechless silence, lying full length in the dust, and she still could not speak when he reached her.

"Put your foot on mine," he said reassuringly; "then swing yourself up behind me if you can. If you can't, I'll pick you up in front."

She tried hard, but she failed; so he put both arms under hers and lifted her.

"Am I welcome?" he asked. And she nodded.

Fresh from killing a man—with a man's blood on his broken sword and the sweat of fighting not yet dry on him—he held a woman in his arms for the first time in his life. His hand had been steady when it struck the blow under Jaimihr's ribs, but now it trembled. His eyes had been stern and blazing less than two minutes before; now they looked down into nothing more dangerous than a woman's eyes and grew strangely softer all at once. His mouth had been a hard, tight line under a scrubby upper lip, but his lips had parted now a little and his smile was a boy's—not nervous or mischievous—a happy boy's.

She smiled, too. Most people did smile when young Cunningham looked pleased with them; but she smiled differently. And he, with that blood still wet on him, bent down and kissed her on the lips. Her answer was as characteristic as his action.

"You look like a blackguard," she said; "but you came, and I knew you would! I told Jaimihr you would, and he laughed at me. I told God you would,

and you came! How long is it since you shaved?
Your chin is all prickly!"

They were interrupted by a roar from the three
waiting squadrons. He had ridden without caring
where he went, and his mare had borne the two of
them to where the squadrons were drawn up with
their rear to the great gap in the wall. The situation suited every Rangar of them! That was, indeed, the way a man should win his woman! They
cheered him, and cheered again, and he grinned
back, knowing that their hearts were in the cheer-
ing and their good will won. Red, then, as a boiled
beet, he rode over to the six-horse carriage and dismounted by her father—picked him up—called two
troopers—and lifted him on to the rear seat of the
great old-fashioned coach.

"Get inside beside him!" he ordered Rosemary,
examining the missionary's head as he spoke. "It's
a scalp wound, and he's stunned—no more. He's
left off bleeding already. Nurse him!" He was
off, then, without another word or a backward glance
for her—off to his men and the gap in the wall
that waited an investigation.

The amazing was discovered then. The treasure
—the fabled, fabulous, enormous Howrah treasure
was no fable. It was there, behind that wall! The
jewels and the bullion in marketable bars that could
have bought an army or a kingdom—the sacred,
secret treasure of twenty troubled generations, that
was guarded in the front by fifty doors and fifty
corridors and three times fifty locks—the door of

whose secret vault was guarded by a cannon, set to explode at the slightest touch—was hidden from the public road at its other side, its rear, by nothing better than a five-foot wall of ill-cemented stone! Cunningham stepped inside over the dismantled masonry and sat down on a chest that held more money's worth than all the Cunninghams in all the world had ever owned, or spent, or owed, or used, or dreamed of!

"Ask Alwa and Mahommed Gunga to come to me here!" he called; and a minute later they stood at attention in front of him.

"Send a hundred men, each with a flag of truce on his lance, to gallop through the city and call on Jaimihr's men to rally to me, if they wish protection against Howrah!"

"Good, sahib! Good!" swore Alwa. "Howrah is the next danger! Make ready to fight Howrah!"

"Attend to my orders, please!" smiled Cunningham, and Alwa did as he was told. Within an hour Jaimihr's men were streaming from the four quarters of the compass, hurrying to be on the winning side, and forming into companies as they were ordered.

Then Cunningham gave another order.

"Alwa-sahib, will you take another flag of truce, please, and ride with not more than two men to Maharajah Howrah. Tell him that I want him here at once to settle about this treasure."

Alwa stared. His mouth opened a little, and he stood like a man bereft of reason by the unexpected.

"Are you not still pledged to support Howrah on his throne?"

"I am, bahadur."

"Would plundering his treasure be in keeping with your promise to him?"

"Nay, sahib. But——"

"Be good enough to take my message to him. Assure him that he may come with ten men without fear of molestation, but guarantee to him that if he comes with more than ten—and with however many more—I will fight, and keep his treasure, both!"

CHAPTER XXXIII

Friends I have sought me of varying nations,
Men of all ranks and of different stations;
   Some are in jail now, and some are deceased.
Two, though, I found to be experts at sundering
Me from my revenue, leaving me wondering
   Which was the costlier—soldier or priest.

A LITTLE more than one hour later, Howrah—sulky and disgruntled, but doing his level best to appear at ease—faced young Cunningham across a table in the treasure-vault. Outside was a row of wagons, drawn by horses and closely guarded by a squadron of the Rangars. Behind Cunningham stood Alwa and Mahommed Gunga; behind the Maharajah were two of his court officials. There were pen and ink and the royal seal between them on the table.

"So, Maharajah-sahib. They are all sealed, and each chest is marked on the outside with its contents; I'm sorry there was no time to weigh the gold, but the number of the ingots ought to be enough. And, of course, you'll understand it wasn't possible to count all those unset stones—that 'ud take a week; but your seal is on that big chest, too, so you'll know if it's been opened. You are certain you can preserve the peace of your state with the army you have?"

"Yes," said Howrah curtly.

"Don't want me to leave a squadron of my men to help you out?"

"No!" He said that even more abruptly.

"Good. Of course, since you won't have to spare men to guard the treasure now, you'll have all the more to keep peace in the district with, won't you? Let me repeat the terms of our bargain; they're written here, but let's be sure there is no mistake. I agree to deliver your treasure into safe keeping until the rebellion is over, and to report to my government that you are friendly disposed toward us. You, in return, guarantee to protect the families and property of all these gentlemen who ride with me. It is mutually agreed that any damage done to their homes during their absence shall be made good out of your treasure, but that should you keep your part of the agreement the treasure shall be handed back to you intact. Is that correct?"

"Yes," said Howrah shifting in his seat uneasily. "Is there anything else?"

"One other thing. I am outmanœuvred, and I have surrendered with the best grace possible. That agreement stands in my name, and no other man's?"

"Certainly."

"The priests of Siva are not parties to it?"

"I've had nothing whatever to do with them," said Cunningham.

"That is all, then, sahib. I am satisfied."

"While we're about it, Maharajah-sahib, let's scotch those priests altogether! McClean-sahib has told me that suttee has been practised here as a regular thing. That's got to stop, and we may as well stop it now. Of course, I shall keep my word about the treasure, and you'll get it back if you live up to the bargain you have made; but my government will know now where it is, and they'll be likely to impose a quite considerable fine on you when the rebellion's over unless this suttee's put an end to. Besides, you couldn't think of a better way of scoring off the priests than by enforcing the law and abolishing the practice. Think that over, Maharajah-sahib."

Howrah swore into his beard, as any ruling potentate might well do at being dictated to by a boy of twenty-two.

"I will do my best, sahib," he answered. "I am with the British—not against them."

"Good for you!—er, I mean, that's right!" He turned to Alwa, and looked straight into his eyes. "Are you satisfied with the guarantee?" he asked.

"Sahib, I am more than satisfied!"

"Good! Oh, and—Maharajah-sahib—since we've fought your battle for you—and lost a few men— and are going to guard your treasure for you, and be your friends, and all that kind of thing—don't you think you'd like to do something for us—not much, but just a little thing?"

"I am in your power. You have but to command."

"Oh, no. I don't want to force anything. We're friends—talking as friends. I ask a favor."

"It is granted, sahib."

"A horse or two, that's all."

"How many horses, sahib?"

"Oh, not more than one each."

The Maharajah pulled a wry face, but bowed assent. It would empty his stables very nearly, but he knew when he could not help himself. Mahommed Gunga clapped a hand to his mouth and left the vault hurriedly.

"You understand this is not a demand, Maharajah-sahib. I take it that you offer me these horses as an act of royal courtesy and as additional proof of friendliness?"

"Surely, sahib."

"My men will be very grateful to you. This will enable them to reach the scene of action with their own horses in good shape. I'm sure it's awfully good of you to have offered them!"

Outside, where the late afternoon sun was gradually letting things cool down, Mahommed Gunga leaned against the wall and roared with laughter, as he explained a few details to the admiring troopers.

"A horse or two, says he! How many? Oh, just a horse or two, Maharajah-sahib—merely a horse apiece! Fifteen hundred horses! A horse or two! Oh—ha-ha-ha-ha-ha-ho! Allah! But that boy will make a better soldier than his father! As a favor, he asked them—no compulsion, mind you—just as a favor! Allah! What is he asking now, I wonder! Ha-ha-ha-ha-ha-ho-ho-ho!"

And inside, with a perfectly straight face and almost ghastly generosity, young Cunningham proceeded to impose on Howrah the transferred, unwelcome, perilous allegiance of Jaimihr's reassembling army. The mere keeping of it in subjection, it was realized by donor and recipient alike, would keep the Maharajah's hands full.

"Are you satisfied that your homes will be safe, now?" he asked Alwa. And Alwa looked him in the eyes and grinned.

CHAPTER XXXIV

Now, fifteen hundred, horse and man,
Reel at the word of one!
Loosed by the brazen trumpet's peal—
Knee to knee and toe on heel—
Troop on troop the squadrons wheel
Outbrazening the sun!

WITHIN a fortnight of the outbreak of the mutiny, men spoke with bated breath about the Act of God. It burst at the moment when India's reins were in the hands of some of the worst incompetents in history. A week found strong men in control of things—the right men, with the right handful behind them.

Some of the men in charge went mad, and were relieved. Some threw up their commands. Some of the worst incompetents were killed by the mutineers, and more than one man who could have changed the course of history for the worse were taken sick and died. Instead of finding themselves faced by spineless nincompoops, the rebels reeled before the sudden, well-timed tactics of real officers with eyes and ears and brains. The mask was off on both sides, and the sudden, stripped efficiency of one was no less disconcerting than the unexpected rebellion of the other.

Byng-bahadur—"Byng the Brigadier"—was in command of a force again within three days of the news of the first massacre; and because he was Byng, with Byng's record, and Byng's ability to handle loyal natives, the men who succeeded to the reins packed him off at once with a free hand, and with no other orders than to hit, hit hard, and keep on hitting.

"Go for them, Byng, old man. Live off the country, keep moving, and don't let 'em guess once what your next move's going to be!"

So Byng recruited as he went, and struck like a brain-controlled tornado at whatever crossed his path. But irreparable damage had been done before the old school was relieved, and Byng—like others—was terribly short of men. Many of his own irregulars were so enraged at having been disbanded at a moment's notice that they refused to return to him. Their honor, as they saw it, had been outraged. Only two British regiments could be spared him, and they were both thinned by sickness from the first. They were Sikhs, who formed the bulk of his headquarterless brigade, and many of them were last-minute friends, who came to him unorganized and almost utterly undrilled.

But Byng was a man of genius, and his bare reputation was enough to offset much in the way of unpreparedness. He coaxed and licked and praised his new men into shape as he went along; within a week he had stormed Deeseera, blowing up their greatest reserve of ammunition and momentarily stunning the rebellion's leaders. But cholera took charge in the city, and two days later found him hurrying out again, to camp where there was uncontaminated water, on rising ground that gave him the command of three main roads. It was there that the rebels cornered him.

They blew up a hundred-yard-long bridge behind him at the one point where a swiftly running river could be crossed, and from two other sides at once mutinied native regiments and thousands from the countryside flocked, hurrying to take a hand in what seemed destined to be Byng's last action. The fact that so many swaggering soldier Sikhs were cornered with him was sufficient in itself to bring out Hindoo and Mohammedan alike.

The mutinous regiments had all been drilled and taught by British officers until they were as nearly perfect as the military knowledge of the day could make them; the fact that they had killed their officers only served to make them savage without detracting much from their efficiency. They had native officers quite capable of taking charge, and sense enough to retain their discipline.

So Byng intrenched himself on the gradual rise, and sent out as many messengers as he could spare to bring reinforcements from whatever source obtainable. Then, when almost none came, he got ready to die where he stood, using all the soldier gift he had to put courage into the last-ditch loyalists who offered to die with him. He had counted most on aid from Cunningham and Mahommed Gunga, but that source seemed to have failed him; and he gave up hope of their arrival when a body of several thousand rebels took up position on his flank and cut off approach from the direction whence Cunningham should come.

The sun blazed down like molten hell on sick and wounded. Rotting carcasses of horses and cattle, killed by the rebels' artillery-fire, lay stenching here and there, and there was no possibility of disposing of them. A day came very soon, indeed, when horse, or occasional transport bullock, was all there was to eat, and a night came when Govind Singh, the leader of the Sikhs, came to him and remonstrated.

The old man had to be carried to Byng's tent, for a round shot had disabled him, and he had himself set down by the tent-door, where the General sat on a camp-stool.

"General-sahib, I have not been asked for advice; I am here to offer it."

The huge black dome of heaven was punctuated by a billion dots of steely white that looked like pin-pricks. All the light there was came from the fitful watch-fires, where even the wagons were being burned now that the meagre supply of rough timber was giving out. The rebels, too, were burning everything on which they could lay their hands, and from between the spaced-out glow of their bonfires came ever and again the spurt of cannon-flame.

"Speak, Govind Singh!"

"Sahib, we have no artillery with which to answer them. We have no food; and the supply of ammu-

nition wanes. Shall we die here like cattle in a
slaughter-house?"

"This is as good as any other place," said Byng.

"Nay, sahib!"

"How, then?"

"In *their* lines is a better place! Here is nothing
better than a shambles, with none but our men falling. They know that our food is giving out—they
know that we lose heavily—they wait. They will
wait for days yet before they close in to finish what
their guns have but begun, and—then—how many
will there be to die desperately, as is fitting?"

"We might get reinforcements in the morning,
Govind Singh."

"And again, we might not, sahib!"

"I sent a number of messengers before we were
shut in."

"Yes, sahib—and to whom? To men who would
ask you to reinforce them if they could get word to
you! To-morrow our rear will be surrounded, too;
they have laid planks across the little streams behind
us, and are preparing to drag guns to that side, too.
Now, sahib, we have fire left in us. We can smite
yet, and do damage while we die. To-morrow night
may find us decimated and without heart for the
finish. I advise you to advance at dawn, sahib!"

That advice came as a great relief to Byng-
bahadur. He had been the first to see the hopeless-
ness of the position, and every instinct that he had
told him to finish matters, not in the last reeking
ditch, but ahead where the enemy would suffer

fearfully while a desperate charge roared into them, to peter out when the last man went down fighting. Surrender was unthinkable, and in any event would have been no good, for the mutineers would be sure to butcher all their prisoners; his only other chance had been to hold out until relief came, and that hope was now forlorn.

A Mohammedan stepped out of blackness and saluted him—a native officer, in charge of a handful of irregular cavalry, whose horses had all been shot.

"Well—what is it?"

"This, sahib. Do we die here? I and my men would prefer to die yonder, where a mutineer or two would pay the price!"

A Ghoorka officer—small as a Japanese and sturdy-looking came up next. The whole thing was evidently preconcerted.

"My men ask leave to show the way into the ranks ahead, General-sahib! They are overweary of this shambles!"

"We will advance at dawn!" said Byng. "Egan—" He turned to a British officer, who was very nearly all the staff he had. "Drag that table up. Let's have some paper here and a pencil, and we'll work out the best plan possible."

He sent for the commanding officers of the British regiments—both of them captains, but the seniors surviving—and a weird scene followed round the lamp set on the tiny table. British, Sikh, Mohammedan, and Ghoorka clustered close to him, and watched as his pencil traced the different positions

and showed the movement that was to make the
morrow's finish, their faces outlined in the lamp's
yellow glow and their breath coming deep and slow
as they agreed on how the greatest damage could be
done the enemy before the last man died.

As he finished, and assigned each leader to his
share in the last assault that any one of them would
take a part in, a streak of light blazed suddenly
across the sky. A shooting-star swept in a wide
parabola to the horizon. A murmur went up from
the wakeful lines, and the silence of the graveyard
followed.

"There is our sign, sahib!" laughed the Mohammedan. The old Sikh nodded and the Ghoorka
grinned. "It is the end!" he said, without a trace
of discouragement.

"Nonsense!" said Byng, his face, too, turned upward.

"What, then, does it mean, sahib?"

"That—it means that God Almighty has relieved
a picket! We're the picket. We're relieved! We
advance at dawn, and we'll get through somehow!
Join your commands, gentlemen, and explain the
details carefully to your men—let's have no mis-
understandings."

The dawn rose gold and beautiful upon a sleepless
camp that reeked and steamed with hell-hot suffering. It showed the rebels stationary, still in
swarming lines, but scouts reported several thousand
of them moving in a body from the flank toward the
British rear.

"What proportion of the rebel force?" asked Byng. "New arrivals, or some of the old ones taking up a new position?"

"The same crowd, sir. They're just moving round to hem us in completely."

"So much the better for us, then! That leaves fewer for us to deal with in front."

As he spoke another man came running to report the arrival of five gallopers, coming hell-bent-for leather, one by one and scattered, with the evident purpose of allowing one man to get through, whatever happened.

"That'll be relief at last!" said Byng-bahadur. And, instead of ordering the advance immediately, he waited, scouring the sky-line with his glasses.

"Yes—dust—lance-heads—one—two—three divisions, coming in a hurry."

Being on rising ground, he saw the distant relieving force much sooner than the rebels did, and he knew that it was help for him on the way some time before the first of the five gallopers careered into the camp, and shouted:

"Cunnigan-bahadur comes with fifteen hundred!"

"Fifteen hundred," muttered Byng. "That merely serves to postpone the finish by an hour or two!"

But he waited; and presently the rebel scouts brought word, and their leaders, too, became aware of reinforcements on the way for somebody. They made the mistake, though, of refusing to believe that any help could be coming for the British, and by the

time that messengers had hurried from the direction
of the British rear, to tell of gallopers who had ridden past them and been swallowed by the shouting
British lines, three squadrons on fresh horses were
close enough to be reckoned dangerous.

"Is that a gun they've got with them?" wondered Byng. "By the lord Harry, no—it's a coach
and six! They're flogging it along like a twelve-
pounder! And what the devil's in those wagons?"

But he had no time for guesswork. The desultory
thunder of the rebel ordnance ceased, and the whole
mass that hemmed him in began to revolve within
itself, and present a new front to the approaching
cavalry.

"Caught on the hop, by God! The whole line
will advance! Trumpeter!"

One trumpet-call blared out and a dozen echoed it.
In a second more a roar went up that is only heard
on battle-fields. It has none of the exultant shout of
joy or of the rage that a mob throws up to heaven;
it is not even anger, as the cities know it, or the
men who riot for advantage. It is a welcome ironically offered up to Death—full-throated, and more
freighted with moral effect on an enemy than a
dozen salvoes of artillery.

The thousands ahead tried hard to turn again and
face two attacks at once; but, though the units were
efficiently controlled, there were none who could
swing the whole. Byng's decimated, forward-rush-
ing fragment of a mixed brigade, tight-reined and
working like a piece of mechanism, struck home into

a mass of men who writhed, and fell away, and shouted to each other. A third of them was out of reach, beyond the British rear; fully another third was camped too far away to bring assistance at the first wild onslaught. Messengers were sent to bring them up, but the messengers were overtaken by a horde who ran.

Then, like arrows driven by the bows of death, three squadrons took them on the flank as Cunningham changed direction suddenly and loosed his full weight at the guns. Instead of standing and serving grape, the rebel gunners tried to get their ordnance away—facing about again too late, when the squadrons were almost on them. Then they died gamely, when gameness served no further purpose. The Rangars rode them down and butchered them, capturing every single gun, and leaving them while they charged again at the rallying hordes ahead.

The strange assortment of horsed wagons and the lumbering six-horse coach took full advantage of the momentary confusion to make at a gallop for the British rear, where they drew up in line behind the Sikhs, who were volleying at short range in the centre.

Byng detached two companies of British soldiers to do their amateur damnedest with the guns, and, for infantry, they did good service with them; fifteen or twenty minutes after the first onslaught the enemy was writhing under the withering attention of his own abandoned ordnance. But the odds were still tremendous, and the weight of numbers made the ultimate outcome of the battle seem a foregone conclusion.

From the British rear heads appeared above the rising ground; the deserted camp was rushed and set alight. The tents blazed like a beacon light, and a moment later the Ghoorkas retaliated by setting fire to such of the rebel camp as had fallen into British hands.

It was those two fires that saved the day. From the sky-line to the rebel rear came the thunder of a salvo of artillery. It was the short bark of twelve-pounders loaded up with blank—a signal—and the rebels did not wait to see whether this was friend or foe. Help from one unexpected source had reached the British; this, they argued, was probably another column moving to the relief, and they drew off in reasonably decent order—harried, pestered, stung, as they attempted to recover camp-equipment or get away with stores and wagons, by Cunningham, Alwa, and Mahommed Gunga.

In another hour the rebel army was a black swarm spreading on the eastern sky-line, and on the far horizon to the north there shone the glint of bayonets and helmet spikes, the dancing gleam of lance-tips, and the dazzle from the long, polished bodies of a dozen guns. A galloper spurred up with a message for Byng.

"You are to join my command," it ran, "for a raid in force on Howrah, where the rebels are supposed to have been concentrating for months past. The idea is to paralyze the vitals of the movement before concentrating somewhere on the road to Delhi, where the rebels are sure to make a most determined stand."

As he read it Mahommed Gunga galloped up to him, grinning like a boy.

"Cunnigan-sahib's respects, General-sahib! He asks leave to call his men off, saying that he has done all the damage possible with only fifteen hundred."

"Yes. Call 'em off and send Cunningham to me. How did he shape?"

"Like a son of Cunnigan-bahadur! General-sahib—salaam!"

"No. Here, you old ruffian—shake hands, will you? Now send Cunningham to me."

Cunningham came up fifteen minutes later, with a Rangar orderly behind him, and did his best to salute as though it were nothing more than an ordinary meeting.

"Oh! Here you are. 'Gratulate you, Cunningham! You came in the nick of time. What kept you?"

"That 'ud take a long time to tell, sir. I've fifteen hundred horses about ten miles from here, sir, left in charge of native levies, and I'd like permission to go and fetch them before the levies make off with them."

"Splendid! Yes, you'd better go for them. What's in the wagons."

"The Howrah treasure, sir!"

"What?"

"The whole of the Howrah treasure, sir! It's held as security. Howrah guarantees to keep the peace and protect the homes of my men. I guaranteed to hand him back the treasure when the show's over, less deductions for damage done!"

"Well, I'm— Who thought of that? You or Mahommed Gunga?"

"Oh, I expect we cooked it up between us, sir."

"H-rrrr-umph! And what's in the six-horse coach?"

"A lady and her father."

"The deuce they are!"

Byng rode up to the lumbering vehicle, signing to Cunningham to follow him.

"General Byng," said Cunningham. "Miss McClean, sir."

A very much dishevelled and very weary-looking young woman with a wealth of chestnut hair leaned through the window and smiled, not at the General but at Cunningham. Byng stared—looked from one to the other of them—and said "Hu-rrrr-umph!" again.

"It was she who made the whole thing possible, sir."

"The very deuce it was!" It began to be evident that Byng was not a ladies' man!

"This is Mr. McClean, sir—Rosemary's father. He helped her put the whole scheme through."

Byng nodded to the missionary and looked back at Rosemary McClean—then from her to Cunningham again.

"Hu-rrrr-umph! Christian names already! More 'gratulations, eh?"

Rosemary's head and shoulders disappeared and Cunningham looked foolish.

"Well! Send Mahommed Gunga for the horses. Ride over there to where you see General Evans's column and tell him the whole story. Take a small escort and the treasure with you. And—ah—er— lemme see—take this carriage, too. Oh, by the bye —you'd better ask General Evans to make some arrangements for Miss McClean. Leave her over there with the treasure. I want you back with my brigade, and I want you to be some sort of use. Can't have love-making with the brigade, Mr. Cunningham!"

The Brigadier rode off with a very perfunctory salute.

"Isn't he a rather curmudgeony sort of officer?" asked Rosemary the moment that his back was turned.

"Oh, no!" laughed Cunningham. "That's Byng- bahadur's little way, that's all. He's quite likely to insist on being best man or something of that sort when the show's all over! Wait here while I fetch the escort."